THE LIFE CHANGING JOURNEY OF NICHOLAS SAVAGE

Rob Wassell

The Life Changing Journey of Nicholas Savage

www.lifechangingjourney.uk

First published in 2021 by RAW Publications
www.rawpublications.co.uk

International Standard Book Number

978-0-9569912-5-6

RAW
Publications

Chapter 1

Trevor Whiting sat in front of a live studio audience staring into the dark lens of a television camera.

He flattened the hair on the side of his head and clasped his hands tightly around a clipboard.

He looked down at handwritten notes and repeated the names of the guests in his mind.

He listened to the countdown in an earpiece.

Five, four, three, two, and — we're live!"

"Hello and welcome to The Debate, with me, Trevor Whiting."

"This evening — my guests are Jenny Blackburn from Friends of the Earth, Jane Craven from the World Health Organisation and Louise Ormrod from the Research Ethics Committee."

The crowd applauded.

"In tonight's debate we discuss the meteoric rise of Nicholas Savage and his incredible journey from complete anonymity to worldwide notoriety."

The crowd murmured.

"We also turn the discussion to the more sensitive issue of whether his actions were ethical and what the repercussions could be for us all."

The atmosphere quickly changed, spurred on by a production manager waving his arms out of shot.

Some of the crowd booed or hissed and others applauded.

"All this and more, right after this ..."

Chapter 2

"Need one cheeseburger," shouted a voice from the tills.

"Two minutes!" Nicholas called out as he tossed a raw beef patty onto the hotplate.

He hated his job — any vegetarian would have — but he needed the money and there weren't an awful lot of opportunities around at the moment.

One final turn of the burger, grab the bun, slap it in, add the cheese — a squirt of ketchup — token gherkin — top the bun — wrap it — done.

"One cheeseburger, ready to go," groaned Nicholas.

He looked at the clock just in time to see the second hand strike the hour. He noticed the manager, Helen, at the front of the shop closing the door.

11 o'clock — thank heavens, the end of another shift.

He turned off the hotplate and carried out his 'end of shift' chores — now firmly programmed in his mind after officially being six months into the job. The company manual had to be followed accurately and to the letter.

After dotting the 'i's and crossing the 't's, his teammates began to scurry out of the door.

As Nicholas followed, he heard a voice call his name.

"One moment please, Nicholas," the manager shouted.

He felt deflated. He knew what was coming.

"We've had this conversation before Nicholas, haven't we?"

"Yes, we have."

"Then you know what I am going to say, don't you?"

"Yes, I do."

"Then what am I going to say?"

"That I need to be an example to my fellow team members."

"And?"

"To be motivated and show a keenness and willingness to work."

"That's right. There are wonderful opportunities here if you want to work for them Nicholas, just think about that."

Nicholas nodded.

"You're seventeen — nearly an adult. Buck your ideas up and you could get any position you want Nicholas. You've got a clever head on your shoulders. I think you just lack motivation. You need a goal."

"Yes, yes. I understand."

"Okay, you can go now. See you tomorrow. Don't be late."

"I won't. Night," Nicholas said and rushed out the door.

As the cool night air hit him, he breathed a sigh of relief. He felt his stomach rumble. He was hungry.

They gave him a budget, but there was no way he could eat at work. He hadn't eaten meat for years, ever since his Mum told him about the Mad Cow Disease outbreak in the nineties. It had given him very vivid and frightening nightmares. The veggie options left a lot to be desired. Instead he would wait until he got home and have a slice of toast or something.

His colleagues had long since vanished, not that he had

anything in common with them. They didn't seem to be on his level.

He glanced around the car park. The usual crowd hung around the far corner in their hot hatchbacks and hoodies. One of them called over. "Oy — speccy!"

He ignored them and kept walking. He heard footsteps running and then felt a hefty shove from behind.

"Speccy. Speccy," one of the lads shouted. He wore a baseball cap, baggy jeans and a loose white sports top with the word 'New York' emblazoned on it.

"Geek boy, let's have a go with your glasses," another boy taunted, wearing similar clothes but with 52 on his shirt. He reached out and tried to pull the glasses off Nicholas's face.

"It's not my fault that I've got bad eyes," Nicholas said.

"Ooooooohhhh, it's not his fault he's got bad eyes!" 52 said and tried again to grab them.

Nicholas pulled away and started to run. The boys made gestures, threw a few insults and gave up.

Nicholas kept running, looked behind and saw that they'd returned to their cars. He stopped a moment to catch his breath and then carried on.

He could walk this route with his eyes closed. He'd worked out the previous night that he'd been this way seventy two times, or one hundred and forty four if you counted the walk to work as well. The journey was exactly 1.2 miles, which meant that he had walked 172.8 miles since he'd started working at Burger Ville.

He had a choice. He could either go straight ahead through the estate or the usual way, around and up Leigh Road.

He'd go through the estate. It was the same distance, but more direct. He just wanted to get home.

He felt his stomach turn over. It was almost like a feeling of dread, but he put it down to hunger.

He sighed. He was fed up. His life was going nowhere. He hated working with the remains of dead animals all day. He hated life. He just wanted things to be — different.

He turned into the estate. It was called the Reary Estate or as the locals referred to it, the 'Dreary Estate'. The grey characterless concrete buildings loomed over a grey central concourse and, despite the residents laying borders of plants, even they seemed to have turned grey.

Towards the centre of the concourse the area opened up with walkways underneath the building and to the sides with more borders and more grey plants. A vague attempt at a water feature was in the centre. It was only a few inches deep so as not to present a hazard for small children.

He heard some kids up ahead, shouting, laughing and cajoling.

"Do it again, do it again," one of them shouted.

"Yeah!" another one cried, "Do it!"

If he just kept his head down and walked around them he'd be fine, he'd seen them before.

They were obviously engrossed in something that would keep their attention away from him.

A crowd of boys were huddled over something on the ground. He couldn't see what it was. He lowered his head and began to walk by.

He heard a shriek, but it didn't sound as though it came from one of the boys.

"Ergh!" one of them shouted, "Don't get it on me!"

Two of the boys jumped back, opening up a gap through which he could see the gruesome object of their amusement.

His heart sank. He felt physically ill but couldn't stop himself. He had to do something.

"Oy, stop it — that's cruel!" Nicholas cried.

One of the boys turned and looked directly at him.

"Fuck off!"

The others took no notice. Nicholas rushed in to intervene.

He didn't even see the punch — but he felt it land — an excruciating pain and then nothing but darkness. He spun and fell.

***

When he awoke, the boys had gone. It took a moment for him to realise where he was. He had a blinding headache and his face throbbed. He felt wet. It was only when he tried to move he realised part of him was lying in the water feature.

He pulled himself out and looked around. There to his side was the cat that the boys had been torturing. He felt sick to his stomach. Poor thing.

He bent down. At first he thought it was dead, it should have been, but it gradually opened its remaining eye and looked directly up at him.

"Sorry, there's nothing I can do," he said as tears began to stream down his cheeks. "I don't think there's anything anyone can do."

He stared at the cat and the cat stared back.

He couldn't let it suffer.

He had to do something.

He dragged its body towards the water feature. A bloody trail smeared across the concrete.

He paused a moment. The cat looked at him. It was as if it knew what he was intending to do — as if it wanted him to do it.

He swallowed hard, took a deep breath and thrust its head into the water.

Its body began to struggle and thrash and then, after about ten seconds, it was calm and still. It had gone. It had passed away.

He couldn't hold back the tears. As he held its lifeless body, he knelt on the ground and sobbed uncontrollably.

Chapter 3

It had been the worst night he'd ever had. He hadn't slept. Every time he closed his eyes all he could see was the cat staring back at him.

He thought how completely helpless it had been. Unable to get away — unable to do anything but accept what was being done to it.

Previously he thought he just hated life, but now he hated people too.

As he walked into the kitchen, there was his Mother, rushing around as usual.

"There you are. I've made your breakfast," his Mother said without looking at him. She was rummaging around, looking for something in her bag.

"Thanks Mum."

Nicholas approached the table. She had made him cornflakes — about twenty minutes ago — the flakes had become mush floating in a pool of slop.

He sat down and pushed the bowl away. He had no appetite anyway.

"What time do you have to be at work?" she said, still foraging in her bag.

"I told you before Mum, 3 o'clock. It's the same time every day and has been for six months."

"Oh yes, silly me," she said and glanced across.

"What the hell happened to your face?" she said, finally giving him attention.

"Oh," he said as he touched the side of his face. "I ran into some boys on the way home. It's fine."

"Does it hurt?"

"No, it looks much worse than it is — it's fine."

"Were they picking on you again?" she said, concerned.

"No they weren't. They were just having a laugh. I walked by, they tried to involve me in their high jinx and I got hit in the face by accident," he said, desperately trying to cover up the real horror of what had happened.

"Oh okay, as long as you're sure," his Mother said, still trying to find whatever she was looking for in her bag.

That was the point, he wasn't sure. He felt that feeling of dread in his stomach again. What did it mean? If only he had paid attention to it last night he may not have gone through the estate. He felt worried, anxious, maybe he just needed to talk to someone about it — and, when you've got a problem, who is the one person you can always turn to?

"Mum, I ..."

"Found it! I've been looking for my door key for the past ten minutes," she said. "Oh my goodness, would you look at the time, I am going to be late for work."

She zipped the bag and flung it over her shoulder.

"Sorry, what were you going to say?"

He saw her eyes glance back at the clock.

"Nothing, Mum."

"Okay see you later. And keep away from those boys tonight."

"But ..." She was gone.

Chapter 4

Nicholas sat down on the sofa and picked up the television remote control.

As the TV sprang to life, horrible images appeared.

He pressed the Info button. It was World War Two in Colour, apparently. All he could see was dead bodies — a mountain of them — it was the holocaust.

The picture changed. It showed people on trains, on their way to the concentration camps. They seemed oblivious to their inevitable doom. They accepted their fate, in many ways just like the cat had done the night before.

His stomach turned over. There was that feeling again. He turned the TV off.

He went to his room and turned on the computer.

As it was booting up, his eyes wandered around the room.

One wall was painted with a jungle scene, another with an ocean, the third with an African savanna and the one with the window a blue sky. His Dad had painted them when he was two, or three, he couldn't remember exactly. It had taken him a long time though, with meticulous detail to recreate the scenes as exactly as possible. He had included as many different types of animal as he could.

The dolphin had always been Nicholas's favourite.

The paint had become a little faded, especially where the sun had bleached it. His Mum had even suggested painting over it at one point, but Nicholas wasn't having any of it. He had very little to remind him of his Father, and this was one thing he could never imagine parting with.

Beside the bed was a small table with just an alarm clock on it.

The white wardrobe and chest of drawers neatly faced each other and stood out in stark contrast to the backdrop of the room. The room was devoid of any clutter and even the antiperspirant, comb and assortment of other items were neatly aligned with labels facing forwards. Behind the wardrobe there was a cupboard in the wall but that had been purposely blocked off as part of his therapy.

The welcome screen flashed up on his computer. He logged in and waited.

His gaze drifted out of the window, it was grey. The first thing he would do when the computer was finally ready would be to check the weather. He'd got soaked walking to work the other day and he didn't fancy that happening again.

The desktop of his computer finally appeared. He launched a browser, typed in www.bbc.co.uk and clicked.

As the main news page appeared, the headline he saw was 'SELFIE DOLPHIN DIES ON BEACH'. Without think-ing he clicked the link. In Argentina, a crowd of people pulled a rare baby dolphin from the sea and posed with it for selfies.

It was dead.

"Oh God — people are sick!" Nicholas groaned and shut the computer back down again.

He looked at the bedside clock. Today was going to be a very long day.

Chapter 5

Nicholas felt exhausted as he persevered, step after step, up the side of the huge sand dune. His feet sank into the sand and with every step forward he slipped back. He looked upwards, the summit was close, so close, yet he kept slipping back.

He became more determined than ever. With each step he dug in his heels. He got higher and higher. The muscles in his legs burned but he had to keep going. He felt an intense driving force spurring him on. He felt excited, motivated and optimistic for the first time in his life.

He just knew that when he reached the top he would find what he was looking for — an answer — the answer.

As he made the final step, he knew he'd done it. He had reached the top. He looked upwards. The sky was blue — not a cloud to be seen. The sun raged. It was hot but he wasn't sweating, he was dry and felt completely comfortable.

He turned around and was taken aback by what he saw. At the bottom of the huge sand dune was a green patchwork of fields that ran off in all directions around him.

Within those fields there were shapes. He looked more closely — they were animals — lots of animals.

There were sheep and elephants, giraffes and tigers, antelope and leopards, all standing next to each other, looking up — looking at him.

Nicholas suddenly realised how he was standing, his arms raised at his sides with his hands outstretched.

He could clearly see the animals below, spreading as far as the eye could see — more animals, of every type imaginable. He looked around. Directly behind him, he saw a train station. At the station were people, all lining up with their bags and suitcases boarding a train. As one train loaded and disappeared into the horizon, another turned up. He looked more closely. The people didn't seem to be alarmed. They were talking amongst themselves as though they were going on a day trip. They had not a care in the world. The animals were herding the people.

A sound caught his attention. He looked around. At the base of the sand dune he saw a dolphin. It was standing on its tail and clapping with its flippers. It was clicking and squeaking. Then other animals began to make a noise. Horses neighed. Lions roared. All around him the animals were shouting and applauding. Then he heard his name — Nicholas — Nicholas — N I C H O L A S!

He was awake.

"Nicholas!" his Mum called out.

"I was trying to wake you," she said. "Didn't you hear me clapping and calling your name?"

"Mum? What?" Nicholas said, dazed.

"I am going to work."

"Okay," Nicholas grumbled.

"Remember to visit your Gran today and check she's okay. She phoned last night in a fluster."

"Yeah okay," Nicholas sighed and then his Mother was gone.

He got out of bed, went to the bathroom and then into the kitchen.

On the table was the usual bowl of mushy cornflakes in slop — he poured it away.

He looked in the fridge to see if his Mum had made him lunch. She hadn't.

He felt like a hamster on a wheel.

He'd get ready and go to his Gran's. That would help take his mind off things.

Chapter 6

It was a fifteen minute walk to his Gran's. For generations the family had always lived close to one another. He walked alongside the terraced houses and counted down. He reached number Twenty.

He knocked on the door and waited.

After a minute the door opened partially.

"Yes?"

"It's me Gran."

"Nicholas! How nice to see you. Come on in," his Gran said opening the door wider.

"You didn't have the chain on," Nicholas said as he walked into the hall.

"I can't be bothered with that. It's too fiddly for my hands. Anyway, why would anyone want to steal from me?"

"That's not the point," Nicholas said. "You should do it anyway."

Nicholas went into the living room and sat down on the sofa opposite a well–worn armchair.

"Would you like a cup of tea?"

"Yes please, Gran."

"Would you like anything to eat?"

"I can make you a sandwich if you like."

"Oh yes please. I am hungry."

"Okay, back in a tick," she replied and went into the kitchen.

Nicholas sat and looked around the room. His Mum had been right, he was overdue for a visit, but it had got boring and slightly uncomfortable. All they talked about were the same old things and some days she didn't even remember who he was. It was upsetting so he'd just got fed up with coming round. And he always sat in the living room while she made the tea, he never helped.

He felt an urge to do something different.

He stood up and went to the kitchen.

"Can I give you a hand?" he asked.

"That would be nice, thank you Nicholas," his Gran said as she poured boiling water from the kettle into a tea pot.

"If you could get the cups and saucers, I'll finish your sandwich. Cheese and pickle okay?"

"Yes, that's great, thanks," it had been his favourite since he was child. In fact, his Gran made him many favourites, including toast under the grill, homemade chips and scrambled egg with brown sauce — that was his real favourite.

Nicholas opened the cupboard and placed two cups and saucers on the side.

"Do you remember when we used to bake cakes, Nicholas?"

"Of course, I remember it well."

"And you used to love licking out the bowl afterwards. You used to make such a big deal."

"'Can I lick the bowl out Gran', you used to insist," she said and chuckled.

"That was the best bit," Nicholas said.

"Oh it's a shame that things have to change," she sighed, as she turned the plate and cut the sandwich diagonally with a knife.

"Gran?"

"Well, look at you, all grown up and me so old that I won't be around much longer."

"Don't say that Gran," Nicholas snapped. He hated it when she talked like that.

"It's true though," she said matter–of–factly.

"I'll take the tea," he said, diverting the conversation while he grabbed the pot. "I'll come back for the tea cups. You go and sit yourself down."

Nicholas's sandwich was waiting for him on the coffee table. He was sure that slices of bread were getting smaller. He could almost fit it into his mouth whole.

"Thanks, Gran."

"You don't look like you're eating enough, you're all skin and bone," She said, concerned.

"I'm okay, just haven't had much of an appetite recently that's all," he replied. He took a bite of sandwich. He paused. It was okay, but the bread was a little dry and the cheese past its best. He thought for a moment about some of the things he saw at work but quickly put it out of his mind — he didn't want to make himself sick.

"Is everything okay?"

Nicholas nodded.

"Work going well?"

Nicholas swallowed. "As well as can be expected, it's only Burger Ville. How about you?" Nicholas asked.

"Oh I'm okay. Just waiting for that day when I don't wake up."

Nicholas groaned.

"Well, life has to end one day, and when you get to my age, that day could come at any time."

"And you're okay with that?" Nicholas asked.

"You accept it when you're older. It's a fact of life."

Nicholas didn't want to think about it — it made him sad.

"You remember Irene?"

"The woman who looked like a puffin?"

His Gran laughed, "Yes, the puffin. Well she's no longer with us."

"That's a real shame."

"Yes, it is. But as I said, it is a fact of life. People live and people die."

Nicholas took another bite from the sandwich.

"It would be a good thing if more people died."

"What?" Nicholas said, not quite believing his ears.

"If more people died," his Gran said. "There are just too many people in this world now. I don't know how we're going to cope. Soon they'll have nowhere to live and nothing to eat. The world needs less people."

Nicholas shook his head.

"In the old days it would have been a disease or famine that wiped people out, nature's way of keeping the population under control, but these days our medicine is so good that we'll soon make people live forever. We need a plague — to thin the herd."

Nicholas didn't know what to say.

"I wouldn't want to live forever. I've had my time. I've

done my job."

"Your job?"

"Yes, my job was to be a good wife to your Grandfather, to bring your Mother into the world and look after you when you were young, so your Mother could go to work and earn money to clothe and feed you."

When his Gran got going, she really got going.

"Now people want everything to be easy, automated and done for them. They don't expect to make an effort for anything. They want everything on tap whenever they desire it."

Nicholas put his plate down on the table.

"And they don't want to work for it. Some would rather sit on their arse all day than do a decent day's work. It's been coming for years. It's what did it in for your Grandad's business."

"Grandad's business?"

"Yes, he was a very successful man — until the unions."

"What do you mean? I don't think you've ever mentioned his business before."

"Oh, it was a very sore subject when your Grandad was alive, so we never spoke about it. I guess old habits die hard and we followed his wish."

"But you can tell me now though?"

"Yes, I guess I can," his Gran said, shifting her weight in the chair. "You can pour," she said, motioning towards the tea pot.

Nicholas leaned forward and poured the tea.

"In business, much of it is being in the right place at the right time with the right idea. Your Grandfather originally worked in a factory. Then one day an acquaintance asked if he could make a specialised tool. During his lunch break he made the tool. The man was so impressed that not only did he pay him what they agreed; he paid a little extra too. Your Grandfather thought that he could be onto something, so he quietly put the word out that he could make tools and the next thing he knew the orders came flooding in."

"And he did this during his lunch?" Nicholas asked.

"Well that was the point. He only had a limited amount of time during lunch, plus he was using someone else's machine, this couldn't go on forever, he had to do something."

"And what did he do?"

"He had to buy his own machine. A small fortune those machines cost. We had very little money and even our life savings wouldn't have covered the whole amount?"

"So what did he do?"

"He packed in his job and we borrowed the money. It was the only thing we could do. We borrowed as much from family and friends as possible and went to the bank for the rest. That way we could pay the bank back a smaller amount, save on interest and pay everyone else back as soon as we could."

"It sounds like a big risk." Nicholas said.

"Yes, it was, very much so, but all business is a risk. You don't know for certain that things will work out, you just have to follow your gut instinct and go with it."

"So what then?"

"He also needed somewhere to work. So he set up the machine in the garage. He worked his socks off, day in, day out, all day, every day — and do you know what? Within two months he'd paid off the bank and in four months he'd paid off everyone else."

"But the orders still came flooding in and the jobs got larger and larger and it got to the point that your Grandfather couldn't cope on his own anymore."

Nicholas drank his tea listening intently. His Gran had told him lots of stories before but never this much about his own Grandad.

"He had to invest in more machines and men to operate those machines. Within the first year he had a total of four machines and three extra men and by the end of the second year nine machines and eight men, including a foreman to manage the workmen."

"Wow, things really took off," Nicholas said.

"That's not all. Within five years the business had a workforce of over a hundred men."

"That's amazing. Were they all manning machines?"

"Oh no, by the time the business got to that size your Grandfather needed other staff as well to do the book keeping, accounts, administration, plus delivery drivers for the vans and lorries."

"I had no idea," Nicholas said, gobsmacked.

"He was a very successful man," His Gran said sipping her tea.

"But you said something about the unions?"

"Yes, that's when things changed," she said frowning.

"Your Grandfather was a clever man and he had set the whole factory to work like a well–oiled clockwork mechanism. Some machines took a while to make things and in some cases there was one man to three machines. He'd set it off running and then the next one and the next one and he'd monitor to make sure they were all doing what they were supposed to be doing. But the unions changed all that."

"How?"

"The first thing they said was there had to be equal pay rights, so that everyone doing the same job must be paid the same. But some people had been there longer than others, some people worked faster than others, some people were just better at their job than others and your Grandfather rewarded everyone honestly and fairly."

"And then what happened?"

"Your Grandfather disagreed so they striked."

"Striked?"

"They all laid down their tools and said they wouldn't work until their demands were met."

"But ... that's blackmail?"

"Exactly, they held him to ransom to get what they wanted."

"He didn't give in did he?"

"He had no choice. When the men weren't working, the business wasn't earning. Products weren't getting made and orders weren't being satisfied and clients got unhappy so they went elsewhere."

"Couldn't he just have sacked them?"

"It was nearly the entire workforce. It would take him months to re–employ people and these were skilled engineers. As I said, he had no choice."

"You said that was the first thing?"

"The second was that some people realised they could get away with not doing much. They were all being paid the same amount and the union gave them protection. One of the men was only producing about a tenth of what he should in a day so your Grandfather sacked him, but guess what?"

"They striked?"

"Yes, they striked. Unfair dismissal they called it and demanded that he be reinstated."

"But he wasn't doing his job properly?"

"I know, but strength in numbers. They were like a pack of hyenas when they got going."

"So what did he do?"

"He re—instated him, he had no choice."

Nicholas shook his head — he just couldn't believe it.

"That's not all though. The third thing is what did it in for the business."

"Third thing! What was that?"

"The final nail in the coffin was when the men demanded that there should be one man to one machine."

"But, I thought you said that some men could operate more than one machine?"

"They could, but this was a rule they insisted on, so guess what?"

"They striked," Nicholas said.

"Yes, they striked. Your Grandfather relented. He had to give in to get productivity back on track but six months later, with the increased staffing costs and lack of productivity overall, the company went into receivership."

"But what about Grandad?"

"Well, he tried to keep the company afloat with our own money, but that was just like trying to use a cork to save a sinking ship. We ran out of money and went bankrupt."

"So Grandad lost everything?"

"We lost everything — I worked in the company too. I was effectively his business partner, we made all the decisions together."

"Wow ..." Nicholas thought about everything his Gran had told him. "So the workmen basically forced their own employer out of business."

"Exactly."

"But why would they do that?"

"Who knows? Perhaps a lack of awareness of the big picture or just plain stupidity."

He could see his Gran disappear in thought for a moment.

"Personally, I always suspected that they revelled in the power the union gave them. They knew they could get what they want without truly understanding the implications of their actions. There was a reason after all that those workers weren't running their own businesses."

Nicholas tried to think of an analogy, "So they bit the hand that fed them."

"That's a very good way of looking at it, yes."

Nicholas shook his head in disbelief, "People are weird."

His Gran nodded.

They had chatted for what seemed like hours when Nicholas noticed the time.

"Sorry Gran, I just realised the time. I've got to go and get ready for work."

"Okay dear," she replied getting up from her chair.

"Don't get up. I'll see myself out," Nicholas said. An idea came to him. "Can I come back tomorrow?"

"Of course, it will be lovely to see you again."

"Great, see you tomorrow. Bye."

Chapter 7

The alarm went off.

Nicholas rubbed his eyes.

He'd had the same dream again last night. He saw himself looking down from the sand dune, the animals below, herding people — it was all so real. He had only had one recurring dream in his life before and that was after his Father died.

His Dad popped into his mind for a second but he quickly pushed the memory aside, it was much too painful.

He got dressed, walked out of his room and into the kitchen.

His Mum seemed a bit more relaxed this morning.

"Morning Nicholas," she said. "I've just made your breakfast."

Nicholas inspected the bowl and to his surprise the cornflakes were still crispy. He sat down and began to tuck in.

"Did you see your Gran yesterday?" his Mum asked.

"Yes, I did," Nicholas replied between mouthfuls. "She was really on the ball."

"Oh that's good. She does have her good and bad days."

"And she talked about Grandad."

"Oh yes, what did she say?"

"She told me about his company and how he built it up

from nothing but went out of business due to the unions."

"Oh yes, that was horrible. It was something we couldn't talk about whilst your Grandad was still alive. "

"Why was that though?" Nicholas asked.

"The whole experience made him ill from stress. I don't think he ever properly recovered from it."

She shifted her position in the chair as the memories came back to her.

"I think he felt embarrassed, that he'd let people down and failed. And those he had trusted and relied upon had betrayed him. He built something himself, with his own hands, he employed people, gave them jobs, a livelihood — but then those same people turned on him and destroyed the very thing he created. After that, he lost faith in humanity."

Nicholas thought for a moment. "I said to Gran, it was as if they bit the hand that fed them."

"Yes, exactly," his Mother smiled.

Nicholas reflected on the conversation.

"It's amazing to think, all those years ago, my Grandad, your Dad, actually made a success of his life, just by his own hard work and determination — before others ruined it of course."

His Mother smiled, "Yes, yes, it is, but then I truly believe that you can be anything you want to be, if you want it enough."

Nicholas finished his breakfast and watched his Mum finish hers.

He had lots of thoughts and questions going around in his mind.

"It was really interesting speaking to Gran about her life." Nicholas said.

"In what way?" his Mother asked.

"Oh, just that usually the conversation has been about me, or work, or incidental stuff, but never about her life. It was fascinating."

"Well, you have to remember she's had quite a life."

"We've never spoken about your life, Mum?" Nicholas said.

"That's true, but I don't have the experience that your Gran does."

Nicholas suspected that she was just being modest.

"I am going to see Gran again today."

"Oh that'll be nice. She does get very lonely and her brain needs the stimulation."

"What do you mean?"

"You know, she really needs something to do, to have company and talk, to think and recall memories. It's important that she keeps her brain active as she gets older."

Nicholas nodded.

"Thanks Mum."

"What for?"

"For breakfast — for everything."

His Mother smiled. "No problem — oh my — look at the time!"

Chapter 8

The front door opened.

"Gran, what did I say yesterday about putting the chain on the door?"

"But I knew you were coming."

"That's not the point. You need to take care. There are some nasty people around."

"Oh, come on in."

Nicholas walked through to the living room. On the coffee table was a leaflet. Something about bricks and walls for the house, "What's this?"

"Some man delivered it yesterday. He said that the bricks on the house were so old that they were absorbing water like a sponge and they need re–coating with something to make them waterproof again."

Nicholas inspected it, "Never heard of that before."

"He sounded convincing though."

"Yeah, but it doesn't mean it's genuine does it?"

"He showed me a little experiment with water and a brick. It did what he said it would. It seemed genuine."

Nicholas got out his phone, "Let me Google it."

"Okay, I'll make the tea. Would you like anything to eat?"

"A sandwich would be great, if that isn't any trouble?"

"No trouble. Back in a minute."

Nicholas tapped the search into his phone and sifted through the results. There were several links to sites about painting exterior walls and using breathable paint but that wasn't what he was after. He changed the search phrase and tried again. Finally, he was getting somewhere.

His Gran walked in with a pot of tea and a sandwich.

"As I thought Gran, it's a con."

"What is?"

"This brickwork leaflet. It's a con."

"Hold on, let me get the tea cups and you can tell me all about it."

Nicholas continued to read other articles until his Gran came back.

"So, it's a con. Bricks are porous and they are supposed to absorb water. It's how bricks work. The water doesn't get into your house as the first course of bricks is on the outside, then you have a cavity wall and then the bricks on the inside. The external bricks absorb the water and they dry out again when it stops raining. There is no need to coat the bricks with anything and by doing so you could actually cause more problems."

His Gran nodded.

"So, when they come back, say you don't want it and turn them away."

"Okay."

"So what are you going to do?"

"I'll turn them away, dear."

"Okay, thank you."

Nicholas put his phone down on the coffee table and sat back.

"How's work?" Gran asked.

"I only saw you yesterday. Same as always."

"As long as you're enjoying it, that's the main thing."

Nicholas wondered if his Gran didn't listen properly or if she was having one of her 'off' days.

"Well, that's the point, I am not enjoying it. I hate going to work."

"Well, can't you get another job?"

"There are no other jobs. The job at Burger Ville is all I could get. There are no jobs around, especially for me with no experience."

"Well maybe you could start your own business like your Grandad."

"Yeah, but what would I do? I have no skills, much less the skills to make a tool like Grandad. I have nothing."

"Determination — that is what your Grandad had. He loved doing a good job and he wanted to please people. You just need to have a think and decide what you're passionate about."

"Nothing."

"There must be something."

"No, nothing."

There was silence. His brain began to wander and all of a sudden the thought of the cat popped into his mind.

"Cruelty to animals," his Gran said.

"What?" Nicholas said, not quite believing his ears.

"Cruelty to animals — that's what someone should do something about."

"That's weird, that is exactly what I was just thinking."

"Was it dear?"

"Yes. I saw some kids being cruel to a cat the other night."

"Oh that's awful, is it okay?"

Nicholas struggled to hold back the emotion, "No — it — died."

"Oh poor thing. They don't do anything to deserve it, do they? They're innocent."

"Yes, that's right ..." Nicholas said. "I was watching a programme last week and it mentioned some whales that had been washed up on a beach."

"Oh yes, I saw that, very sad."

"Yes, exactly — and it's becoming more common — they think the sounds made from ships, submarines and various types of equipment are making the oceans so noisy that it interferes with the whales' navigation systems, so they end up swimming into areas they shouldn't be and get trapped."

"Poor whales," Gran said. "Something I've always wondered about is fishing."

"In what way?"

"Well, you have hundreds or even thousands of fishing boats that go out every day with their massive nets, hauling in tons and tons of fish. If they're over quota they have to throw some of them back because they can't sell them."

"It's such a waste," Nicholas said.

"Yes, it is. But, how can that keep going on?"

"Fishing?" Nicholas asked.

"Over–fishing. Taking the fish out of the sea in such great numbers. Do that day in and day out and eventually there won't be any fish left to make new fish."

"That's a good point, it's obvious when you think of it," Nicholas said. He remembered the report he had seen on the BBC website. "Did you see the story on the news about the baby dolphin with people posing for selfies?"

"Selfies?" his Gran asked.

"You know, when people take a photo of themselves on their phone?"

"Oh, the one in Argentina wasn't it?"

"Yes, that's it."

"That was so cruel."

"Yes, it was."

"They don't have much going for them really do they?" His Gran said in a matter—of—fact kind of way.

"What, dolphins?"

"Humans!"

Nicholas thought for a moment, "Not really Gran, no."

"It was their world before ours." Gran said.

Nicholas pondered his Gran's words — she was a wise old bird.

Out of the blue, his Gran had an idea.

"That's what you should do."

"What's that?" Nicholas asked.

"Help save the animals."

As soon as his Gran had spoken his stomach turned over — there was a strange familiarity about her suggestion — something he couldn't quite place — help save the animals.

"What do you mean?" Nicholas asked.

"Do something to help save the animals."

"But there are groups out there who already do that, The World Wildlife Fund, RSPCA — there must be hundreds of them."

"Yes, but they're obviously not doing a very good job if

the animals keep suffering."

She had a point. Again, there was something familiar, as though it made a partial connection in his mind that he couldn't complete.

"I just don't know where I would start."

"Neither did your Grandad when he started his business. Just break the whole thing down into smaller and easier to achieve tasks and work through them one at a time."

"But what about time?"

"You're lucky. You work in the evenings, which means your mornings are free. You can do everything you need to do before work."

"But how would it make money?"

"Charitable donations. If people are giving to the other groups that exist, they'll give money to you."

"And why would people want to support me?"

"When you talk about Burger Ville you talk about it being boring and tedious. When I asked you what other jobs were out there, you said there were none. When I asked you why don't you form your own business, you said you have no skills and no experience. But, when you spoke about the animals, you spoke with passion. Passion, determination and the desire to make a difference is what will make people support you."

"Wow," Nicholas said. He hadn't thought about it like that. He hadn't realised he was passionate about anything.

His Gran had made some excellent points, but then he thought of probably the biggest hurdle of them all.

"But what about finance, I have no money and I'd need money to get it off the ground."

"I'll loan you the money."

"What?"

"Well, if it wasn't for family your Grandad wouldn't have been able to get his business started."

"But?"

"You can pay me back when you can, just as you would any other investor."

"I don't know what to say."

"I need to see a business plan though, with how much you need to borrow and a breakdown of what the money will be used for."

"But I've never written a business plan. I wouldn't know where to start."

"Then research it. You have the world's information at your fingertips with that 'netty' thing on your phone."

"Yes, I suppose I have. We're lucky these days, but what on earth would you have done in your day — there was no internet then, was there?"

"We would have gone to the library and borrowed books and probably paid specialists for their services."

"Wow, that would have taken even more time and money."

"Exactly, nowadays you can do anything you put your mind to much more easily than we ever could."

"Yes, Gran, you're right, it is easier now."

"Well there you go then."

Nicholas had been so engrossed in their discussion that his tea had gone cold and he'd forgotten to eat his sandwich.

"For the first time in my life I feel inspired and motivated."

"Excellent! I can see the same look on your face that I saw on your Grandad's all those years ago."

Nicholas smiled.

"Sorry I let my tea get cold but I'll take my sandwich and eat it on the way home."

"Are you going already?"

"Yes, I want to make a start on this straight away."

"Okay dear."

"Thanks Gran." Nicholas grabbed the sandwich, "Thanks for everything."

***

Nicholas had a spring in his step.

He chewed his way through the bread and cheese. It was slightly beyond its best but he didn't care, he felt inspired.

He struggled to connect his thoughts.

He remembered his Gran saying 'help save the animals', what was it? Why did this feel so familiar to him — then like a bolt of lightning — it hit him — his dream!

"The animals!" Nicholas said aloud. He looked around to make sure no one had heard his outburst.

The animals. In his dream.

Now it was all starting to make sense.

This is what he was destined to do.

He quickened his pace and rushed home.

Chapter 9

It was early on Saturday morning and Nicholas was already up and on his computer, researching and writing the business plan that his Gran had asked him to put together.

He could hardly concentrate at work last night. His mind kept drifting. He felt slightly sorry for some customers with overdone burgers, but only slightly. He had hardly slept either, with thoughts going around in his mind, the thrill, the excitement — why had he never experienced these feelings before?

Because he had never done anything like this before — that's why.

He was surprised at how easy and straightforward he had found it, so far. Just as his Gran had suggested — break it down into smaller tasks and do each one at a time.

What is a business plan? was his first question:

A business plan is a formal statement of business goals, reasons they are attainable, and plans for reaching them. It may also contain background information about the organization or team attempting to reach those goals.

"Thank you Google and Wikipedia," Nicholas said aloud. That made sense. He had to convince his Gran that this was going to work.

He knew his business goal; it was to help save the animals, but as he continued to write, it naturally began to expand and he realised that in order to save the animals, he also had to save their eco–systems, which in turn meant he needed to — "Save the planet!" Nicholas said aloud.

There was a knock at the door and his Mum walked in.

"Nicholas?" His Mum said with a pile of washing in her arms, "Are you okay?"

"Er, yes, fine thanks."

"I thought I heard you say something."

"Oh yes, talking to myself."

His Mum looked around. She noticed the computer and scribbled notes on a pad beside. She sensed his excited mood.

"What are you up to?"

"I am writing a business plan for a new venture."

"Really, what is it?"

"I don't want to say anything just yet. Let me finish it and then you can read it and tell me what you think. That way it won't spoil the surprise."

His Mother smiled, impressed by his enthusiasm. "Okay, I look forward to that."

She closed the door and let him get on with it.

Nicholas momentarily lost his train of thought but it didn't take long for it to return.

He kept typing, the words flowing automatically.

He kept searching, one result linking on to another and another. He researched trusts, charities, trustees and their obligations, so much information at his fingertips.

He kept reading and taking in the fascinating information in front of him.

Time passed.

Chapter 10

It was Monday. The weekend had gone in a flash and Nicholas stood at his Gran's front door.

He rang the bell and waited for his Gran to open the door. He was excited. He held the business plan tightly in his hand.

The door opened partially, the chain was on.

"Who is it?" a voice called out?

"It's me Gran, it's Nicholas."

"Who?"

"Nicholas, your Grandson."

It took a moment to register. "Hold on," his Gran said.

Something didn't feel right but he hoped it was just that his Gran was having a bit of an 'off' day.

"Hi Gran, I've done it, I've put the business plan together," Nicholas said as the door opened.

He rushed in.

"I spent the whole weekend on it as I had to do so much research on things I didn't know, like how charities work plus so much investigation into examples where I believe the charity could help."

Nicholas hurried through to the living room and sat down.

His Gran entered, slowly, sheepishly — something definitely wasn't right.

"Gran, what is it?"

"Something happened at the weekend," she said as she sat down.

"What do you mean, something happened? What happened?"

"You remember those brick people, the ones who left the leaflet?"

Nicholas nodded.

"Well, I did as you suggested and turned them away, but later in the day two men turned up to say that they'd noticed a problem with my roof. "

Nicholas didn't like the sound of where this was going.

"They said they could sort it out there and then for £10, otherwise if it wasn't done, it would get worse and it could cost thousands."

"What did you do, Gran?"

"I let them in."

"And then what happened?"

"They said they needed to go up into the attic so I told them where it was and they went up. I could hear the loft hatch open so I know they went up there."

"But you did watch what they were up to?"

"No, I left them to it."

"Oh Gran — So, what happened?"

His Gran gave him a look that was a combination of guilt, disappointment and regret.

"Did they take anything?"

"Well, all my jewellery was still where it was."

"I'd even left my watch on the side because of this rash on my wrist, so, although they had been through my bedroom, I think I was fortunate — it could have been worse."

"What did they take, Gran?"

She hung her head in shame, "They took the money."

"The money? What do you mean — the money?"

"They took my savings."

"You kept money in the house?"

"Yes, of course."

"But that's what banks are for."

"But what if I needed to get access to it?" his Gran said.

"But that's what cash machines are for and withdrawals over the counter."

"Yes but you can only take out a certain amount each day and they ask so many questions about what the money is for, what are you going to do with it, where did you get it in the first place. I just don't like banks these days."

Nicholas took a deep breath and realised there was no point in saying anything else.

He sighed, "How much did they take?"

"Ten ..." his Gran mumbled.

"Sorry, I didn't hear that properly — how much?"

"Ten thousand pounds."

"Ten thousand pounds!? — you kept ten thousand pounds in your bedroom?"

Nicholas didn't know what to say.

He'd gone from sheer excitement when he stepped through the door to utter astonishment and disappointment. He opened the pages of the business plan in his lap and turned to the last page. There, underlined, was a figure that he had meticulously calculated over the weekend. He didn't want to be greedy and he didn't want to be unrealistic.

It was the bare minimum he needed to get the project underway.

He listened to his Gran's voice going around and around in his head, "ten thousand pounds — ten thousand pounds", he looked at the figure again — he just couldn't believe it — £10,000.

"Anyway, enough about my bad news, what about your plan, you say you've finished it?"

"What?" Nicholas hadn't heard her properly.

"Your business plan," his Gran gestured to the paper he was holding in his hands.

Nicholas closed the pages, "I don't think it's the right time to discuss it now." He tossed it onto the coffee table.

"Anyway, what did the police say?"

"I didn't phone them."

"What? You were burgled and you didn't phone the police!"

"It's my own silly fault for letting them in."

"But you at least told Mum, right?"

"I didn't want to bother her with it."

"Oh what? You've got to tell Mum. I'll phone her now."

"But, she'll be at work."

Nicholas shook his head, got out his phone and dialled.

It rang. He imagined his Mum hearing her phone ring and then rummaging around in her bag. She answered.

"Hi Mum, sorry to trouble you at work but I need to talk to you," Nicholas said.

"Gran let two men in the house and they stole her money," he relayed the story to his Mother.

"Er, hold on."

"When did this happen?" Nicholas said looking at his Gran.

"It was about four o'clock on Saturday afternoon." Gran replied.

"Four o'clock on Saturday afternoon."

"Okay, Okay. Yes, I'll do that. Yep, will do. Okay. Bye Mum."

Nicholas hung up.

"She said phone the police."

"Okay," Gran said, she realised it wasn't worth arguing.

***

Nicholas opened the door.

It wasn't an emergency by any means but it had taken nearly three hours for them to arrive.

"We had a report of a burglary, are you the victim?" The burly policeman asked, his expression clearly indicating he thought Nicholas was too young to be the homeowner.

"No, it's my Gran, come on in." Nicholas said opening the door for the policeman who towered above him and his female colleague.

"I phoned nearly three hours ago," Nicolas said.

"We're very busy and under–resourced," the officer said, indicating he was unsure of where he should be going.

"Through the door on the right," Nicholas pointed.

The officer nodded and removed his hat.

Nicholas followed them in.

"The police are here."

"Would you like a cup of tea?" Gran said, preparing to stand.

"It's okay love, you sit down, we're fine."

"Do you mind if we sit?" the policeman asked.

"Oh yes, please do — and help yourself to a biscuit if you want," Gran said gesturing to a plate of chocolate digestives.

The policeman and his colleague sat on the sofa, "Thanks."

The female officer took out a little black book and a pencil and made a few notes.

Nicholas sat on the arm of his Gran's chair and placed his hand on her shoulder to comfort her.

"We've had a report of a burglary. Apparently some money was taken. Can you tell me about it please?"

"On Saturday afternoon at four o'clock, two men called at the door saying that they had noticed a problem with my roof. They said they could fix it for ten pounds and that if they didn't it could get worse and end up costing me thousands."

The female officer made notes.

"And then?" the policeman asked.

"I let them in. They said they needed to get into the attic so I told them where it was and let them get on with it. They were up there quite a while and they were definitely in the attic cause I could hear the loft hatch go and them moving around. Then, when they had finished, they said they were all done and left."

"And did you pay them?" The policeman asked.

"Yes, ten pounds as agreed."

"And then what happened?"

"I went up later, probably about six o'clock to put some washing away and noticed that some of the things in my bedroom had been moved. I looked in my wardrobe and my money had gone."

"How much?"

"Ten thousand pounds."

The female officer stopped writing with her pencil hovering over the page. "Sorry madam, did you say ten thousand pounds?"

"Yes, all my savings."

"You do realise that is what banks are for, to look after your money," the policeman said.

"That's exactly what Nicholas said earlier."

"And you are?" the policeman looked at Nicholas and asked.

"I am Nicholas."

"I gathered that. What relation are you?"

"Oh I see — Grandson."

The female officer noted.

"Can you remember what the men looked like?" the policeman asked.

"Oh yes, I've got a photographic memory. The first one was ..."

"It's okay love. I'll ask for an artist to come round and take more details. We'll also ask your neighbours if they saw anything."

The policeman looked at his colleague in case she wanted to add anything.

"Was there anything else leading up to the event that seemed out of place or odd?" the female officer asked.

"No, I don't think so," his Gran said.

Nicholas raised his hand, "There were the other men who

came round, about the bricks Gran. They left a leaflet."

"Oh yes, the men about the bricks in the walls," his Gran remembered.

"Yes," Nicholas said. "I Googled it, it's a scam where they coat your bricks to stop them absorbing water."

"Oh yes, we've had reports of them recently. They're a scout team for the burglars. Sent on ahead to find potential victims. It's probably what's happened here," the female officer said, making notes.

"Do you still have the leaflet?" The policeman asked.

"Er, yes, it's in the recycling," Gran replied.

"I'll get it," Nicholas said.

There was an uneasy silence.

Gran kneaded her hands whilst the female police officer put her book away in her pocket.

The policeman picked up a biscuit and took a bite. It broke in half and landed on the floor. He looked at his colleague, pulled a face, picked up the broken biscuit and put it on the edge of the table.

"Well, at least I got my roof fixed."

"Sorry?" the policeman asked.

Nicholas walked back in wondering what they were talking about.

"If there is one thing to get out of this, at least I got my roof fixed."

"No, you don't understand, there was no problem with your roof. You were a victim of a clever scam. The brick people try it on but also act as scouts to make sure you were vulnerable. The roof people were the actual criminals. It's all a scam. They just wanted your money."

Gran was visibly shaken. "Oh my ..."

Nicholas placed a supportive hand on her shoulder and then handed the leaflet to the policeman.

"Thank you. We'll send this to the lab for tests. It all helps."

The policeman and his colleague stood up.

"When do you think you'll get my money back?" Gran asked.

"I'm sorry to have to say that you'll probably never see it again," the policeman bent down in front of her. "Even if we do catch these people, we need evidence against them. Even if we do find the money, there is nothing to actually link it to you. It's your word against theirs. Sorry."

"Oh dear, I was going to help Nicholas with his new project."

Gran became even more shaken. She looked at the policeman, she looked at Nicholas. It was as though all her hopes had been taken away.

The policeman looked at Nicholas, shrugged and shook his head.

"Thank you for coming," Nicholas said. "Good luck."

"We'll see ourselves out."

Nicholas sat back down on the sofa and heard the front door close. An uncomfortable silence followed, neither wanting to speak for fear of saying the wrong thing.

"Sorry Nicholas, I've let you down."

"No you haven't Gran, don't be silly."

Another silence followed.

Nicholas noticed the broken biscuit and the crumbs on the floor.

"Look, he's made a mess on the floor. Where's the vacuum cleaner?" Nicholas said.

"It's in the cupboard under the stairs."

"Oh ..." Nicholas stopped dead in his tracks, a feeling of anxiety rushing through him.

His Gran looked at him perplexed but then it dawned on her.

"Sorry Nicholas, I wasn't thinking. Don't worry, I'll do it."

Nicholas took a number of deep breaths and regained control of his breathing.

"I'd better go. I'll give Mum an update and I need to get ready for work."

"I didn't think you started till later?"

"Yes, but I've got a few things to do first."

"Okay dear, you have a good day."

"Oh and Gran."

"Yes?"

"Just remember to keep the chain on at all times."

"Oh yes, dear, I won't make the same mistake twice."

Nicholas left closing the front door behind him.

As he stepped out into the street he looked around waiting a moment for his heart to stop racing. When he had arrived earlier he had been so full of hope and excitement and now he felt empty, disappointed and full of resentment at the mean, horrible, nasty bastards who could take money from his Gran.

Chapter 11

Nicholas woke up. He'd had the most bizarre dream.

He had dreamt that he was the judge in court. They had caught the two men who had taken his Gran's money and it was his responsibility to try them. The evidence was irrefutable and yet they had both pleaded not guilty. They had said that his Gran had paid them ten thousand pounds in cash to repair the roof and her mind had been in a muddle thinking it was just ten pounds. Their lawyer had pleaded their case and now it was time to hear from the jury.

He remembered doing a double–take in his dream when he realised the jury consisted of animals sitting upright in the jury box stalls with disapproving expressions on their animal faces. He asked them for their verdict and a unanimous 'guilty' was given.

The sentencing was swift, harsh and satisfying.

"Your actions were despicable and callous. I sentence you to death for picking on a defenceless and vulnerable old lady — take them away!" Nicholas ordered.

He had felt something brush against him. He looked round and there was a dolphin, standing next to him with its flipper resting on his shoulder. Then the flipper slapped him round the face and he woke up with a start.

He had been lying on his arm and his hand had gone dead. He'd obviously moved in his sleep and his hand had brushed his face. It had made him jump.

He'd had so many odd dreams of late that he'd even asked his Mum about them. She told him that the brain can often try to tell you things in your sleep. It can give you answers to questions, guidance on what to do or where to turn, but he was still confused by what it all meant.

He looked at the clock — breakfast time.

***

"You're up early."

"Woke up early. Did you speak to Gran last night?"

"Yes, I did," his Mum replied. "Thank you for calling the police and being with her when they arrived. She puts up this front of being brave and capable but when you get old you lose confidence. It happens to everyone."

"That's okay. Was she alright?" Nicholas asked as he sat down and poured some cornflakes into a bowl.

"A bit shocked I think, and disappointed."

"Disappointed?" Nicholas asked.

"Because she couldn't help you with your new venture."

Nicholas shrugged.

"She told me all about it too."

Nicholas snapped his head to look at her, "But she doesn't know anything about it yet."

"Obviously she does, she explained it all to me."

Nicholas shook his head, but how? He had taken the business plan but then he had phoned the police and …

"Oh of course, I left the business plan on the coffee table."

"Your Gran was very impressed and so am I. To think that my Nicholas could come up with such a professional document and enterprising vision of what he wants to do. Well done."

Nicholas couldn't remember the last time his Mother had been so complimentary about him. He blushed.

"Only one problem though, I need money to get it going."

"Yes, she mentioned that too, and that is why she is so disappointed. Especially when the police told her that, even if they caught the criminals, she wouldn't get the money back."

Nicholas nodded whilst he ate.

"I only wish ..." his Mother stopped short and rubbed her eye.

He knew what she was going to say, 'I only wish your Father was here.' She didn't say it often but when she did, it was an emotional reminder of a very big hole in their lives.

They sat in silence for a few minutes. It was as though his Mother had been plucking up the courage to say something. She finally spoke.

"Money isn't a good topic at the moment."

"Why's that?"

"I haven't told you this, because I didn't want to worry you, but they're having some problems at work. They've got to make some cutbacks to save money and we've had to re-apply for our jobs."

"Reapply?"

"Yes, basically they interview us for our existing positions."

Nicholas wanted to make sure he understood this correctly, "So they interview you for the jobs you're already doing, even though you're already doing them?"

"Yes, that's right."

"But, what's the point?"

"I suspect it's to prevent them having to make a difficult decision themselves."

"In what way?"

"Well, being a manager isn't easy. You need to be firm and make tough decisions at difficult times all in the best interests of the company. I suspect that the managers — and my manager in particular — are struggling with having to make a decision, so they're leaving it to the Human Resources department to carry out this process for them."

"Getting someone else to do the dirty work for them, you mean," Nicholas said.

"Yes, basically."

"So when is your interview?"

"Last week."

Nicholas remembered, "So that explains why you were all tense and rushing around that morning."

"Yes, that's right. I was really nervous."

"But you've been doing your job for ..." Nicholas tried to think.

"Thirteen years," his Mother added.

"Thirteen years," he repeated, staggered that it had been the majority of his life.

"I read recently whilst I was researching the business plan that it takes ten years of doing something before you can be considered to be an expert, and you've been doing your job for thirteen years. Anyway, I thought it was you who kept the company running?"

"It is, but that's what life is like, unfair. My boss has only been there six months and I think he feels threatened by me as I've been there so long and I know so much — much more than him."

Nicholas butted in, "So why didn't they make you the manager?"

"Because I am not a man."

"But that doesn't make sense, what difference does that make?"

"Well the MD is an older gentleman who believes that the key people should be men."

"But surely that's discrimination?"

"It is, but it goes on regardless and it's difficult to prove, it's just the way it is."

"That's unfair."

His Mother nodded.

"And when do you find out?"

"Today."

"Today? Okay, well, I am sure you'll be alright."

His Mum smiled. His naivety was sweet but she knew otherwise. She felt sick with worry.

"I'd better go. It'll show that I'm keen and willing if I'm there early," his Mother said as she checked her bag and grabbed her coat.

"Okay Mum, see you later — good luck."

She kissed her fingers, touched his cheek and left.

He rubbed his face with the back of his hand as he heard the front door shut. He sat staring at the remaining flakes of corn in his bowl. He had a feeling that things were about to change.

Chapter 12

Nicholas rang the bell and waited.

After a minute, his Gran opened the door and he was pleasantly surprised to see the chain still on.

"It's me Gran, its Nicholas."

"Oh hello Nicholas, come on in."

She fumbled with the chain and opened the door. He walked in.

"I've got a visitor today, she's in the living room, but it's okay, you can go through."

Nicholas was intrigued as he stepped into the living room.

"Ahh, Mrs. Lorenz. Hello, I haven't seen you for ages."

"Oh hello Nicholas. Haven't you got tall, you're all grown–up, a young man."

"Don't get up," Nicholas said sitting down beside her on the sofa.

"There is more tea in the pot, I'll get another cup," his Gran said.

"I hear you're working for a big multi–national company?" Mrs. Lorenz said.

"Burger Ville — I work for Burger Ville," Nicholas remarked.

"But they've got outlets across the world?" She said.

"Yes, I suppose that is one way of looking at it."

His Gran walked back in with a cup."

"Here you are Nicholas."

"Thanks, Gran," Nicholas said and poured himself a cup of tea from the pot.

His Gran chuckled, "Do you remember when you used to sip tea out of the saucer? You were so small then. Do you remember that Ava?"

"Yes Lil, I remember when he was small, yes, how could I forget." Mrs. Lorenz said and reached out to squeeze his cheek.

Nicholas recoiled and forced a smile.

"So, how are you Mrs. Lorenz?"

"Oh, I could be worse. Hearing is going, eyes are going, can't walk as far as I used to but I mustn't grumble. I am lucky to be around considering."

"Do you remember when ..."

His Gran and Mrs Lorenz began to reminisce.

He had heard the stories before, of how her family had escaped the Nazi's during the Second World War. Many of their friends and family had gone on trains to the concentration camps.

Mrs Lorenz and her parents narrowly avoided being captured by the SS. They were trying to escape Germany by hiding underneath a blanket in the back of a farmer's cart. It was delivering hay to a nearby village where the resistance had strong support. It was stopped at a checkpoint when a young Nazi soldier found them whilst carrying out an inspection.

Apparently he had looked shocked and unsure of what to do. Thankfully he let them go but if he had alerted his senior officer they would almost certainly have been shot.

Nicholas sipped his tea and listened to their stories. It was a fascinating insight into a different generation. It was such a simple existence, with no TV, no mobiles, no computers and certainly no internet — he just couldn't imagine it.

"Anyway, I must be off," Mrs Lorenz said.

"Sorry, I hope I haven't intruded?" Nicholas said, worried that he had disrupted their plans.

"Oh no, I need to get the bus, I've got an appointment at the hospital."

"How long has it been, Ava?" Gran asked.

"I had to wait three months for the referral and then four months for the appointment — they just can't seem to cope. I joked to your Gran I'd be dead before I had the appointment," Ava chuckled.

Nicholas smiled. He didn't think it was that funny.

Mrs Lorenz struggled to stand and Nicholas helped her to her feet.

"Do you need any help?"

"I'll be fine dear. The bus stop is just a few doors along."

"Well, thanks for popping by Ava."

"Nice to see you Lil', I'll pop in again next week."

Nicholas sat back down as he listened to the chattering voices from the hallway and then the front door closed.

"Now then Nicholas, what are you going to do?" his Gran said as she walked back into the room and eased herself into the chair.

"What do you mean?"

"I have no money to lend you, so what are you going to do?"

Nicholas shrugged his shoulders.

"What does that mean?" His Gran asked.

"Well, there is no point now is there?" Nicholas replied and shrugged his shoulders again.

"You've written an excellent business plan. You clearly understand what you want to do and how you want to do it — of course there is a point."

"But I can't do it without money."

"Exactly, so get the money."

Nicholas was confused. They were going around in circles.

"But you said it yourself. You don't have the money to lend me."

"And what if I hadn't had the money in the first place or even suggested it, what would you have done then?"

"Erm, well ..." Nicholas thought for a moment, "I guess I might not have even written the business plan or even talked about the project in the first place."

"Exactly, so call it fate, call it whatever you like but consider that everything that happens, happens for a reason — now, what are you going to do about it?"

Nicholas felt as though he was on the spot, "I don't know." He thought about his Grandfather and his business and how he had borrowed money from family and the bank. "I'll try the bank."

"There you go. You've got your answer."

Chapter 13

Nicholas sat in the end chair of three, waiting for the bank's Business Development Adviser to become available. He was nervous. He remembered opening a savings account with his Dad when he was about twelve. Maybe he didn't have a concept of nerves at that age, or maybe it was just because his Dad had been with him. He looked at the empty chair beside him. He really missed his Father.

He had made an appointment for ten o'clock but apparently previous meetings had run on and it was now ten–fifteen.

He looked around. He remembered his Gran saying that banks don't look like banks anymore but he didn't know what they used to look like to make the comparison. He saw a very smart and modern interior with lots of curves, painted white. It reminded him very much of an interior he saw at Ikea when he last went with his Mum.

"Mr Savage?" A voice called out from his side.

"Yes, that's me."

"My name is Maciej. This way please," the man said, his accent being a little tricky to follow.

Nicholas stood up and followed the young man who had called his name.

He appeared to be only a little older than him so Nicholas presumed he must be on work experience and perhaps he was being taken to see the Business Development Adviser in his office.

They walked around a curved partition and sat down. Nicholas noticed a name plate on the desk, Maciej Winogrodzki, Business Development Adviser.

Nicholas had a deep suspicion this wasn't going to go well.

The man tapped on a computer keyboard, clicked his mouse, typed a few things and eventually turned to him.

"How can I help you?"

"Thank you for seeing me. I would like a business loan for my new venture," Nicholas said, smiling profusely and handing the man his business plan document.

The man placed the business plan on the desk, tapped on a computer keyboard and moved the mouse.

"We have a number of different lending products available dependent on your specific needs, including a Base Rate Loan, a Fixed Rate Loan, a Commercial Fixed Rate Loan and an SME Fixed Rate Loan ..."

Maciej continued to speak, flicking his eyes between the computer screen and Nicholas, reading from what was obviously a script.

Nicholas felt himself drifting off. He hadn't heard what he wanted. Why offer something without knowing what he intends to do.

Maciej finally finished and seemed to be awaiting his response.

"Do any of those products interest you?"

"Don't you want to know more about what I am intending to do?"

"I am sorry?" Maciej replied.

"Don't you want to know about my business plan?" Nicholas said, gesturing to the document on the desk.

"We haven't got to that stage yet, I need to know what product you are interested in."

"Well, I presume by product you mean loan, but how do I know what loan I want, I was hoping you could tell me what loan I need."

"It doesn't work that way, I need to know what product you are interested in."

Nicholas was starting to lose his patience. He had got it from his Dad, his Mum had told him. Woe betide anyone who didn't make sense in front of his Dad and woe betide Maciej if this continued.

Nicholas took a deep breath.

"I need a loan."

"And which of our business loan products are you interested in?"

"I'd like to borrow ten thousand pounds."

"Which product, the Base Rate Loan, the Fixed Rate Loan, the ..."

"Maciej," Nicholas did the best to pronounce his name, "You don't need to tell me again. I just need your standard, basic, simple business loan."

"That would be either the Base Rate Loan or the Fixed Rate Loan."

"I'll go for the Fixed Rate."

"Okay, so that is the Fixed Rate Loan for our Business

Loan product," Maciej said as he tapped the responses into the computer.

"And how much are you looking to borrow and over what term?"

"I've already said. Ten thousand pounds and term, er, say two years?"

"Ten thousand pounds," the man repeated, tapping on his keyboard. "Over two years."

"And what do you want the money for?"

"To help fund a new business venture."

The man tapped on his keyboard and closely inspected the computer screen for what questions to ask next.

"And what is the nature of the business?"

"To help save animals."

The man looked at him, "Like a zoo?"

"A zoo? No. It's all in the business plan," Nicholas snapped.

"But I haven't seen your business plan."

"It's there in front of you!"

"I haven't read it."

"I know you haven't read it, I am trying to say that all the answers to your questions are in the business plan sitting in front of you — right there," Nicholas growled.

"The business plan will accompany your application where head office will make a decision as to whether to approve your loan or not."

"So you don't decide yourself?"

"No, that is not my job. My job is to take your details against which to process your application."

Nicholas was deflated, "I see."

"Would you like to continue with your application?"

"Yes, I would."

Maciej looked at the screen and read back through the application as if to remind himself where they were in the process.

"So, you are starting a zoo?"

"No, it's not a zoo — it's a charity to ..."

"We do not lend to charities," Maciej interrupted.

"What?"

"It is our policy not to lend to charities. We do not have any products available to you."

"Why?"

"I don't know why."

"But you are the ..." Nicholas checked the name tag on the desk, "Business Development Adviser — advise me!"

Maciej turned to his screen, tapped a key and read from his help guide: "It is our policy to not lend to charities, trusts or charitable organisations as usually income cannot be guaranteed as the organisation is reliant upon the generosity of others." Maciej continued, "A charitable ..."

"That's fine, you've told me enough," Nicholas said. "You realise it would have saved a lot of time if you'd just looked at the business plan."

"The business plan supports the application and is sent to head office ..."

"Yes, yes, you told me that, it's just — well, what does it say on the front of the business plan."

"I am sorry?"

"On the front page of the business plan, right in front of you, what does it say?"

The man looked down and read from the front page: "A charitable organisation to help save animals and make a valuable contribution to the prevention of further damage to our planet, by Nicholas Savage."

The man looked up.

"Yes, it says here that it is a charitable organisation."

Nicholas looked at him with a 'told you so' expression on his face.

"It is our policy to not lend to charities."

"I know, you've told me."

Nicholas sighed.

"Look, Maciej, how long have you been doing this job?"

"I am sorry?"

"How long have you been employed by this bank doing this job?"

"I have been Business Development Adviser for six months and before that as a teller for twelve months."

"Right, so you've been with the bank now for eighteen months, so you know quite a bit about banks and money and loans I presume?"

"Yes, that is correct."

"Right then, so without reading from scripts or advising me on company policy, just talk to me now as an experienced bank and loan person."

Maciej just stared at him.

"In your experience, would there be any bank out there, anywhere, at all, that is likely to offer me a loan for a charitable organisation?"

Nicholas watched as Maciej fought against the instinct to quote bank scripture.

In his mind, he encouraged the man to respond. Finally, he spoke.

"There are specialist lenders who provide loans to charities but normally they would be guaranteed by assets or guarantors."

"Thank you Maciej, that is very helpful."

"Also, previous experience would be taken into consideration. You are very young, you probably don't have any experience in business or running a charity, that may go against you — if you will forgive me for saying."

Nicholas was annoyed, but he finally appreciated the honesty.

"That's fine. In those two sentences you've been more helpful than in this whole session — thank you."

"You're welcome," Maciej smiled and nodded. "Is there anything else that I can help you with today?"

"No Maciej, I think that is enough for one day."

Nicholas grabbed his business plan, stood up and left.

Chapter 14

Nicholas flopped onto the sofa.

"So, how did you get on, yesterday, at the bank?" His Gran asked.

"It was a nightmare!"

"How come?"

"To coin a phrase that you've often used, it was like pulling teeth."

She laughed. "Everything is a nightmare these days, if it's not some automated phone system, you have to use the internet or you have to deal with people who don't know what they are talking about."

"That's what it was like. He just kept reading from a script and wouldn't read the plan."

"He didn't even read the business plan?"

"No, it was to accompany the product application."

"Product?" His Gran thought she had misheard him.

"Yes, product, that's what they call it.

"But why don't they just call it a loan?"

"They call it a loan too, but it's a product, apparently."

"See why I don't like banks. They don't even look like banks anymore."

"I thought of you saying that whilst I was waiting. So what did they look like?"

"Well, I worked in a bank for a while when your Grand-father's business went under. Our bank had wooden panelling, benches against the walls, tall tables so you could write your paying–in slips standing up and about fourteen cash desks, and I worked in one of those positions."

"It's not like that anymore. Modern, white, plastic, curves — it reminded me more like a showroom out of Ikea."

"I don't really know what that is?"

"Ikea, the furniture store."

His Gran shook her head. "Oh, and the smell — it smelled of old wood, and money."

"This one just smelled of cleaning products, like carpet cleaner. We don't really use cash much these days."

There was an uncomfortable silence as the thought of the missing ten thousand pounds coincidentally flashed through both of their minds.

"Anyway, the loan, did you get it?"

"No, they don't lend to charities."

"I suspected that would be the case," his Gran said.

"What?"

"I suspected that they wouldn't give you the loan."

"Then why did you let me go through with it?" Nicholas asked in disbelief.

"Because you need the experience."

"What do you mean?"

"Okay — How did you feel when you were waiting at the bank?"

Nicholas wasn't sure where this was going but thought he'd play along.

"Nervous."

"You were nervous. Yet, you went ahead and did it anyway, so what does that tell you about yourself?"

"That I can do things?"

"Yes, despite being nervous or never having done something before, you can do it."

Nicholas nodded, she had a point.

"And, how did you find the experience?"

"Erm, frustrating, infuriating and disappointing."

"Disappointing, why?"

"Because it wasted both of our time."

"And this is what business is like, full of frustration when things don't turn out the way you want, or being reliant on others who let you down and waste your time."

Nicholas nodded, she was right.

"And, importantly, how did you feel after the meeting?"

"After?"

"Yes, after the meeting, having been given the decision that they wouldn't lend you the money."

"Er, I guess it made me more determined to try to get the money from somewhere else, to show them I can do it regardless of my age and experience."

"You see. Compare that to how you felt two days ago sitting where you are now on the sofa."

Nicholas realised, she had a point, a very good point.

"If I had said, don't bother, they won't lend it to you, you would have accepted what I said and not had this experience, this very experience that has left you more motivated to make it happen."

Nicholas smiled.

"You said regardless of your age and experience?" His

Gran remembered.

"Yes, that's what he said, I am young and I have no experience."

"Well, what he doesn't know is that you are wiser than your years, largely due to you spending more time with me and your parents than with others your own age. Use that to your advantage."

"Use it how?"

"Show people how mature you are, it will help you stand out."

"What people?"

"When the time comes, you will know."

Nicholas always felt slightly infuriated when his Gran spoke in riddles.

"When he criticised your age and experience, how did you feel?"

"Annoyed — No, more than that — Angry."

"Criticism can be very difficult to take, but just remember it is just one person's view, rightly or wrongly, it is just their opinion. Whilst it might affect how they do business with you or how they perceive you, it can't hurt you. But, do listen to what they say, as it may help you change your approach or adjust something to work in your favour."

"Okay, I will."

"Your business plan was excellent by the way — very well written."

"Thank you, I'd put a lot of time into it. All weekend."

"I can see that, but, it does need improving in a few areas."

"Really, where's that?"

"A name, the charity needs a proper name."

"Okay. And what else?"

"It didn't say much about you."

"There isn't much to say?"

"Is there not?"

"Like the man at the bank said, I don't have any experience?"

"But you have vision and passion and the determination to make this work, to make a difference. You write so much about what you will do and how you will do it but not why you are doing it."

Nicholas listened.

"You will be the face and the name behind this charity — you will be why it succeeds. You will be its figurehead, the statesman, you will be doing interviews and talks and you will travel the world."

"But — how do you know that?"

"Instinct. Intuition. Gut feeling."

"Wow ..."

"But, remember — it's up to you to make it happen."

Nicholas nodded and smiled, "Gran, how did you get to be so wise?"

She laughed, "Wise? I don't know about that."

"More knowledge than wisdom — when it was clear your Grandfather's company was becoming more successful, I went to evening college to study business — plus I did a lot of research using books from the library."

She thought for a moment, "The most important thing of all though is experience."

"Experience?"

"Yes. If you think about it, your entire future is shaped by your experiences, so try to put yourself in as many situations as possible and you will become more experienced and ultimately much wiser for it."

Nicholas thought about that for a moment, "Experience — I will — thank you."

Chapter 15

Nicholas was having so much fun creating the business plan that work was now just a distraction. He opened the back door to the restaurant. The familiar odour of cleaning products and chips hit the back of his nose.

He took off his hoodie, rolled it up and put it in his locker. He heard a voice from behind call his name.

"Nicholas. I need you on the counter tonight," his manager said.

"I prefer to cook."

"The counter please, as soon as you're ready, we're busy. It's good experience."

"But ..." there was that word his Gran used — experience — it changed his mind.

"Yes, okay, just coming."

Nicholas rushed over and tapped his personnel number into the till.

"Yes sir, what can I get you?"

He took the order and processed it, then another and another. There was one good thing about working on the tills he realised, the passage of time, it went so quickly. He'd been there an hour and it had gone in a flash.

"You're doing well Nicholas," his manager said.

"The only thing is though — try not to carry too many things at once."

"Sorry, what do you mean?"

"I noticed that often you walk back with several items in your hand, a box of nuggets and a shake for instance. If you carry one at a time back to the counter you won't drop them."

"But I haven't dropped anything?"

"I know, I am just saying, the less you carry, the less chance you may drop something."

"But I won't drop anything because I won't let go of it and going back twice to the same area would be wasting my time when I could easily be carrying them both."

"But that is what I am asking you to do."

"But it's inefficient."

His manager gave him a look and he knew what was going to come out of her mouth next.

"That's an order, Nicholas."

"Yes, Boss," Nicholas replied and turned to serve the next customer.

"Yes madam, what can I get you?"

Nicholas walked back and forth between the counter and the shelves, mumbling under his breath about how inefficient his service had now become. Sure it was only six feet or so, but that wasn't the point, it was the principle, he was now less efficient than he had been previously.

As he served people on auto–pilot, his mind returned to some of the things his Gran said about not being able to trust others.

He heard raised voices from the front of the restaurant.

"Wanker!"

There was a youth, probably early twenties and tall, wearing a vest and covered in tattoos. He was squabbling with another man, shorter, chubbier and with a mean looking face.

"Go Baz, hit him — hit him!" the girl with him encouraged.

The man with tattoos grabbed the shorter man. They began to wrestle.

People at nearby tables picked up their food and moved away. Those on the other side of the restaurant tried their best to keep their conversation going with one eye on the trouble.

They were shouting and swearing and working their way closer towards the counter.

Nicholas looked at his boss who was trembling with fear. She was trying to speak but no words came out. She brought her hands to her chest and he saw her pull out a necklace from under her top. She played with it between her fingers but he couldn't quite see what it was.

He looked back at the commotion in front of him. The girl was egging them on, the two men throwing punches at each other.

Someone had to make a move and yet no–one was doing anything.

Nicholas felt his stomach turn over, he had to do something.

"BAZ!" Nicholas shouted.

The tall man with the vest and the tattoos stopped throwing punches and looked over.

The shorter man stopped struggling.

The man looked at Nicholas as if trying to place his face.

"Baz? It's you isn't it?" Nicholas said with wide eyes and a big smile.

He let the shorter man fall to the floor and walked over to the till.

"Do I know you?" he snarled.

"It's me, Nic! It's been so long I can't even remember — how's things!?" Nicholas said enthusiastically.

"Er, yeah, good — you?" The man said with a confused expression.

"Great, thanks." Nicholas leaned forward and whispered, "Don't tell the boss, but whatever you want — on the house."

The man's grimace turned into a smile, "Alright, mate, yeah." He turned to his girlfriend, "What d'you want babe?"

They were so distracted they didn't see the shorter man scurry out of the restaurant and into the darkness outside.

Nicholas grabbed the food, handed him the bag and winked. "Good to see you again. Laters mate."

The man nodded and grabbed the bag. "Cheers mate."

It was as if the whole restaurant breathed a sigh of relief as they left.

Nicholas watched the door close behind them and heard his name called from behind.

"Nicholas, do you have a moment please," his manager said.

He sighed. What is it this time? I'm probably going to get into trouble for giving the food away for free.

"What just happened in there …"

Nicholas interrupted, "Yes, sorry."

"What do you mean sorry?"

"For giving away free food."

"No, not at all, you did the right thing. In fact, what I was going to say is, well done, I am very impressed. You defused that whole situation with intelligence, clever–thinking and bravery."

"What?" Nicholas couldn't quite believe that he was actually being praised.

"You read the situation and acted in a way that I don't think I could ever have done. I was useless. I'm just ..."

Nicholas looked down at the necklace dangling from her neck. It was a crucifix.

"... I'm just so impressed. I am going to recommend you for management training."

Nicholas felt like a new person.

Before he knew it a word left his mouth.

"No."

"No? What do you mean, no?"

"I don't want to."

"But, you can't say that."

"Why not, are you going to say it's an order that I do management training?"

"No, but it's a great opportunity."

"Only if you want to be a manager at a Burger Ville Restaurant."

"But I thought a goal would help you?"

"I'm fed up of this place," Nicholas said.

"What do you want to do then?"

"I want to help save the animals and the planet."

"What?"

He wasn't sure what had come over him. He felt confident, inflated and positive.

"I quit."

"If you quit, you won't get paid."

"You'll pay me up to the last complete hour otherwise I'll take you to a tribunal," Nicholas snapped.

His manager was shocked. She took a step back, "Nicholas, what's got into you?"

"It's not Nicholas, its Nic!"

Nicholas turned, walked out the back, grabbed his hoodie from his locker and slammed the door behind him.

As he stood outside he took a deep breath — he felt alive.

He looked up at the Heavens. It was clear and, despite the outside lights, he could just about make out a few stars twinkling against the night sky.

He heard a car engine rev and voices in the distance.

"Oy speccy!" a voice called out from the other side of the car park.

"Fuck off! I'm not in the mood!" Nicholas shouted and stabbed a finger in their direction.

A tense pause was followed.

"Oooooh, he's not in the mood," shouted one of the boys.

They laughed and continued joking amongst themselves.

Nicholas threw back his shoulders. He was sure he'd gained another inch in height.

***

After about ten minutes he realised where he was and stopped.

Again, he had two choices. He could either go the longer way via Leigh Road, or through the Reary Estate.

He remembered the previous experience and a shudder ran through him, but tonight he was a new man.

He carried on walking towards the Reary Estate.

He looked up at the dreary buildings as he walked out into the central concourse. He could hear voices ahead. It was the same lads as before. He felt nervous and apprehensive, yet something was driving him and he allowed himself to be taken along by it.

He pulled his hoodie up over his head and strode with confidence.

He was almost upon them and could hear their voices clearly.

He knew they could hear him coming as his footsteps echoed off the concrete.

When he came into view, they stopped talking and turned to look at him.

Nicholas felt a lump in his throat. He swallowed hard as one of the boys stood up, preparing himself for whatever might happen next.

"Alright!" Nicholas shouted and nodded.

"Yeah," the boy said.

"Alright mate," another said.

"Yeah, alright," said another.

The boy sat back down and they carried on chatting.

Nicholas smiled to himself and, as he strutted out of the estate, he felt unstoppable.

Chapter 16

"Morning. Sleep alright?" His Mother asked as he walked into the kitchen.

"Yes, thanks Mum. I had the best night's sleep in ages."

Her son seemed different. He had a certain glow about him that she hadn't seen before.

"Is everything okay?"

"Yes, everything is fine thank you. I quit my job last night."

"What?"

"I quit my job."

"Yes, I heard what you said. I just can't believe what you did. Why did you quit your job?"

"I was sick of the place."

"I know you didn't like it there, but it's a job, you need to earn money."

"Yes, but all the time I am working there, I can't concentrate on my new venture."

"But it takes a long time to set up a business, and it isn't even a business, it's a charity, you won't even get paid will you?"

"Of course I'll get paid," Nicholas said, his confidence slightly shaken, as it occurred to him things were possibly a little more complicated than he had first thought.

"I don't want to put you off, but you have to be realistic, we all have to earn money."

Nicholas felt annoyed and angry. "I will make a success of this."

"I am sure you will Nicholas, but you can't just take risks like this," his Mother said, almost in tears. "Not at this time."

"What do you mean, not at this time?"

"I've lost my job," she said, beginning to cry.

"What? But, I thought everything was okay. You said that everything was okay."

"I am working my notice. I've got until the end of the week."

"You should have said. I wouldn't have quit."

"But you have," she sighed. "You did what you thought was right. You did what was right for you."

Nicholas rose to his feet.

"I will make a success of this Mum, I promise I will."

"I know you will Nicholas, I know you will."

"All ventures are a risk, life is a risk, and it's not Nicholas — it's Nic!"

He stormed out of the kitchen and back to his room.

He opened up his laptop, loaded his business plan and set to work refining more detail.

Chapter 17

Nicholas felt his stomach rumble. He looked down at the time — 1.30pm, and he hadn't had any breakfast, no wonder he was hungry.

He left the room and went to the kitchen. It had been a very productive day so far. He had an extensive 'to do' list and had worked through most of the points. He had two significant issues left — firstly where to get the money from and secondly what to call the charity.

There were plenty of grant opportunities and even funding from organisations like the Lottery, but it required a vast amount of forms to be filled out and it could take months or even years to get anywhere. He knew the banks wouldn't lend to him and it wasn't a venture that would attract investment from a business angel. He decided that he could only get this off the ground through the generosity of people willing to donate to his cause.

He rummaged through the cupboards in the kitchen. He grabbed a breakfast bar, some biscuits and a coke, that should keep him going.

He sat back down on the bed and opened the can. *First — a name*, he thought to himself as he swigged the drink.

He walked over to the window and leant on the ledge

He looked up at the blue sky. The fluffy white clouds interlaced into a pattern that looked like a cotton–wool quilt.

As he gazed down he could see the park in the distance and the tall green trees which moved ever so slightly in the light breeze. The natural beauty contrasted starkly with the grey office blocks and the nearby houses with their grey roofs, grey roads and grey pavements — dreary–ville.

He sat back down at the computer and thought about how the sky and clouds made him feel. He considered his project and the positivity he drew from it. He reflected on the feelings of happiness, joy and elation. He Googled a few keywords and noted the results.

Then Helen, the manager at Burger Ville, came into his thoughts and he remembered the necklace around her neck — a crucifix. He had never been religious. It just didn't seem at all logical that there could be someone who wanted us all to suffer so much and to bring so much horror to the world. What is Christian about that? He Googled some other keywords and jotted down a few more notes.

He pondered for a moment, Googled something else and after a flash of inspiration smiled with quiet satisfaction — I've got it!

He made some adjustments to his business plan.

Second — donation, he thought as he ripped open the breakfast bar wrapper and took a bite.

He Googled some phrases, 'charity donations', 'charity donor', 'give money to charities' but the results didn't help.

There were topics on 'how to account for tax with donations', definitions of what a donation is and even documents from the Charity Commission on how charities should work. He needed to rephrase his search. He typed in 'generous benefactor' — that helped, then 'generous benefactor charity donations', then 'generous benefactor charity donations movie stars', then he found it, "thank you Google!" — A Wikipedia article entitled 'List of philanthropists'.

As he scrolled through the page, some notable names caught his eye, including Bill Gates and Warren Buffet, but those were big names and almost certainly unreachable by the likes of him. Bono was another and then one specific, Leonardo DiCaprio. Why should that name have such an impact he wondered?

He Googled 'leonardo dicaprio london' and looked through the results. "Oh my God!" Nicholas said aloud, "It's tonight!"

He read the news article. Leonardo DiCaprio is one of the producers of a film with its opening night in London tonight and he will be appearing with other celebrity guests at the Odeon in Leicester Square for the premiere.

He searched for 'leonardo dicaprio charity work' and found out more about his dedication to good causes. Nicholas was amazed at how closely Mr. DiCaprio's ideas and concepts were aligned with his own visions for the future.

His stomach turned over again, he had a strange feeling inside.

It would take him about forty minutes to get across town and then another ten minutes to the cinema.

From what he could make out, people would start to turn up within an hour of the film starting so he had to be on his way by six.

He needed to make sure that his business plan was as solid as possible, so he started from the beginning and read back through.

He looked at the clock, it was quarter to five, so now the last thing to do was print out his business plan.

He turned on the printer and waited for it to finish its self–test. He plugged the USB cable into his computer and waited and waited. Then after a minute it came up 'Device not recognised'.

"What? It worked last time."

He unplugged it and tried again. Same error. "This is odd."

He clicked into the Printers folder and could see the printer listed as disconnected, even though it was connected. He unplugged it and tried it in a different port. Same error. He looked at the time.

He uninstalled the printer and re–installed it, same error. He looked at the time.

He was starting to get very frustrated and very worried. How could he expect Leonardo DiCaprio to pay any attention if he didn't have a copy of his business plan to show that he was serious.

He downloaded the latest drivers and tried again. Same error. "Oh my God, I don't believe this!" Nicholas shouted in desperation.

What can I do?

He had an idea.

He fumbled through a drawer and grabbed a USB memory stick in the shape of a cheeseburger that he'd been given at a Burger Ville seminar and plugged it in. After a nervous wait, the device was recognised. He saved the document onto the stick, unplugged it and grabbed his coat.

It was now nearly twenty past five and for what he had in mind he had to hurry.

Chapter 18

Nicholas ran down the high street and saw the sign he was looking for — an Estate Agent. He rushed in. There were people sat at every desk but he aimed directly for the desk nearest the door.

"Hello, can you help me please."

The young woman behind the desk looked up. "We'll be closing in a minute, is there a particular property that you were interested in?"

"Er, no, I need your help." He looked at her name tag. "Rachel, I need a document printed," Nicholas said as he held the memory stick in front of him.

"Sorry, I can't do that."

"Why not?"

"It's against company policy."

"Why?"

"It might have a virus on it."

"But, it hasn't, it's empty apart from my document."

"Sorry, it's against company policy, I'm not allowed."

Nicholas slumped into the chair in front of her and looked up at the clock. It was twenty eight minutes past five and he knew everywhere would be closing in two minutes.

"What is it anyway?" Rachel asked.

"All my hopes and dreams and the opportunity to save the animals and the planet."

"It's what?"

Nicholas looked down at the memory stick and sighed.

"I am setting up a charitable organisation to help save the animals and the planet and I was going to give it to Leonardo DiCaprio tonight. My printer's packed up and I can't print it."

He expected a response but didn't get one.

He looked up. Rachel had a shocked expression on her face.

"Did you say you're seeing Leonardo DiCaprio tonight?"

Nicholas thought about the question for a moment, "Yes, I am seeing Leonardo DiCaprio tonight." It was true, in a manner of speaking.

"Oh my God — oh my God. I love Leo. I've seen all his films. Did you see the Revenant? What did you think, wasn't it incredible?"

Nicholas didn't want to admit that he hadn't seen it. "What can I say? He's an incredible man."

"Yes, you're right, he is incredible," Rachel replied, over the moon to meet someone on her wavelength.

She looked around to make sure no–one was looking and held out her hand.

"Quick, give it to me."

Nicholas handed her the memory stick. She reached under the desk and plugged it in.

"Just one copy, yes?" Rachel said. Her tone indicating that was all he was getting.

"Yes please, just one copy for Leo."

Rachel beamed a wide smile and sent the document to print. After a second the printer burst to life and Rachel rushed over to guard the pages that were being churned from the machine.

She held the documents close to her body as she returned to her desk. Her colleagues were busily shutting down their computers and getting ready to go home.

"Here you go sir, this is the information you requested," Rachel said aloud as she handed him the print out. "If you would like to see the property just let us know and we can arrange a viewing."

Nicholas took the document from her. "Thank you very much for this, it really means a lot to me — and to Leo."

"You're very welcome."

Nicholas stood up to leave.

"Can you do something for me please," Rachel said.

"Of course."

"Tell Leo that Rachel Connolly is his number one fan and sends her love."

Nicholas smiled, "Of course."

One of Rachel's colleagues held the door open for him as he left.

He breathed a sigh of relief and hurried back home.

Chapter 19

"Coat, keys, money and business plan," Nicholas said as he ticked everything off his mental checklist.

His Mum was at some kind of leaving event and wouldn't be home till late so he'd written her a note.

```
Off to try to talk to Leonardo DiCaprio to ask
for his help with the charity. See you later.
```

He closed the door behind him and rushed down the stairs.

The whole printer experience had put him behind schedule and he was desperate to get the train.

He held the business plan firmly in his hands. He didn't want to turn up with loose pieces of paper but thankfully he'd managed to rip out the contents of a Burger Ville employment documentation folder and put his business plan inside. It was brown, not the colour he would have chosen, but at least it helped keep the documents safe and looked reasonably professional.

He looked at the time on his phone.

He had five minutes until the train arrived and he had a six minute walk — his stride broke into a run.

Chapter 20

By the time Nicholas arrived at Leicester Square there were crowds of people screaming and chanting Leo's name.

He stood at the back and stared.

It was at least twenty deep.

He sighed.

Has Leo already arrived?

How do I even get to talk to him if he hasn't?

How will I ever get to the front?

He looked down at the business plan in his hand, looked back up at the crowd and rushed forward.

"Let me through please," Nicholas asked firmly and to his surprise, they did. The more he requested, the further he got. "Coming through," he said and before he knew it, he was at the front.

He placed a hand on the barrier and watched a smartly dressed man walking up the carpet.

He had no idea whether he was an actor or a member of the production crew.

A woman screamed to his left, desperately trying to attract the attention of the man walking up the carpet.

"Who is that?" Nicholas shouted above the noise of the crowd.

"No idea," she said and carried on shouting to the man to look over.

Nicholas shrugged his shoulders and turned to the girl standing on his other side.

"Has Leo turned up yet?"

"No, not yet," She replied. "He's normally one of the last to arrive."

"Are you a big Leo fan?"

"Oh yes, I'm his number one fan," she replied and continued calling to the man on the carpet.

That makes two of you, Nicholas thought to himself.

Nicholas waited, and waited.

His ears were pounded by screams from all around.

People walked up the red carpet he didn't recognise and he was sure that most of the crowd didn't recognise either.

He was constantly being shoved and pushed in every direction. He held the business plan close to his chest with one hand whilst holding onto the barrier with the other. He had to protect his position at the front of the crowd.

The whole experience was strangely hypnotic. He almost felt himself drifting off. The screams and cries were all blending into each other. The rhythmic motion of his body being pushed from side to side until, suddenly, the atmosphere changed — it became electric!

Nicholas leaned over the barrier and looked to his left.

He could see him — Leonardio DiCaprio. He had arrived and was smiling and waving at the crowds.

He couldn't believe it.

He had never seen a movie star in the flesh and his reaction surprised him.

His stomach was in knots. His pulse was racing.

He felt a hot flush of excitement and before he knew it, he started to call out Leo's name.

The screams were now ear–piercing. He'd struggle to be heard. Part of him thought that maybe there was no point and perhaps he should try to do this another way, but what other way? If he was going to get Leo's attention, he had to do something.

"Leonardo, I want to save the animals and the planet, will you help me?"

Leonardo was shaking hands and posing for photos with the crowd but he was on the other side of the carpet, he wasn't even coming close. He needed to make Leonardo look over — he'd wave the business plan in its sickly brown folder.

Nicholas raised his arm as high as he could and shouted, "Leonardo, I want to save the animals and the planet, will you help me?"

Still nothing. Yet he kept waving and waving.

Then suddenly Leo looked over, directly at him.

"LEONARDO, I WANT TO SAVE THE ANIMALS AND THE PLANET, WILL YOU HELP ME!" Nicholas shouted so loud that it hurt his throat — but had it worked?

Eye contact was lost. Leo looked away and carried on mingling with the crowds. He reached the end of the line near the entrance to the cinema.

Nicholas felt a wave of disappointment as he watched the opportunity pass and all his hope with it.

Then Leo turned and walked over to Nicholas's side of the carpet.

He smiled, shook hands and moved along the line.

He moved closer and closer.

He was now just five people way. "Leonardo, will you help me save the animals and the planet?"

Leonardo glanced across and looked away.

He carried on signing autographs but stepped closer and closer until at last he was looking Nicholas directly in the eye.

"Say again please," Leonardo said loudly.

"Leonardo, would you help me save the animals and the planet?"

"How old are you kid?" Leonardo asked.

"Seventeen," Nicholas replied not quite believing that this was happening to him.

"What's your name?"

"Nic Savage."

"And who do you work for?"

"No—one, I am doing this on my own."

Leonardo was struggling to hear over the noise of the crowd and moved a little closer.

"I am trying to setup a charity to save the animals and the planet, but I need help, hopefully, your help."

Leonardo placed his head just inches away from his.

"And why are you doing this?"

"Because I feel that other organisations talk the talk but don't actually get anything done."

Leonardo stepped back as if pondering a thought, smiled, stepped closer and reached into his pocket.

"Call my secretary in the morning. We'll set up a meeting."

Nicholas took the card and reeled in shock as he watched the world–famous movie–star Leonardo DiCaprio wave to fans and then disappear into the building.

"What did he give you?" shouted the girl next to him.

"That's not fair, I want one," shouted someone else.

"Get it off him," shouted another.

Before he knew it, he was being pushed and shoved in all directions again. He struggled and finally manoeuvred his way through the desperate grab of the crowd.

With Leonardo's card firmly in his hand and his business plan lost to one of his adoring fans, all he wanted to do was to get home, let the realisation of what just happened sink in and try to fix the damn printer so he could print another copy of the business plan.

Chapter 21

Nicholas had been up until 1am and still his Mother hadn't returned.

By the time he'd awoken in the morning she had already left for work.

He hoped she was okay.

He sat fiddling with the phone in one hand and the business card in the other wondering what time it would be convenient to phone. *Was 9.30am too early?*

He wouldn't know if he didn't try.

He dialled the number.

Someone answered.

"Oh hello, Leonardo DiCaprio asked me to call on this number to arrange a meeting."

"Is this Nic Savage?"

"Yes it is," Nicholas said, surprised and honoured that he should know his name.

"You're setting up a charity to save animals and the planet and would like Leonardo's help, is that right?"

"Yes, that's right."

"Well, you realise that Leo gets asked all the time for help, money, donations, favours, etc. etc. — it happens every day."

"Yes, I can imagine."

"So what makes your project different?"

"Well, as I said to mister DiCaprio, I feel that existing organisations talk the talk but don't actually get anything done. I want to change that, I want to make a real difference, I want to get things done."

"Okay, hold on."

The line went silent. Nicholas held the phone tightly, his hand trembling.

"Nic?"

"Yes. I'm here."

"Leo is due to fly back to the US today ..." the voice said.

In that moment, Nicholas felt the bottom drop out of his stomach. First the door of opportunity had been opened and now it seemed it was about to be firmly shut in his face. He heard the man say something else but didn't quite catch what he'd said.

"Sorry, can you repeat that please?" Nicholas asked, his voice more subdued.

"Can you get to the Mandarin Oriental hotel in Knightsbridge by midday?"

Nicholas felt as if he'd been slapped by a very big hand — or was that a flipper?

"The Mandarin Hotel? Knightsbridge? Midday? Today?" he repeated.

"Yes, is that okay?"

Nicholas looked at the time. It was 10am. "Yes, I can be there."

"Great. Ask for Mr DiCaprio at the desk."

The line went dead.

Nicholas hung up and stared at the phone in disbelief.

Chapter 22

Nicholas held a freshly printed copy of the business plan firmly between his fingers.

It had taken him two hours to resolve the problem with the computer last night. Thank heavens he'd been able to fix it. It would have been embarrassing to go back and see Leo's number–one fan Rachel.

Nicholas had never even been to Knightsbridge before and was marvelling at all the expensive shops. There were clothes in windows that didn't even have prices on. He couldn't imagine how much they cost.

He'd arrived early and had walked past the Mandarin Oriental hotel four times already.

He looked at his phone. It was nearly time — just a few minutes to go.

His stomach was churning.

He was overcome with excitement.

He couldn't believe it.

He was about to meet with Leonardo DiCaprio — the world–famous movie star — in person.

He still hadn't got over the surreal experience of talking to him last night, but to actually be asked to meet with him was really something else.

He thought for a moment about some of the things his

Gran had said and how he had got to this point. She had said 'it's up to you to make it happen'. Nicholas smiled at the thought.

He felt the phone vibrate in his pocket.

He grabbed it imagining the worst — Leonardo was calling to cancel the meeting as something else had come up in his busy life. He looked at the screen. Thankfully it was just the alarm he had set to remind him when it was two minutes before midday.

He put his nerves to one side, swallowed hard and walked into the reception.

The hotel was amazing and despite the urge to stare in awe, he tried to appear professional so he approached the desk confidently.

"My name's Nic Savage. Leonardo DiCaprio is expecting me."

"Yes sir, you can go straight up. Mr DiCaprio is in the Presidential Suite."

"Thank you," Nicholas replied and turned towards the lifts.

As Nicholas approached the lift, the door opened and a couple walked out. They nodded to Nicholas. He nodded back. Pressed the button and watched the door close.

Leonardo DiCaprio. Knightsbridge. Hyde Park. Presidential Suite — it was like a dream.

The doors opened and Nicholas stepped into the corridor.

He stood in front of the door marked Presidential Suite.
Here we go.

Nicholas knocked on the door and waited.

After about thirty seconds a man opened the door.

"Nic?"

"Yes, Nic Savage. Hello."

"Hi, I'm Ben, I am mister DiCaprio's personal secretary. Come on in."

"Thank you," Nicholas said and walked in.

Nicholas had never seen a hotel room like this before — it looked more like a home than a hotel room.

Then he noticed Leonardo. He was on the phone. He waved, turned his back and walked into the bedroom where he continued his call.

Ben led Nicholas into the main sitting room area which had two armchairs, two sofas, tables, lamps and even a fireplace. It was probably larger than the entire flat he lived in with his Mum.

"Please take a seat, Mr DiCaprio shouldn't be long."

"Thank you."

Nicholas sat down and marvelled at the décor and how everything was very tasteful and not at all ostentatious.

He sat looking around, lost in his own thoughts whilst he held the business plan tightly in his hands.

Thankfully he'd managed to find another folder. This time it was orange instead of brown. It was from a project he did at school. It was a little grubby, but it was all he could find.

"Nic. Sorry to keep you waiting," said a voice from behind.

Nicholas stood up and was approached by Leonardo DiCaprio's large 6ft frame. He held out his hand.

Nicholas reached out and shook it.

"Mister DiCaprio, it's a pleasure to finally meet you properly,"

"Call me Leo," he said.

"But, your personal secretary calls you Mister DiCaprio?"

"Yes, but he's paid to — call me Leo."

He sat heavily into the sofa opposite, crossed his legs and placed his hands together.

"Okay kid, tell me all about your ambitious venture."

"Well ..."

"Actually, hold on a second," Leonardo said and called out, "Ben? Ben?"

Within two seconds, his personal secretary appeared. "Yes, mister DiCaprio?"

Leonardo turned to Nicholas, "I'm hungry, are you? Want some food?"

"Er, yes, please. Thank you."

"Get us some lunch will you, a selection of stuff, you know what I like."

"Yes, sir," Ben said and disappeared into the bedroom.

"They've got a great kitchen. Heston Blumenthal has a restaurant here — great food. Anyway, sorry, I interrupted, carry on."

"Well, firstly, thank you for your time, I know you're a busy man," Nicholas said.

Leonardo brushed it away with a gesture of his hand.

"I've produced a business plan if you'd like to see it."

Leonardo reached out and took the plan from him.

"I am putting together a charitable organisation ..." Nicholas stopped talking as he noticed Leonardo skim read the first page then skip all the other pages and turn directly to the last page.

"Why did you do that?"

Leonardo looked up. "I figured most of it was just waffle and what you really wanted would be on the last page."

Nicholas didn't know what to say.

"I was right, ten thousand English pounds, that's all you want?"

"Yes," Nicholas replied.

"Ten grand?"

"Yes," Nicholas replied adamantly.

"It's not enough," Leonardo said and tossed the business plan back at him.

"What?"

"It's not enough. There is no way you can set up a charitable organisation with just ten grand."

"Yes you're right, I know I'll need more eventually, but I wanted to get the organisation off the ground, and if you look at the initial costs to get the charity operational, then it comes to ten thousand pounds."

"You know what makes a successful actor?"

Nicholas shook his head.

"One becomes the character."

Nicholas listened.

"I become the character, in that world, in that situation — I am one with the character. I feel it, I touch it — I believe it. You need to believe it. You need to be your charity."

"I am."

"No, think big Nic, think big!" Leonardo gestured with his hands.

"To really make a success of this you're going to need a property, you're going to need people, experts who will be working with you. If you want to really make things happen, you'll need them to negotiate, open doors, whatever, but it will always be your charity and your face, therefore you are the character and you need to live it and breathe it."

Nicholas nodded.

"You know that I have the Leonardo DiCaprio Foundation don't you."

Nicholas nodded again.

"Well ..." Leonardo continued to talk and Nicholas listened intently.

After a little while, there was a knock at the door. Ben walked through from the bedroom and opened it.

"Mister DiCaprio, lunch is here."

"Great, bring it through," Leonardo beckoned.

"You're gonna love this kid."

Nicholas swivelled round and saw a hostess trolley being wheeled into the room with a selection of delicious looking food. The waiter brought it alongside the sofa, said something to Ben and disappeared.

"Wow, this looks great, thank you."

"Tuck in," Leonardo said.

"What do you do for a job?" Leonardo asked and took a bite of a small sandwich.

"Well, I used to work at Burger Ville but I packed it in so that I could concentrate one hundred percent on this project."

"Well that's some remarkable faith considering you haven't even got it off the ground yet."

"True, but nothing ventured, nothing gained, and it won't succeed if I don't put my full effort into it."

Leonardo nodded and continued to eat.

"What made you want to do this?"

Nicholas thought for a moment. "I guess I am just sick of it all. We are effectively the custodians of this planet and we're destroying it. We have a responsibility and we've lost sight of how to live in equilibrium with our environment. We're taking from it more than it can produce, we are killing it with poisons and waste and we're hurting and killing the animals that we share it with and who were here long before we were."

Leonardo put down his plate and wiped his mouth with a napkin. He sat forward and pointed his finger, "And that is why I am going to back you kid. You just spoke with more passion, determination and eloquence than I have heard from some politicians. You got it kid, that's your speech, that's what's gonna win you support."

Nicholas was gobsmacked.

"What made you choose the name Rapture?"

"Rapture means joy, bliss, happiness, pleasure, all of the things that nature makes us feel. I want people to feel at one with their environment again and to have those feelings about their planet."

"Very good," Leonardo said.

"And what made you choose the colour orange?"

"Er ..." Nicholas didn't know how to answer.

"It's a good colour. It's a nice shade of orange. It symbolises enthusiasm, happiness, determination and success. It's a great choice!"

Nicholas hadn't the heart to tell him that it was a lucky find from the back of a cupboard.

"And what's this?" Leonardo said pointing at the doodle on the front cover.

"Er, it's just a rough drawing. I thought it would be symbolic to our cause," Nicholas said. In fact, he'd drawn it at school and hadn't realised its significance until now.

Leonardo, pondered the image for a moment, nodded and threw it back at him.

"I want you to rewrite your business plan. I want you to factor in a nice office. Nothing too fancy, you don't want to waste money, but it needs to be presentable and worthy of a world—leading charity.

"World—leading?" Nicholas clarified.

"If you want to save the planet, you need to be a world—leader," Leonardo replied before picking up his pace again.

"You're going to need staff to help you, a personal assistant, experts — people who have worked in charities before. You'll make a big splash with this so we can head—hunt some people from WWF, Greenpeace and other similar organisations. I have a few names in mind."

Nicholas sat spellbound, his head was reeling.

"Budget for half a mil' first year, one mil', second and two mil' third."

"Sorry, mil? Do you mean million?"

"Yes," Leonardo replied matter—of—factly.

"Half a million first year, one million second and two million in the third year."

"But ..." Nicholas said, finding it difficult to get his words out.

Leonardo sat waiting for his response.

"But, it's going to take an awful lot of charitable donations to pay you back, it could take years."

Leonardo started laughing. Nicholas was worried that he'd missed the joke.

"It's not a loan kid," Leonard said. "It's an investment."

"An investment — in the charity?"

"No kid — an investment in you!"

Leonardo sat forward even further this time.

"I don't invest in business plans, I invest in people and you've won my heart kid and my wallet, just like you'll win others too. You'll go places with this kid, you've got it, and I see that."

"I don't know what to say?"

"Just say that you'll get the revised business plan back to me tomorrow night. Let me and the lawyers look over it and we'll get back to you ASAP."

"I will."

"I like to move fast kid, you're gonna have to keep up."

"I will."

"You still got the card I gave you?"

"Er, yes, it's here," Nicholas said as he fumbled in his pocket and pulled out the creased card.

"Damn, what you been doing with it?"

"It was your fans last night at the premiere. They tried to grab it from me."

Leonardo chuckled, wrote something on the reverse of it and handed it back.

"That's my personal email address. Get it to me by midnight tomorrow, UK time, that's 4pm in LA."

"I am meeting the lawyers at five so make sure it's not late."

"I won't let you down."

"You won't be letting me down kid — you'll be letting yourself down."

Nicholas nodded.

"Have you had enough to eat?"

"Yes, thank you, that was delicious."

"Okay, well I don't wish to be rude but I've got a few more calls to make and my flight is out of Heathrow at ten past four so I gotta get moving."

"Of course, thank you so much for your time and for your support and belief in me," Nicholas said standing up to leave.

"Any problems, you've got my number and I look forward to your email by midnight tomorrow," Leonardo said as he placed a firm hand on his shoulder and squeezed.

They shook hands and before he knew it, Nicholas was outside in the corridor with the door closed behind him.

Wow — did I just dream all that?

Chapter 23

Nicholas arrived home.

His Mum was already back from work. Her shoes were by the door.

He walked into the kitchen where his Mum was sitting. She looked away as he entered.

"Mum you're home early, are you okay?"

"I'm okay," she said, her voice trembling.

"What is it?"

She turned, her eyes were red, she'd been crying.

"I had an argument with my boss. He told me to go home and not come back. Not even to see out the rest of my notice period. It was so humiliating," she said, tears welling up in her eyes.

Nicholas sat down at the table.

"What did you argue about?"

"Redundancy pay. I was expecting around a month's salary for each year I worked there, so around £25,000 but he said all I will be getting is statutory redundancy which works out at £5,550."

"Oh dear, I'm sorry Mum."

"I thought that I'd be able to keep us going for nearly a year if we tightened our belts and that I could even give you the £10,000 you need for your project — but with what I'll get, it'll be ..." she started crying again.

"No Mum, it's going to be okay."

His Mum looked up through teary eyes and blew her nose.

"It's going to be okay, did you see my note?"

"Note, what note?"

"I left it by the door so you would see it when you came in."

"No, I didn't see a note, what did it say?"

Nicholas went to look in the hall. He had put it on the key table just inside the door but it wasn't there. He looked on the floor then finally caught sight of it. It had obviously blown off when the door opened and landed in a shoe. He picked it up and hurried back into the kitchen.

He handed his Mum the note.

She read it.

"Wow, you saw Leonardo DiCaprio?"

"I saw him last night. He asked me to arrange a meeting and I've just come back from his hotel in Knightsbridge."

"Wow! What did he say?"

"He loves the idea and wants to invest in the charity."

"Ahh, bless him. Still, I suppose ten thousand pounds is a drop in the ocean to him."

"No Mum, half a million in the first year, one million in the second year and two million in the third year."

His Mother was visibly stunned. He could see her mouth the word million.

Nicholas nodded. "Yes Mum — million — it's amazing isn't it."

"Yes, Nicholas, it really is, well done you — very well done."

It was as though a switch had been turned on and Nicholas had activated high energy mode.

"I need to revise my business plan and email it to Leo by midnight tomorrow."

"Leo?"

"Yes, that's what he asked me to call him. And ..."

She listened to him reel off all the things he had to do and how much potential and opportunity there was. How Leonardo said that he was investing in him and how he believed in him so much. She couldn't believe it, her son. She started to cry again, but not out of sadness for losing her job, this time they were tears of joy for her son, the chairman of a world–leading charitable organisation funded by his new friend and backer Leo.

Chapter 24

Nicholas was deep in thought.

There was a knock at the door.

His Mother walked in.

"Nicholas, do you know what time it is?"

"Erm?" He had no idea. He looked down at the clock in the corner of his computer screen.

"It's 2am," his Mother said.

"I didn't realise. What are you doing up at this time?" Nicholas said.

"I couldn't sleep — part worry and part excitement I guess."

"Well, guess what ... I've included you in this."

"In your plan?"

"Yes. Leo said that I need to have a good team of people around me. You need a job and I need a personal assistant, you could be my personal assistant."

"That's very sweet dear but I couldn't be your PA," his Mother said as she sat on the bed.

"You need someone impartial, someone who isn't related to you, someone you can talk to as employer to employee, not son to mother."

"Oh, but ..."

"I really appreciate the thought, but you'll understand when you've got your own PA."

Nicholas looked disappointed.

"How's it coming along?"

"I've got two problems."

"What's that?"

"Firstly, I am not eighteen yet and that means I can't legally take out some types of contract, including tenancy for a building, at least not without a parent, guardian or sponsor's assurance."

"Won't Leo be your sponsor?"

"I don't know, I didn't want to be presumptuous," Nicholas said.

"Well, if Leo can't do it, then I will, so put me down, that covers that."

Nicholas smiled and made a note on the pad beside him.

"What was the other problem?"

"I can't get my head around this formula in this spreadsheet."

"Ahh, you know what that will be don't you?"

"What?"

"Tiredness — because it's late."

"But I have to get this done."

"Leo said you had to email it to him by midnight tomorrow night which gives you all day tomorrow to work on it."

"But ..."

"The brain becomes much less effective the more tired you get, and, after a good night's sleep, you wait and see, the answer will come to you in a jiffy."

"Yeah, okay, I am tired."

"There you go," his Mum said. "Good night and see you in the morning."

"Okay Mum."

"Oh and one more thing."

"Yes Mum?"

"I am so very proud of you."

Nicholas smiled and blushed.

"Night Mum."

Chapter 25

Nicholas felt queasy. He wasn't really comfortable on boats. He tried to move but he couldn't, something was pushing up against him. He turned his head to see a panda. It looked at him and growled. He tried to move to his left, but couldn't. He looked round to see a jaguar, it snarled. He looked across to see an orangutan, it howled. Packed into the little boat were lots of animals, including a lemur, an eagle, a gorilla — then he heard a sound, then again and again.

Instinctively he reached out and silenced the alarm.

He opened his eyes.

The alarm clock had been given to him by his Dad. He had picked it up from a junk shop. It used to be a fox hunting scene, apparently, but his Father had removed the horses and the dogs and attached a model of a wooden boat to the base. He had then placed figurines of animals into the boat. The piercing sound of the alarm was in fact the horn of the hunt, but his Father had referred to it as the the 'call of the clarion'.

He remembered the story his Dad used to tell him to help him sleep — that the animals were on the boat and they were helping each other to survive.

The panda's eyes acted like binoculars and helped it look

for hazards in the sea ahead. The orangutan was good at seafaring and was able to read the weather and the tides. The jaguar was good at fishing and would catch food for them to eat. The eagle would fly off and look for land. The lemur would attend to any problems with the boat and the gorilla was the second in command. The dolphin at the stern was the captain, it was holding a trumpet — or as his Father called it — the clarion.

***

His Mum was sitting in the kitchen sipping tea and reading the news on her phone when Nicholas rushed in.

"I could hear that alarm clock in here," she said. "Why don't you get rid of it?"

"I can't get rid of it, it's from Dad — I could never get rid of it — anyway, Mum — you were right."

"I was?" She said, wondering what he was referring to.

"The spreadsheet — the formula. I worked it out in no time this morning. I just needed a clear head."

"There you go, you see."

"And do you need to do much more on it?"

"Probably about two hours, but its half–eight now so that gives me all day."

"You should be fine then, well done."

Nicholas opened a cupboard and grabbed a breakfast bar.

"No cornflakes today?"

"No thanks Mum, I'll just have this in my room and get it finished."

"Okay," his Mum said. "In fact, hang on a moment."

Nicholas turned.

"I just wanted you to know that I am very proud of you."

"Oh, stop it."

"No, really — I have a feeling that this is going to be the making of you."

Nicholas shrugged his shoulders.

"Be aware though, it is likely to be a roller–coaster ride and your feet may not touch the ground over the next few months."

Nicholas scrunched his face up. "But, how can you know that?"

"I've always been quite sensitive to such things. Call it gut feel or intuition. I just wanted you to know. When the time arises just listen to what your gut instinct tells you — listen to what your intuition tells you and follow your heart. I really couldn't be more proud."

"Er, thanks," Nicholas didn't know what else to say. With a red face, he took his breakfast and went back to his room.

Chapter 26

Nicholas was on a mission.

There was something he needed to do.

His Mum caught him about to leave the flat.

"All done?"

"Yes, Mum — all done."

"How do you feel?"

"Nervous, worried, apprehensive — excited," Nicholas admitted.

"Well, you produced a very professional document, it's all in the hands of fate now," his Mum said.

"Yes, I guess it is."

"One moment you're working in Burger Ville and next minute you're producing professional documents for millionaire movie stars to back you on 'world–class' ventures."

Nicholas smiled.

"If you can achieve all this in just a week or so, what can you achieve in months or even years? Part of me is excited, but part of me is worried too."

"But you've no reason to be worried, Mum."

"I know, but I am — very ..."

Nicholas brushed the comment aside.

"Gonna pop out for a bit, Mum," Nicholas said tying his shoes.

He grabbed his coat and before his Mum had a chance to answer, he had left.

He hadn't wanted to tell her where he was going, he wanted it to be a surprise.

It was only a short walk to the parade of shops down the road. A mixture of businesses including a charity shop, a shop that sold model railways, a kebab house, Chinese takeway, Indian restaurant, another charity shop, two estate agents, a Subway sandwich shop and his destination, the barber shop.

He was nervous, very nervous.

He hadn't done this before. He knew what to expect, he had seen it in films or on TV, but he had never been through it himself.

He reached for the door, swallowed hard and walked in.

The door hit a little bell above it and everyone looked round as he entered.

There were four chairs, three were occupied and the fourth vacant but he couldn't see a barber standing by it.

His heart was racing.

He didn't know how this worked.

What he should do or what he should say.

He'd just watch, and learn.

There were seats by the window. He sat and waited.

After a few minutes a girl appeared and called him over.

He hesitated a second. She was cute.

He blushed slightly, walked over and sat down.

"Hello, I'm Bex."

"Hi, I'm Nicholas."

"I haven't seen you here before. Where do you usually get your hair cut?" She said as she draped a cover over his chest and fastened it around his neck.

"Oh, nearby, but you're my local," Nicholas replied, not wanting to admit that his Mother had cut his hair since he'd been born.

"What would you like?"

"Sorry?"

"What style would you like?"

"Oh I see," Nicholas didn't know what to say, he didn't really have a style. "To be honest, I am not sure. I want something — different. I am trying to re–invent myself."

Bex stood back and raised her hand to her chin. She looked at the sides of his head, the back of his head and his reflection in the mirror.

"Could you remove your glasses please?"

Nicholas reached up and in that moment took one last look at himself in the mirror. His 'pudding bowl' haircut covering his ears with fringe just above his eyes soon to be a thing of the past.

"Do you want something low maintenance?"

In that moment, he remembered the times when he had been out with his Mum when he was younger and she would lick her hand and flatten the hair on his head — he'd hated that.

"Yes please, low maintenance."

"Okay, I have something in mind. Let me know if you're not happy with the way it's going."

Nicholas didn't want to admit that he couldn't see anything without his glasses.

She started snipping at his hair.

He wasn't sure quite how this was going to turn out but the fate of his hair was very much in Bex's hands.

***

"Okay, finished."

Nicholas was snapped from his day dream.

"Gel?"

He'd never worn gel. His instinct was to say no, but a little voice inside told him otherwise.

"Yes, please."

She grabbed a jar from the shelf in front, dipped her fingers inside and coated them in gel. She rubbed her hands together and gently massaged the gel into his hair.

It felt nice, really nice.

Just as he thought he was going to float from the chair, she stopped.

"All done. What do you think?"

Nicholas grabbed his glasses from his lap. He hesitated a moment before putting them on.

What was he going to look like?

Would he like what he saw?

He put them on.

"Wow, it's brilliant."

"Happy?"

"Yes, it's just what I wanted."

"A smart, modern style?" Bex asked.

"Yes, and to be — different," Nicholas replied.

"Thanks, Bex."

"You're welcome, Nicholas."

"Actually, I prefer Nic."

"Okay, you're welcome, Nic."

Chapter 27

Nicholas looked out of the window at the London skyline in front of him.

He still couldn't get it straight in his head that this was his office — this was his charity — this was his life now.

As he stood marvelling at the view, he remembered what his Mum had said just three months earlier — *You're in for a roller–coaster ride — She'd been right — Why are Mothers always right?*

A voice spoke from behind him.

"Mr Savage — I have — I have a mister DiCaprio on the line," Megan said, with just a tell–tale hint of excitement in her voice.

"Thank you Megan, can you put him through please."

Nicholas walked over to his desk, sat down and picked up the phone.

"Hey Leo, how are you?"

"Good thanks Nic, how's things?"

"Really good thank you, brilliant in fact."

"How did you get on with the latest round of donations?" Leo asked.

"Very good. Seven out of the big ten are on board and we plan to target a further fifty big fish in the next week."

"And priorities?"

"We have a meeting in ..." Nicholas looked at the clock on the wall, "exactly fifteen minutes to finalise that list."

"And budget? How are you doing for money?"

"Yep, completely on top of that — I was able to shave some of the costs based on the projection so well within budget and plenty of money left. As soon as the payments clear we'll be flying."

Nicholas could hear laughter coming from the other end of the line. "Why are you laughing?"

"Just you kid. How old did you say you were again?"

"I had my eighteenth birthday last week," Nicholas replied matter–of–factly.

"I am very impressed, well done," Leonardo replied. "We've just wrapped up shooting for the night, it's late and I have an early start tomorrow. I need my sleep. 'Night kid."

Before Nicholas had a chance to answer, the line went dead.

He put the phone down and smiled.

The last few months had been so busy he had just been swept along by it. It seemed that only now could he sit back and realise just how far he had come.

The executive chair reclined as he shifted his body weight. It wasn't leather — it was an eco–friendly fabric with wool stuffing. The wool was a by–product of sheep shearing from local UK farms, just the message that Rapture wanted to deliver.

The desk in front of him was handmade by an artisan who specialised in reclaimed wood. It was made out of re-cycled scaffold boards apparently, but you wouldn't know it to look at it.

He put his hands behind his head and spun around in the chair. He watched the view of his office sweep past: the sofa and two chairs at one end, the full length floor to ceiling windows at the other. His desk and the small table with four chairs were in the middle of the room with the 'driftwood' bookcase which contained directories, guides and brochures.

He looked up at the clock made out of recycled plastic and metal — ten minutes to go.

This was to be an important meeting for the team. They'd been thrashing out a list of projects over the past few weeks and they were going to decide what the priorities should be. They had limited resources and they couldn't afford to spread themselves too thinly.

He had employed a very mixed–bunch team.

Megan Partridge, Personal Assistant, 24 years of age and so heavily made up and immaculately presented she looked like a doll.

She had previously been the PA to a Chief Executive of a bank. He remembered her saying at the interview how she had been in the job since she was 18 but it had opened her eyes to how greedy and ruthless banks could be. When she had heard about this position she had jumped at the chance. She felt that this was her opportunity to do something good in her life and help make a difference. He'd liked that. It's what had made her stand out amongst forty–seven other applicants.

That had been a very intense week. In some respects, she was the best of a bad bunch. She had issues, but her heart was in the right place.

He had been surprised at how long things could take. He needed a PA, someone to help organise himself better. He thought he could just find a few and choose the best one, but nothing was ever that easy. First there was deciding on the job description, package and remuneration. Then placing the advert, arranging and scheduling the interviews, not to mention the interview stage itself and having to wait for Megan to work her notice before she could even start.

He hadn't planned on doing his own admin for seven weeks but that's how long it took in the end.

Eight minutes.

Alexandra Haynes was the complete polar opposite. She never wore make–up. He had remembered overhearing her say that she didn't need to wear make–up. She wanted to be judged by her actions and not what she looked like. Even her black hair was cut short so that she didn't need to waste any time getting ready in the mornings. She was very direct and her Australian accent made her come across as quite aggressive sometimes, although he knew that was not her intention. She had previously been involved with Greenpeace and in particular some newsworthy actions against Japanese whaling ships and shark fin fisherman.

That's the story that touched him most — hearing that over one hundred million sharks each year have their fins cut off whilst they are alive and are then tossed back into the ocean to simply sink to the bottom and die.

Humans are sick.

Summer Bevan was another down to earth girl. She wore very little make–up, kept her blonde hair in a ponytail and often dressed in khaki. She had come directly from the

Wildlife Conservation Society where she had been instrumental in helping protect animal species in Africa.

He remembered at her interview she referred to her embarrassment about her fellow US countrymen and the big game hunting in Zimbabwe. He had assumed she was talking about previous generations of 'white hunter' but he couldn't believe it when she clarified that it is happening right now on special hunting tours, where you can pay to kill lions, buffalo, zebra, leopards and even elephants.

Nicholas was lost for words — who in this day and age would want to kill these remarkable animals — humans really are sick.

Four minutes to go.

Romain Fournier was French Canadian and spent much of his time campaigning against seal hunting. He had told Nicholas that it was regarded as one of the largest slaughters on the planet, as anywhere between one hundred thousand and half a million baby seals between three weeks and three months old are clubbed to death or shot. Sometimes the seals aren't even dead when they are skinned and left to die, their carcasses to rot on the ice. Romain had started crying during the interview — he had seen such horror and was so keen to change things, and yet still it goes on.

Joshua Sanderson was a mysterious character who wouldn't reveal some of the things he'd done. Nicholas didn't know whether to be intrigued or worried, but, having known him a little while by now, he suspected it was to do with animal rights activism and break–ins at medical laboratories. Educated at Oxford and from a family of lawyers, he shunned his family to try to make a difference and that is one of the key things that had made him stand out.

Nicholas owed thanks to Leo for all the introductions to these individuals who now formed his team, some of whom had had rocky beginnings. They were all incredibly strong characters, who had seen how evil and cruel man could be — but together, they needed to be strong — set on one goal — to help save our planet.

One minute. It was time.

Nicholas picked up his pad and a pen and made his way to the meeting room.

The team were present with the exception of Summer.

"Where's Summer?" Nicholas asked.

"She's just finishing a call," Joshua said, she's been on hold to South America for ages trying to get permission for your visit.

Again, Nicholas couldn't believe how long things took to sort out. He figured the Brazilians didn't take too kindly to being told what to do. They had agreed to curtail their deforestation operations by an agreed amount and yet, far from decreasing, it seemed their operations were on the increase.

Megan walked in with drinks and placed them on the table.

"Thank you Megan," Nicholas said taking his seat at the head of the table. It was a well–appointed conference room with a large recycled meeting table and chairs and a projector which pointed at a flat white–painted wall.

"Sorry I'm late," Summer said rushing into the room and sitting down.

Megan closed the door behind her and sat in a chair nearby.

"No problem. Any luck?"

"Sorry Nic, no luck at all. It was really nice of my contact to speak to me so early but he says he can't do anything."

"That's disappointing." Nicholas sighed, "Anyway, we're here to discuss priorities."

"It is a shame," Romain said, "I think Brazil was the favourite for all of us. Without the forests we are all doomed anyway."

There were murmurs of agreement from around the table.

"I know, but at this rate we're going to need a miracle to get us there," Nicholas said. "Alex? What's on the list?"

Alexandra looked down at her pad, turned to a previous page, then another, another and then back again.

"Japan's whaling continues, despite Greenpeace efforts. We could make some impact there perhaps, especially around the fact that they've been slaughtering pregnant whales."

Nicholas nodded, "Okay, next."

"Illegal poaching in Africa, elephants, rhino's, they're all disappearing at an alarming rate, plus the news recently about the locals killing endangered animals for bush meat."

"And ..." Summer said, banging her hand on the table, "We need to do something about those fucking hunting tours!"

Nicholas agreed. She had after all seen things first hand.

Nicholas gestured to Alexandra to move on.

"The good news is that panda numbers are increasing but not to the point that they can be reclassified from endangered to vulnerable."

"That's really good to hear. If that is the case we can move that down the priority list. What else?" Nicholas asked.

Summer sat forward and spoke, "There is a big debate at the moment about whether we should still have Zoos — this was topical a while back when a child fell into the enclosure in Cincinatti and Harambe the gorilla was shot."

"That was such a shame. That gorilla was seventeen years old. They could have done something else I am sure, tranquilizer, distraction ... something," Joshua said.

"If I remember correctly, wasn't there a similar incident years ago where the gorilla actually cared for the child until help came?" Romain said.

"Yes, you're right," Alex replied, "These animals are much more sensitive and compassionate than people realise."

Alex turned her pages again and scanned the list, pausing momentarily to review certain items.

"How many pages of issues do you have there, Alex?"

Alexandra looked up, "Four — double sided."

"And how many issues per page?"

"Two columns per page," Alex replied.

Nicholas was trying to make a point, "and how many in total?"

"Four pages, double–sided, eight in total, two columns, with ..." Alexandra quickly counted the lines, "thirty two lines per page is ..." she did a quick calculation in her head, "five hundred and twelve issues, or thereabouts."

"Five hundred and twelve!" Joshua said.

"Yes, the list includes things like poisoning of falcons, otter habitats as well as the big stuff like plastic in the oceans and chemicals in rivers," Alexandra added.

"It makes you despair doesn't it?" Summer said.

Everyone nodded their heads.

"And the cause of all of it ..." Joshua said philosophically, "Humans."

The team lowered their heads, sharing a joint feeling of shame towards their race.

For a moment they were all silent. Romain shifted his weight in the chair and spoke.

"There is something that has always baffled me about humans."

"What's that Romain?" Nicholas asked.

"Humans are the most intelligent species and yet, given all the knowledge and awareness we have of what we are doing to the planet, we still do it. It is almost like, oh, how do you say in English? In French it is 'Ne mordez pas la main qui vous nourrit',"

Nicholas didn't speak French, but in a flash, he remembered his Gran telling him about his Grandad's business and the strikes that contributed to its demise.

"Do not bite the hand that feeds you."

"Yes, yes, that is exactly it," Romain said. "It is crazy, is it not. It would be like burning your home to keep warm. You are warm for a while but then you have no home."

Everyone around the table nodded and agreed.

Outside the office the phone rang. Megan quietly left the room to answer it.

"I still think the deforestation in South America is what needs our attention most urgently," Romain said.

Everyone agreed.

Nicholas stood up. "Yes, I agree too, but it's no good if

none of us can get into the country to do anything about it. We'll have to choose something else. Unless we do try to do more than one task at a time. But then we run the risk of spreading ourselves too thinly as we've already discussed."

Megan walked back in.

"Sorry to interrupt Nic, but there is a man downstairs who would like to see you."

"Does he have an appointment?"

"No but he did say that it's important and that it would be worth your while to see him."

"What's his name?"

"Larry Bell. He has an American accent."

"An American?" Romain said, "Perhaps Summer knows him?"

Summer looked at him with a bemused expression on her face, "What?"

"It was a joke," Romain said.

Nicholas was initially tempted to ask Megan to tell the man to go away but a voice in his head told him not to.

"Okay Meg, tell him I'll see him, send him up. You guys go through these five hundred plus issues and find me a fitting replacement to the rainforest issue."

"Yes, will do," Alexandra said.

"Certainly," Romain replied.

Joshua nodded and Summer pondered the question.

***

Nicholas sat down in his office and waited.

After a couple of minutes, Megan appeared with a man.

Nicholas guessed around mid–fifties, although he wasn't good with ages, anyone older than fifty just looked old.

"Hello Nicholas."

"Call me Nic. You are Larry Bell?"

"Yes, Larry Bell. Thank you for seeing me Nic. I appreciate that you must be very busy."

Nicholas beckoned him to sit.

"Would you like a drink?"

"Just water please." Larry said smiling at Megan.

"Two waters please, Megan," Nicholas sat down.

"What can I do for you?"

"Well, Nic, I hope it is more a case of what I can do for you."

Nicholas sat back in his chair, not sure quite how to take the man's unannounced visit and overly confident attitude.

Megan appeared with the drinks and put them on the desk.

"Thank you my dear," Larry said. His accent was intriguing. It sounded like a combination of an American western drawl with a hint of Portuguese."

"Go on."

Megan left the room and closed the door behind her.

"I've been watching you and what you're doing here with a great deal of interest. I'm impressed, very impressed. It's rare to see someone of your young age, if you don't mind me saying, doing something so charitable and with so much potential."

Nicholas wondered where this was going, "Sorry, I am a little confused."

"Well that's it. I want to help bring out your potential."

"You want to help bring out my potential?"

"Yes. I want to help you Nic."

"Help me — how?"

"I'd like to help you and your team achieve your potential."

"Sorry, I am having a little difficulty following you. If you are after a job, I think you've got things round the wrong way. We don't have any positions open at the moment," Nicholas's patience had just about run out. He stood, "Thank you for coming in ..."

"Nic, sorry, we've got off on the wrong foot. My apologies, I am too forward, but that's just my nature, I get things done, I am a problem solver."

"A problem solver?"

"Yes, please, sit down and just give me five more minutes of your time."

Nicholas looked into his eyes and saw something which convinced him to sit.

"I used to work for the US Government as a Diplomatic Attaché. That meant I would travel the world liaising with other governments and countries' leaders to reach diplomatic solutions to diplomatic problems. That was my official title, but effectively I was just a trouble shooter. When there were problems, they'd send me in and I'd sort them out."

Nicholas's interest was piqued.

"As the years went by I grew disenchanted with the powers that be and realised everyone is in it for their own specific gains. I wanted to help make a difference by putting my skills and knowledge to good use."

Nicholas was impressed with what he was hearing.

"Have you ever worked in South America?"

"Yes, I have, I spent twenty years there on and off. In Venezuela, Colombia, Bolivia ..."

Nicholas interrupted.

"Brazil?"

"... and Brazil."

"That's interesting as we have a problem that needs solving — we can't get into Brazil. The issue of rainforest deforestation is a primary priority of ours but we can't do anything if we can't get in."

Larry raised his hands in a 'there you go' kind of way, "And that sounds like something I can help you with."

"You can get us in?"

"I'm sure of it."

Larry stood up and buttoned his tweed jacket.

"Can you give me a few days and I'll get back to you."

Nicholas stood, "Er, yes — of course."

Larry turned to leave.

"But you haven't said what you want in return?"

"Let me show you what I can do first and then we can discuss things further."

Nicholas shrugged his shoulders. "Okay."

Larry left.

***

When Nicholas returned to the meeting room, the team were continuing to debate priorities.

"Who was that?" Romain asked.

Nicholas sat down. "Some guy called Larry Bell. He used to work for the US Government and he thinks that he can get us into South America."

"Really? That's fantastic," Alexandra said.

"Excellent," Romain said.

"Wow," Joshua said, "What an amazing coincidence he should turn up."

Nicholas sat back in his chair, there was that feeling in his stomach again, "Yes, it was an amazing coincidence."

Chapter 28

Nicholas sat at his desk fighting off the urge to go to the toilet while he tried to finish a press release.

So many things had happened over the past few months. He could hardly believe they were real. One thing he found staggering and also rather satisfying was how everything he wrote got quoted word for word in newspapers and magazines across the world.

As his fingers hovered over the keyboard he could hold the urge no longer. He got up.

Outside his office is where Megan sat, but she was not at her desk.

The long meeting room was on one side of the corridor and four offices were on the other.

The toilets were at the end and around the corner.

As he walked past the offices he could hear a raised voice — it was Summer. She had a fiery temper at times, so he thought nothing more of it and walked to the end of the corridor.

The men's toilets were right next door to the ladies' and as he walked by he could have sworn he heard Megan's voice cry out.

Nicholas tapped the door with his knuckles.

"Hello? Megan, are you okay?"

No answer.

"Meg?"

Still no answer.

He pushed the door open looked inside.

"Megan, is that you? Is everything okay?"

"Nic? Yes, I'm okay," Megan said tearfully.

Clearly everything was not okay. Nicholas walked in.

Megan was standing in front of the washbasins. She was very upset, her mascara had run in streaks down her perfectly made–up face and her mobile phone was on the floor.

Nicholas bent down and picked it up. He turned it over — it seemed fine.

"What's the matter?"

"Nothing."

"Obviously there is — what's up? You can tell me Meg," Nicholas said softly.

"You'll think it's silly."

"No I won't. Did you drop your phone?"

"No, I threw it."

"You threw your phone? Why?"

"I couldn't get it right."

"Sorry, you couldn't get what right?"

"My pose," Megan said.

"Your pose?"

"I was posing for a selfie and it just wouldn't come out right."

"Oh I see," Nicholas said, not wanting to admit that he didn't see at all.

"But why take a selfie in the toilet?"

"It's the only place where there are mirrors behind me."

Nicholas looked at the mirror and where she was standing and tried to imagine what type of photo she had been trying to take.

Megan could see he was confused.

"You don't understand. I have to keep up my image," Megan snapped.

"That's fine, Meg. I wasn't judging you."

Megan gently dabbed the tears from her face. Looking at herself in the mirror was making her even more distressed.

"They have to see me at my best."

Nicholas was still confused, "Sorry, who has to see you at your best?"

Alex walked in.

"What's going on?" Alex said, wondering what she'd walked in on.

"Hi Alex — Meg's a bit upset. She dropped her phone and thought she'd broken it."

"Oh Meg, poor you — are you okay?" Alex rushed over.

"I'll leave you girls to it," Nicholas said.

He left the toilets and opened the next door along.

He was now desperate to take care of something for himself.

Chapter 29

Nicholas was almost finished with his press release when there was a knock at the door.

Megan walked in.

"Can I have a word?"

"Yes, of course," Nicholas said. "Come in and sit down."

Meg sat down. She was sheepish and embarrassed.

"Sorry about earlier."

"That's okay, are you feeling better?"

"Yes," Megan nodded. "Thank you for being kind and picking up my phone. It was silly."

"That's okay," Nicholas said. He didn't want to say how foolish he thought she had been.

"I don't know what I would have done if I'd broken my phone."

Nicholas understood. What if someone had needed to get in contact with her in an emergency, or ...

"It's my life. It's the most important thing in the world."

Nicholas was taken aback. His phone was important to him but it wasn't the most important thing in the world.

"I don't know what I'd do if I couldn't update my followers."

"Your followers?"

"I've got over five thousand followers on Instagram, they have to see me at my best," Megan snapped.

"Who are these followers?"

"I dunno — just people."

"How many photos do you take a day?"

"Depends."

"On?"

"Just depends — a few."

"And you post all of them to Instagram?"

She cocked her head to one side and looked at him like he was stupid.

"I post about ten a day but it might take ten or twenty attempts to get the best picture."

Nicholas realised she meant 'per picture', did some quick mental arithmetic and worked out that she must be taking hundreds of photos a day.

"Anyway, I just wanted to say thanks."

"No problem," Nicholas didn't know what else to say.

Megan got up and left.

No wonder she was away from her desk so often — now it all made sense.

He turned his attention back to his press release and read it through from the beginning. He made a few alterations and was just about to read through one final time when there was another knock on his door.

It was Joshua.

Nicholas waved him in.

"You got a sec, Nic?"

"Yes, of course. Take a seat."

He'd always liked Josh. Even though there was something worrying about his secret past, they had always got on well.

Joshua sat.

"How can I help?"

"I'd like to give my notice," Joshua said outright.

"What?"

"My notice — I'd like to hand it in."

"I heard you," Nicholas said. "I just didn't want to believe what you said."

Joshua stared at the floor.

"But you've only been with us — what is it — four weeks, why do you want to leave?"

"This stuff is too big picture. I need to get my teeth into something specific which is why I feel I have to go."

"Go where?"

"Animal Rights UK."

"What do you mean — too big picture?"

"You're looking at world issues and climate change, but I want to concentrate more on issues that affect animals in the UK."

"Yes, we are dealing with world issues — but you knew what you were getting into when you joined."

"Yes, I know, but I've changed my mind. That's all."

You've changed your mind? That's all is it? Nicholas couldn't believe what he was hearing.

"I can tell you've made up your mind so I won't try to change it. Can you let me have it in writing please and your notice period is four weeks from today."

"Oh I told them I would start on Monday."

"You told them what? But you signed a contract. Your notice period is four weeks."

"So? Does that mean I can't go on Monday?"

"Well, what about the projects you've been dealing with, they will all need to be handed over. We will have to tell other groups that you'll be going and let them know who the next point of contact will be — it will take time to reorganise."

Joshua shrugged his shoulders.

Nicholas expected more.

"Does the rest of the team know?"

"Yes, I told them already."

"But you should have discussed it with me first."

"Yeah but you couldn't have stopped me going."

"That's not the point, it's just ..."

Nicholas sighed.

"Make sure that all your projects are shared equally amongst the others. Give me a list of each project and who you've handed it over to. I also want a list of the primary contacts at the groups you've been liaising with by the end of the day. I will email them personally to let them know you're leaving and to reassure them their projects will be in–hand."

Joshua nodded.

"By the end of the day," Nicholas said firmly.

"Yes, a list by the end of the day."

Nicholas nodded.

Joshua got up and left.

Nicholas was very disappointed.

He turned his attention back to the press release.

The phone rang.

He sighed.

"Yes, Meg?"

"I've got HSBC on the phone about a payment that you made earlier?" Meg said.

"Okay, put them through."

"Hello, is that Nicholas Savage?" The voice was somewhat difficult to follow.

"Yes, it is."

"This is HSBC. You attempted to make a payment earlier today ..."

Nicholas started to speak but the voice continued.

"... and we need to ask you some questions as part of our on-going efforts to combat fraudulent activity."

"Is this regarding my ..." Nicholas tried in vain to interrupt the voice.

"Sorry," Nicholas said, "There appears to be a delay on the line, are you in the UK?"

After a moment, the voice replied, "I am speaking from Hyderabad in India."

"That explains the delay then. Is this regarding my payment to Amazon earlier?"

"I am sorry, but before I can talk to you about activity on your account, I need you to answer some security questions."

"Okay," Nicholas replied.

"Can you tell me first, second and fifth letters of the password on your account?"

Nicholas thought for a moment, "Erm, I don't think I have one?"

"When you set up your telephone banking you would have specified a password to be used on your account, what is the first, second and fifth letters of the password on your account?"

"I am sure I don't have one. I don't think I ever set one up."

"According to the system there is a password on your account, what is the first, second and fifth letters of the password on your account?"

Nicholas was getting impatient. He took a deep breath.

"I can't remember. What can we do if I can't remember?"

"I can reset your password if you would like?"

"You'll have to because I can't remember what it is."

"Before I can reset your password, I need to ask you a number of security questions."

Here we go again.

Nicholas managed to answer all the questions including his date of birth, registered card address and details from the card. He even managed to come up with a memorable password that he was sure he wouldn't forget.

"Can you confirm the amount of the payment?"

"One moment," Nicholas said as he quickly tried to find the email confirmation. "Ahh, here it is — it was exactly forty–three pounds and ninety–nine pence."

"And who was the payment to?"

"Amazon."

"I am sorry but that is not quite correct, can you tell me who the payment was to please?"

Nicholas was a little worried that maybe his account had been hacked. He looked at the email again.

"Definitely Amazon, I've got the email confirmation here."

"Can you be more specific?"

Specific? How can I be more specific? Nicholas thought to himself as he triple–checked the email.

"Erm, at the bottom of the email it says Amazon EU Sarl — does that help?"

"Yes, that is it, thank you."

"So, what now?"

"We'll let the payment go through."

"Thank you."

"Is there anything else I can help you with today?"

"Er, you phoned me, not the other way around?"

"Yes, but are there any other HSBC products you might be interested in today?"

I'm not going through that again.

"No, thank you. That's enough. Thanks for your help. Good bye."

The voice said goodbye and Nicholas put the phone down.

He was just about to go back to the press release when he noticed an email come in from Amazon — apparently there had been a problem trying to take payment from his card and unless he took action the order wouldn't be placed.

"Oh for God's sake!" he said aloud.

The phone rang again.

"Meg, what is it now?"

"Sorry Nic, but I have Esmeralda DaFoe on the line from the WWF?"

"Oh right, I wasn't expecting a call from Esmeralda, I wonder ..."

"Hello?" a voice said.

"Hello? Meg?"

"No, this is Esmeralda DaFoe from the WWF, is that Nic Savage?"

"Sorry, Esmeralda, it appears my PA put your call through without telling me."

He sat back in his chair, "How can I help you?"

"I've just had an email from Joshua saying that he's leaving. I can't believe you didn't tell me yourself."

Nicholas sighed, quietly and deeply.

"Sorry Esmeralda, he wasn't meant to do that. I was going to email you later, to explain the situation personally."

There was a knock on the door. He glanced up, it was Joshua. Nicholas waved him in.

"I hope this isn't going to jeopardise our Tiger project in Nepal. We have targets to reach to coincide with the Chinese year of the tiger in 2022."

"It won't. Joshua will be handing over to another member of the team."

"Who?" Esmeralda said.

From that Nicholas concluded that Joshua hadn't mentioned it in the email.

"All that will be in my email, you have my word."

Nicholas could hear Esmeralda sigh on the other end of the line.

"Thank you, Nic. I knew I could count on you. Leo speaks very highly of you."

"Leo's very kind — thank you. I'll email you later and talk to you again very soon."

"Goodbye, Nic."

"Goodbye, Esmeralda," Nicholas said putting the phone down.

Joshua sat opposite him.

"I specifically told you to give me the list and I would email everybody."

"I thought it would be easier if I just did it."

"But that is not what I asked — Joshua," Nicholas said, sitting forward in his chair with his arms on the desk.

"We're working with some big name organisations, major players in the world of environmental protection, animal welfare and climate control. As I have explained before, I want us to be at the centre of all this, to help these organisations achieve their goals, to be a major player ourselves and how can I do that properly when Esmeralda DaFoe phones up from the WWF criticising us for not having our act together."

Joshua stared blankly. Nicholas jumped out of his seat angrily.

"This woman is on the board of directors at the WWF. She sits right next to Leonardo DiCaprio, our sponsor — our supporter — the very person we owe all this to," Nicholas said, gesturing to the office and everything around him, his face growing redder and redder by the second.

Joshua sank into the chair.

Nicholas grew another two inches in height.

"It's exactly this kind of irresponsible behaviour and disregard for working practices and direct instructions that really fucking pisses me off. You said you had a new job to go to — well, you can go now!" Nicholas snapped with his finger pointing to the door.

Joshua knew there was nothing he could say. He walked out.

Nicholas sat down and took some deep breaths. He was fuming. He felt hot, flushed, angry and disappointed. He picked up the phone and dialled Meg. It rang and rang.

He looked up. She wasn't at her desk.

He had a pretty good idea where she might be.

He stormed down the corridor towards the toilets. He pushed the door of the ladies' open.

"Meg?" Nic snapped.

Meg hesitated and then replied, "Yes?"

"What are you doing in there?"

She hesitated again, "I am taking photos."

"Meg, I don't pay you to take photos of yourself, I pay you to work. Joshua will be leaving immediately. Can you ensure that he only leaves with his belongings and no company property — and if you fail to carry out these instructions, you will be leaving too!"

"Also, make sure everyone, including you, are in the meeting room in five minutes."

The response was timid: "Okay, Nic."

Nicholas let go of the door and stormed back to his office.

He stood in front of the window and looked out at the world.

His heart was racing. He started to breathe deeply, concentrating on the air filling his lungs. He held his breath for two seconds and then breathed out — just as his psychotherapist had taught him years earlier.

It worked. He felt much calmer. Still disappointed, but calmer.

He sat down. He only had a few minutes. He desperately wanted to finish the press release otherwise he would miss the deadline and that would be a disaster.

He had promises to keep and expectations to meet and people around him weren't helping.

He saw an email from Amazon saying the order had failed. He'd deal with it later. If one order failed he would simply order another. Their order cut—off time was later than this press release was due and he had to prioritise accordingly.

He flicked between windows on his computer back to the press release. He'd already read it in detail earlier so a quick rescan to ensure nothing had changed would be fine.

It was fine — sent.

Nicholas stood up, took another deep breath and walked to the board room.

The team, minus the now absent Josh were present — the room was in silence.

They all watched Nicholas approach the end of the table. He stood behind his chair.

They were quiet and uncertain of what was to come next.

Nicholas stood a moment and gathered his thoughts.

"Josh has left. I know you know that already because he told you he was leaving before he told me. That's fine, I don't necessarily mind he told you first but what does upset me is that he has let us all down."

He continued.

"We have a notice period for a reason, to help ensure a smooth transition and handover of the projects he was working on. He was intending to leave by the end of today which gives us no time to do any of that properly. He has already told some of the charities he's leaving and they're fretting because they think we've let them down. Just one small action can have huge ramifications on how people perceive us and obviously their opinion is crucial — they must be able to trust us."

"I want us to be seen as professional, knowledgeable and experienced and most of all as making a valuable contribution to the welfare of this planet, its habitat and its animals. I can't do that on my own, I need a team — I need you."

Nicholas wiped a tear from the corner of his eye. He hadn't realised how deeply this had affected him.

"Nic?"

Nicholas looked up.

"We don't agree with what Josh did. You're right, he let us all down and that annoys us too," Romain said.

"We didn't know he was intending to leave and we won't let you down Nic," Summer said.

"We're right behind you Nic, all the way," Alex said.

Nicholas smiled. "Thank you guys, that really means a lot."

"Does anyone know where he was going?" Summer asked.

"Animal Action," Romain replied. "He said they get things done and don't just talk about it — his words — not mine."

Nicholas nodded and looked over to the chair nearest the door.

Megan had her head lowered and was scribbling on her notepad — hopefully taking notes.

He looked up and noticed writing on the board.

"What's that?"

"Josh did it before he left," Summer replied.

Nicholas walked around the table and looked at the board.

Around the edges Josh had made reference to animals and the issues affecting them. Not everything from their list but certainly the major ones. He followed the writing all the way around the board, each reference having an arrow that pointed to the centre of the board, all back to one common denominator.

"Do you want me to rub it off Nic?" Summer asked.

"No, leave it, it's powerful — it's accurate."

Chapter 30

Nicholas hoped today would be less eventful than the day before.

He looked at the clock — nine fifty.

Rebecca Plumpton from Care for the Wild International was due to arrive at any minute.

He was reading information from their website when the phone rang — it was Meg.

"Is Rebecca here?"

"Yes, shall I make her a drink and seat her in the conference room?"

"Yes, please — tell her I'll be through in a minute and could you ask Summer to join us and could you come and take notes please."

"Will do, Nic," Meg said and hung up.

Nicholas had been in early to try and catch up with his email list advising various organisations of Josh's departure. He'd done pretty well, only a handful left to go.

***

Nicholas walked into the meeting room.

"Rebecca, very nice to see you."

Rebecca stood up and beamed a smile, "Very nice to see you too Nic, I have been looking forward to meeting you."

Nicholas smiled, pulled a chair from underneath the table and sat down beside her.

Meg appeared with Summer.

"This is Meg, my loyal and trusty PA," Nicholas said, gesturing towards Megan. "And, Summer Bevan, who is exceptionally well experienced and has done a lot of work in Africa."

They said their pleasantries and sat down.

"I was looking at your diagram on the board," Rebecca said, pointing to Josh's drawing on the whiteboard. "It sends a strong message doesn't it."

"It certainly does, Rebecca."

"Are those all your projects?"

"Some of them, yes," Nicholas said.

Rebecca gasped to think they were working on so many projects. It made the word in capital letters in the middle all the more overwhelming.

"Thank you for seeing me. I wanted to bring you up to date with what's happening with us and to find out more about your plans and how you might be able to help."

"Okay, sure — fire away."

"Care for the Wild International has recently merged with the Born Free Foundation. Together we are stronger and more capable and can pool our resources to work on projects at home, including Badgers and Marine Mammals, Brown Bears in Greece as well as other projects in Europe and Africa."

"Was there a specific project that you feel we can help with?" Nic asked. He was already aware of the merger and many of the projects they were involved in.

"Well, specifically Africa and bush meat. I read your piece in Wildlife magazine and how this is something you're targeting," Rebecca said, pointing to where it was written on the board.

"Yes it is. It was Summer who wrote that article." Nicholas gestured towards its author.

"It was very good," Rebecca said.

"Thank you," Summer replied. "Did you know we're working with the Bushmeat Crisis Task Force?"

"No, I don't remember reading that in the article?"

"It was only confirmed yesterday. Nic is very keen for us to be a facilitator, helping organisations work together more effectively and exploit mutual opportunities."

"That's right," Nicholas said walking around the table. "Thank you, Summer."

"There are so many organisations out there, all doing their best to help spread the word about the plight of animals, the environment and the climate, each one doing their own individual thing, trying to reach their audience and achieve their objectives."

"And this is where I want Rapture to help."

"I want us to help organisations like Care for the Wild — or Born Free as it is now and the Bushmeat Crisis Task Force. To introduce them to each other, to bring them together and help them collaborate. I want to provide the tools and systems to help project manage what is going on, who is doing what, when and how it is being done. So that every organisation can work as efficiently as possible with minimal duplication of effort and maximum return on charitable investment."

Nicholas stood at the head of the table visibly animated.

"I want us all to use the resources that we have at our

fingertips — the internet, social media, mobile phone apps — everything we can to help get the message out and make as many people as possible realise this is OUR planet and we ALL have a responsibility to look after it and every living thing that we share it with."

Rebecca sat spellbound. She had read about Nicholas in the papers and she had seen him interviewed on television, but this is the first time she was able to see and hear his passion first–hand.

Rebecca stood up and started clapping.

Nicholas blushed.

"He's incredibly convincing isn't he," Summer said.

"Yes, he is," Rebecca replied.

Nicholas waved the comment aside, "I just want to make a difference, that's all."

"And that is why everyone wants to work with you, Nic," Rebecca said. "You also mentioned your project management system."

"Yes, Clarion — it should be online in a week or two."

"Clarion? That's an interesting name, it means trumpet doesn't it?"

"Yes — an old war trumpet. I had to come up with a name for the project and I thought that was appropriate. It's a clarion call to groups across the world to help them communicate with each other."

"A war trumpet?" Rebecca said. "Interesting — I suppose it is a war in a way," she said looking at the whiteboard.

Their combined gaze fell on the white board and the single word written in the middle, the cause of all of the problems — HUMANS.

Chapter 31

Nicholas yawned as he sat at his desk.

He felt like it should be midday yet it was only eight forty–five. He'd been at work since five thirty. His Mum had been worried that he was working too many hours but things needed to get done.

Joshua leaving meant he had to pick up the pieces and emails, phone messages and even hand written letters were arriving every day.

Nicholas glanced over at the small table. Scattered on it were at least another hundred letters that still needed to be opened. He was popular, people wanted to meet him and do interviews, but what they wanted most was money or an introduction to Leo.

He didn't want to just give money away. There was plenty of money to go around, but some of it was being wasted and some efforts were being duplicated. What he wanted was to give help and support and that is why he had created Clarion.

He hadn't heard from the development team all week. His idea was simple, get people to contribute their skills to help showcase their work.

Rapture wasn't paying for the system — but Rapture was

giving the developers of the system what money couldn't buy: publicity and promotion on a global stage that would in turn help them to make money from the work that came off the back of it — with other groups and charities across the world, if they wanted it.

It was a win–win situation for everyone, but the lack of updates concerned him.

The system should be in final testing this week and was due to go live in two weeks.

He had done his research and offered the opportunity to a company that had already produced a similar web–based project management system.

The current version worked on the basis that all projects belonged to the charity, but Nic had wanted an extra level added to make it a tiered system.

Rapture would oversee and coordinate everything. The individual groups and charities would be in the middle and projects could be divided amongst groups thereby sharing information in a secure environment and collaborating in the most efficient way possible.

He liked the fact that the software already had a risk register built into it which allowed groups to assign resources based on threat levels to species or environment.

Additional features included categorisation, tasks, scheduling, approval, sign–off and even target scoring and measures, together with full management reporting and statistical analysis.

When Nic had asked about adding the extra layer on top, the reply had been a very confident 'yes'.

He knew they started early. He picked up the phone.

"Hello, is Mike there please?

"Yes, it's Mike speaking, how can I help?" A cheery voice said on the other end of the line.

"Hi Mike, It's Nic Savage from Rapture."

"Oh, hi Nic, how are you?" Mike said — Nic detected a change in the tone of his voice.

"I am just phoning for an update as we were expecting Clarion to be in testing this week."

"I'm so glad you called. I was going to call you later today," Mike said.

"Er, we've just got a few issues that we're trying to sort out."

"What type of issues?"

"Just some problems with the extra project layer that we're adding."

"I presume this is going to delay the project?"

"Yes," was Mike's simple reply.

"And ... by how long?"

"About another two ..." Mike mumbled.

"Another two weeks did you say? That's okay, we can work around that," Nic replied positively.

"Er, no — two months," Mike replied.

"Two months! That more than doubles the estimated development time," Nic said, raising his voice.

Mike didn't reply.

"You said you could do what we needed to make it work."

"And we can," Mike said.

"You can in two months," Nicholas said and sighed, "You said it was 'Easy' — your words."

"It's not quite as easy as we thought."

"Two months is one hell of a delay. I've been trying to manage the expectations of some of the biggest charities and environment groups in the world — the WWF, Greenpeace, The Rainforest Trust, Friends of the Earth — this is just," Nicholas was so angry he couldn't find the word, " — humiliating!"

"Sorry, Nic, we just underestimated the amount of work involved."

Nicholas's brain went into overdrive. Thoughts and ideas rushed into his mind.

Nicholas took a deep breath and spoke.

"Okay, Mike, what do you have that does work?"

"All the middle tier stuff works, basically it's the Rapture level, the ability to oversee projects, reporting, statistics, all the high level stuff," Mike did his best to cover off all the positives.

"So we at Rapture don't have the high level view, but we could still log–in at each organisation or group level to manage what is going on?"

"Yes, that's right."

"In my opinion then, there is no reason to delay going live. The organisations, groups and other charities wouldn't see our level anyway so, as far as they are concerned, there would be no missing functionality?"

"Er, that's right."

"So, can you envisage a problem going live with what you do have?"

"Well, only that it would be incomplete according to the specification."

"Specification aside, we need to deliver what we agreed

within the promised timeframe. This would allow us to achieve that."

"Yes it would."

"Then that is what we'll do."

"Mike, why didn't you suggest this as a compromise solution?"

"Er, I don't know — because the project isn't complete as per the specification."

Nicholas ignored the comment. "So, can you get the most current working version up and ready with logins across to us by this afternoon so we can continue testing?"

"Yes, Nic," Mike replied.

"Okay, I'll expect them later. Thank you."

"Okay, Nic."

Nicholas hung up.

***

"Would you like a drink, Nic?" Megan asked distracting him from his computer.

"Oh yes, thank you — tea, please," Nicholas replied.

"Before you go Meg, I've been trying to remember the name of that person at PETA that Rebecca recommended we speak to at our meeting the other day. I've checked the minutes but it's not in there?"

"I probably couldn't remember the name."

"That's fine, can you bring your notes please and let me know."

"Er, yes, I'll try to remember."

Meg left and Nicholas turned his attention back to his computer.

In a few minutes Meg appeared with a cup of tea in one hand and her pad in the other.

"Here you go Nic, your tea."

"Thanks Meg. Did you find the name?"

"I haven't remembered yet."

Nicholas was confused. "You don't have to remember, just refer to your notes."

Meg appeared sheepish.

"Can you just check your notes, now, please."

She kept the pad close to her chest and flicked through.

"No, not here."

"What do you mean, not there, you can't have checked it thoroughly enough. Check again."

Meg flicked through her pad once again and spent a little more time checking.

"Nope, sorry."

"Meg you're meant to write everything down, not just the main parts of the discussion — let me see."

Meg recoiled a step, "Er, you won't be able to read my writing."

"I'm sure I can."

She placed the pad behind her back.

"No, it's private."

"Meg? What do you mean it's private? They are the notes to our meetings — they're not private."

"They're private to me."

"Meg, I really don't understand what is going on — give me the pad please."

Meg didn't know what to do.

"Meg, your pad is company property and the meetings

were on company time. Give me the pad now!"

Meg lowered her head, took a step closer and handed the pad to him.

He opened it. Inside were page after page of drawings.

"Drawings?"

Meg nodded.

"So, in every meeting we have, you don't take notes, you draw?"

Meg became defensive. "I always write the date at the top and the attendees as you'll see," Meg said, pointing to the pad.

"But obviously we need to know the detail of the meeting and everything we've discussed — that's the whole point of taking notes."

"I always listen and pay attention — that is how I write the meeting minutes."

"You do it from memory?"

"Yes, from memory and pictures."

"So that's what you meant earlier when you said you'd try to remember the name."

"Yes, I will remember, just give me time."

"You're meant to take minutes to record everything so that you won't be reliant on your memory."

"But I've got an excellent memory."

"That's not good enough," Nicholas snapped.

"Everything that we do here is done for a reason, a very good reason. As a charitable organisation we need to be responsible for everything we do and we are answerable to the Charity Commission. We have to abide by certain rules and regulations. One of these is that we have to keep very accurate minutes of any meetings we have. This is a legal requirement and we are bound to it by law. If there was ever an investigation they could consult our records, including your notes — so they are most definitely not private and it is crucial that you take them down precisely!" Nicholas said pointing at the pad.

"Oh, I didn't know that," Meg replied.

"And, you don't need to. There is so much I have to do to ensure that everything works here and that we are legally compliant. I have a huge responsibility to get it all right, which is why I have been here since five–fucking–thirty this morning. I need a team that can help and support me and I need that team to do what I ask them to do, when I ask them to do it — okay?"

Meg nodded.

"So, Meg." Nicholas threw the pad back at her. "Get a new pad and make proper notes from now on — understand?"

Meg caught the pad and nodded. "Yes Nic, I understand."

She closed the door behind her.

Nicholas walked over to the window and took a very deep breath.

Chapter 32

"Nic, I've got two parcels here from Amazon for you?"

"Thanks, Meg. Can you put them on the table please."

"Yes, sure," Meg said, struggling with the two boxes.

Nicholas finished writing his email and pressed send. He looked up.

He had expected an order from Amazon but not in two boxes and certainly not that size of box.

He grabbed a pair of scissors, carefully sliced through the tape on either end and opened one of the boxes. It was a brand new backpack for his upcoming trip to South America, if Larry was able to pull things off — but why such a large box, you could easily have fitted three backpacks inside.

He turned to the other box. It was the same size and the same weight.

He suspected what had happened.

He opened the box.

Another backpack.

HSBC had called to query the payment but had obviously let it go through. Then presumably Amazon hadn't updated their system in time, so the payment failure email had probably already been sent. Consequently when he re-ordered it later it was assumed to be a second order for a second backpack.

Nicholas sighed — nothing was ever easy.

He left the other backpack on the table in its box.

He returned to his desk and forwarded the original order confirmation to Megan with his login details and asked her to return the other backpack.

The phone rang.

Nicholas picked it up.

"Hi Nic, Larry Bell is here to see you, would you like to see him?"

"Yes, please Meg."

"Okay, one minute," Meg replied and hung up.

Larry walked into the office full of smiles and elation.

"You're in."

"What?" Nicholas said standing up.

"You're going to South America. Pack your bags — I hope your passport is current."

"I am?"

"Well, technically it's we. We go tomorrow."

"We? Tomorrow? That soon?"

"Yes, I'll have to come with you — my contact will be expecting it. And you said you wanted to get into South America, and I've done it for you."

Nicholas wanted to know more. "Please sit."

Larry nodded, unbuttoned his jacket and sat down.

"As I said, I've got good contacts in South America. I spoke to one of them, Pablo, in Brazil and he has arranged for two of us to get a special business visa."

"I was hoping it would be me and one of my team."

"I've known Pablo for nearly twenty years, we go way back together. He insists that I escort you as part of the business visa arrangement and I can only get two issued."

"Is that normal?"

"In South America, nothing is normal. Pablo doesn't know you, but he knows me and he insists that I am there too."

"Okay, I suppose that makes sense. A business visa?"

"We could have gone for a temporary visa and said that it was for research purposes but they get a little twitchy if they feel someone might want to meddle in their affairs — on the other hand, everyone wants more business."

"Okay, makes sense," Nic replied.

"Pablo will meet us at the airport with the visas."

Nicholas was surprised and impressed by the speed at which these arrangements had been made.

"Er, thank you," was all he could say.

"You're welcome."

"But you still haven't told me what you want in return?"

"I've got to that stage in life where I'd like to give something back and what you're doing here is amazing. All I ask is that you cover the flight and expenses and I am happy to help."

Nicholas thought for a moment, weighing everything up, "Sounds great, let's do it."

"No problem," Larry said. "It's the Amazonian rainforest you're covering primarily isn't it?"

"Er, yes it is," Nicholas replied, amazed at how well informed he was.

"Okay, the area we'll want to go to is north of Mato Grosso in the West of Brazil. You'll need to get a flight from Heathrow to Manaus."

Heathrow to Manaus, Nicholas repeated in his mind so as not to forget.

"I am flying back to the States tonight, but get your PA to phone me with your arrival time and I'll meet you at the airport in Manaus," Larry said as he stood up. He reached into his jacket and pulled out his business card.

"I need to organise a cameraman to record footage of the expedition."

"Don't worry, I've already thought of that. Do you know Dominic Howard?"

Nicholas shook his head.

"He's already out there and he's very good. And besides, I've only got permission for you and me to get into the country."

"Oh, okay."

Larry smiled and opened the door to leave, "See you in a couple of days."

Nicholas looked down at the business card, turned it over and back again. All it had on it was his name and a mobile number.

When Nicholas looked up, Larry had gone.

There was that feeling in his stomach again. What did it mean?

He knew one thing though, they'd got their big break and he was finally going to South America.

Megan walked in.

"Everything okay?"

Nicholas looked down at the card again. "Yes. Yes, everything is fine. Can you assemble the team in the meeting room please — I have something important to report."

Chapter 33

Nicholas walked along the pavement counting down the numbers to his Gran's.

Despite being so busy with Rapture, he made sure he visited his Gran at least once a week. After all, if it hadn't been for her, none of this would ever have happened.

He reached the front door, rang the bell and waited — and waited.

The door opened. The chain was on.

"Who is it?" a voice called out from behind.

"It's me, Gran. It's Nicholas."

"Not today thank you," his Gran said and closed the door.

Nicholas sighed and rang the bell again.

The door opened.

"Hello, Lillian, my name is Nicholas and I am the son of Angela Savage, your daughter."

A moment passed while his Gran thought things over, "Nicholas, how nice to see you. Come on in."

She removed the chain and opened the door.

"Would you like a cup of tea and a sandwich?"

"A cup of tea would be nice, no sandwich thank you. I've already had lunch."

"Okay. Go and sit yourself down and I'll be back in a minute."

Nicholas went into the living room and looked around. His Gran was becoming more forgetful and the deterioration had been swift. He looked at the clock on the mantelpiece. It was three thirty. He'd knocked off early to see his Gran and still have time to pack. Then he could go into work tomorrow and leave directly from the office. He noticed an object beside the clock — it was a shoe. What was a shoe doing on the mantelpiece?

After a few minutes, his Gran walked in with a tray.

Nicholas jumped up to help and grabbed the tray, "Here, let me help you."

"Thank you," she said and sat down.

As he was putting the tray on the table, Nicholas noticed there were two slices of bread wedged in his cup.

He sat down. She was definitely getting worse. She had her 'off days' a lot more frequently now, but his Mother wasn't there often enough to see it. Her new job was keeping her so busy. Even though she felt awful, she just couldn't find the time to go round.

He had an idea. He pulled out his phone, selected the camera and set it to record.

"I'm just checking something on my phone, one second. I'm having trouble getting a signal," Nicholas said as his Gran smiled, seeming to stare right through him.

He waved the phone around making sure he recorded the cup, the shoe on the mantelpiece and his Gran staring into space.

"Oh, I've just noticed you've forgotten the milk."

"You sit there. I'll go and get some."

He grabbed his cup and went into the kitchen. He threw the bread in the bin and rinsed the cup under the tap. He opened the fridge but there wasn't any milk. The ham had gone off, the cheese was unwrapped and there was her other shoe.

He kept the phone recording all the time.

"Mum, I'm recording this to show you how much worse Gran is getting. You don't often get to see her this bad when you come round so hopefully this might help," he whispered into the phone.

He removed the shoe, wrapped the cheese and threw the ham away.

He was about to walk out of the kitchen when he noticed a bowl of water on the floor and the back door wide open. He made sure he captured that too and closed and locked the back door.

He filled his cup with water and walked back into the living room.

She was still staring into space and smiling.

"Everything okay Gran?"

She became animated as though a switch had been flicked.

"Yes, everything is fine thank you."

"What day is it today Gran?" Nicholas asked as he sat down.

She thought about it for a moment and seemed to struggle, "I am surprised you're asking me Nicholas, you should know."

"I just wondered if you knew Gran."

She thought about it again, "I can't seem to think. You know what it's like when you get to my age. Every day seems to be the same anyway."

Nicholas was worried but there didn't seem to be an awful lot he could do about it at that time. He'd talk to his Mum and see what she thought, especially after he'd shown her the video.

His Gran just sat, smiling.

"I am going to South America, Gran."

No response.

"Gran — I said I am going to South America."

"Oh, we used to love it there. We'd often go when your Mum was young."

"What?" Nicholas said. He never knew they'd been to South America.

"We used to rent a little cottage just near the mouth of the river. It overlooked the castle. Your Mum's most favourite places to go were Frenchman's Bay with the cliffs and Sandhaven Beach where the sand seemed to stretch forever," Gran said disappearing into thought. "Oh they were lovely times."

"In South America?"

"South America, yes."

"Are you sure you mean South America, five thousand miles away?"

His Gran looked confused.

"No, you're right, it must be the other South America — the journey definitely wasn't that long — imagine all that distance, in your Grandfather's Morris Oxford."

"There is only one South America."

Nicholas watched her face. She was really struggling and he could see she was starting to get panicky.

"It was definitely South something."

Nicholas racked his brains, "You don't mean South Shields do you?"

"Yes, yes, that's it — South Shields, we used to go on holiday there."

Now it makes sense.

"What was the castle like?" Nicholas asked — amazed at how one minute she seemed so vague and the next able to recall memories from years ago.

"Its full name is Tynmouth Priory and Castle. It was a bit of a ruin but there was still a lot left of it. You could make out the walls and the huge windows. There were a lot of graves there too. It was quite a magical place."

"Sounds lovely. I'll have to try and go," Nicholas smiled.

His Gran had drifted off again.

He checked the phone to make sure it was still recording.

"Can you remember where I said I was going?"

"Going? You're going to South Shields. Make sure you visit the castle — and Sandhaven Beach — the sand stretches for miles."

He felt a touch of sadness and stopped recording. He'd captured enough to make the point.

They sat in silence for the rest of the time.

He drank his cup of water and said goodbye.

As he closed the door behind him, he couldn't help think that he may not be able to have any more meaningful discussions with his wise old Gran.

Chapter 34

The tube train screeched on its tracks and sparks flashed on the walls of the tunnel.

Daylight flooded the carriage as it emerged from the tunnel on its way to Heathrow airport.

Nicholas had lost count of the number of stops as he'd been busy trying to read a book that he'd brought with him. It was called Pearl of Wisdom. He didn't read that often and had forgotten how much he'd been enjoying it. It was about the Special Intelligence Agency and one of their agents who was embroiled in a mysterious case.

He looked up. A man opposite was fast asleep with a hand down his trousers.

He looked around. Everyone was in their own little world, mostly immersed in their mobile phones.

He turned back to his book and continued to read.

A voice called out and then another. Further along the carriage a man and a woman began to argue, seemingly about who was going to change their baby's nappy. The child was screaming and crying. It was obviously in discomfort, yet its parents were more concerned about which one of them was going to be inconvenienced by their baby's needs. That would involve diverting their attention from their phones.

The train pulled into the next station, Nicholas looked up. They had arrived at Hounslow Central, three stops to go.

Some people got off and some people got on. He turned his attention back to his book as the doors closed and the train pulled away.

He could hear a sound getting louder and louder. The racket was coming from the next carriage. The door opened and a man appeared singing at the top of his voice and thrashing an acoustic guitar with all his might. He kept pausing in front of people. They kept their attention on their phones. They didn't look up, pretending he didn't exist.

Nicholas looked to his left, no–one looked. He looked to his right, the couple were still arguing and the baby was crying even louder due to the commotion heading in its direction.

Despite no–one paying any attention, the man continued to walk through the carriage shouting and strumming loudly on the guitar.

Nicholas wondered when this hell was going to end.

The man opposite woke up. He obviously had no idea where he was for a moment. Then he realised where his hand was and quickly pulled it from his trousers. He stared at it for a moment, smelled it, and went back to sleep.

Nicholas sighed and tried to continue with his book.

The train finally pulled into the next station, Hounslow West. The man stopped singing, rushed to the door, shouted "Thanks everybody — see you next time," and jumped out onto the platform.

People walked on with their bags and suitcases. A smartly dressed man got on, dragging his suitcase behind him.

Nicholas desperately tried to focus on his book until his attention was snatched away by the case hitting his leg. "Ouch" Nicholas said. The man looked down and scowled as if to say 'how dare he interfere with his suitcase'. Nicholas rubbed his leg. The man walked off dragging his case carelessly behind him.

A group of teenagers, probably from China, sat next to him and opposite in the few empty seats available. They started to converse in very loud voices. One of them was looking for something on her phone. She laughed loudly and showed the screen to her friends. Each one of them laughed, more loudly than the one before. They continued to chatter and laugh at the top of their voices, so much so that he couldn't concentrate on his book any longer — just as he'd reached another exciting bit too! He reluctantly stuffed it into his backpack.

He looked out of the window and watched the outskirts of London zoom past. The train began to slow down and pull into Hatton Cross. *One more stop to go, thank heavens.*

The train doors closed. All seats were now taken and standing passengers shuffled and nudged each other into position.

A woman stood in front of him with a briefcase in her hand. Every time the train jolted it hit him in the leg. He tried to move but there was nowhere to move to and, to cap it all, the woman next to him huffed when he tried to reposition his elbow.

He could hear a commotion erupting from the other end of the carriage. Raised voices, words uttered, people making noises of disgust and trying to move further along the carriage. Finally the man and woman had stopped bickering and even the baby had stopped crying — then it hit him: the worst smell that he had ever smelled in his life. Everyone around him reacted at the same time.

"Ergh, what the hell is that smell?" Nicholas said aloud hoping that someone would answer.

"They're changing the baby's nappy," someone shouted.

"You shouldn't be doing that in here," another voice said.

"That's disgusting," said another.

Nicholas held his nose but it wasn't really helping. It felt like the baby's excrement was coating the back of his throat. He could almost taste it.

The Chinese girls were making loud sounds of disgust.

People were pushing and shoving each other towards the other end of the carriage but there was nowhere to go.

Nicholas continued to hold his nose. He looked at the tube map above the window opposite. Just one more station to go and it couldn't come quickly enough.

The woman with the briefcase had almost fallen onto him twice as people tried to push past.

She continued to bang his leg. He looked up. She didn't look well.

She held her briefcase tightly with one hand and let go of the rail with the other. She placed the hand over her mouth. She started to wretch and gag — she was going to vomit.

A voice in Nicholas's head shouted "MOVE!"

Without a further thought, he grabbed his backpack and prised himself out of his seat. At that same moment, the woman was sick in the exact place where he had just been sitting.

Some vomit splashed onto the arm of the woman who'd been next to him and the Chinese girls leapt up out of their seats squealing their disgust.

Nicholas turned his head, this was revolting. In this short journey he'd seen enough to put him off ever getting on a train again — *where was this bloody station!*

Chapter 35

Nicholas had finally arrived at Heathrow, Terminal 3.

He was booked on the American Airlines flight to Manaus departing at 17:15.

He hadn't admitted to anyone that he'd never flown before. He was excited, worried, nervous and, at times, terrified. He didn't know where to go or what to do.

He made sure he was early, with time to spare.

He would observe and follow everyone else's lead.

Megan had already done the on−line check−in and the new backpack met the carry on dimensions for baggage. All he needed to do was to head for the departure gate, apparently.

He stood for a moment and looked around. The first thing that surprised him was just how big the place was. He'd never seen a ceiling so high. It felt more like an indoor sports stadium than what he'd expected an airport to look like. And everything was so white, and shiny.

He noticed a lot of people walking in a specific direction towards a sign, Departures, he headed the same way.

Up ahead people were queuing to go through security. They were removing their belts and emptying their pockets. They placed these items into black trays which then went into the x–ray machine together with their bags. He also noticed that some people were removing their shoes. He looked down at his walking boots and secretly hoped that he wouldn't have to remove them as there were so many eyelets, it would take ages to take them off and put them back on again.

He shuffled forward. More people joined the queue behind him. He felt something strike the back of his leg. He looked down. It was a small bag on wheels. He looked up. The man behind simply stared back.

The process was slow. It was lucky that he'd allowed plenty of time but nevertheless the time seemed to be going quite quickly. He realised he'd been at the airport twenty five minutes already.

The couple in front moved forward and one of the airport staff signalled him over with a controlling swipe of his hand.

"Belt off and items from your pockets in the tray. Bag in the tray." The man snapped. He looked down, "Boots off."

Inside his head Nicholas groaned. He bent down and began to untie his laces — remove the knot, loosen the top loop, then the one underneath that, and the one underneath that. Someone behind him let out a huge sigh.

He was getting agitated, as he knew he was holding the other people up, but he took a deep breath. He had time and the other people were having to go through the same process. He finally loosened his boots enough to take them off. He put them in another tray and pushed it forward. Another member of the security staff snatched it from him and pushed it into the machine.

He stood in socked feet and noticed the next thing people did was to walk through the security gate.

He walked through and stopped, expecting something to happen, but nothing did.

A stern faced security guard signalled him to move to the side and collect his items from the x—ray machine.

Others before him were scrambling to lift the trays off the conveyor and to a table at the end where they put their belts and shoes back on. Nicholas didn't shove, he lined up and watched his bag and boots appear from the rear of the machine.

He lifted the tray with his bag off the conveyor, walked over and put it onto the table. By the time he'd gone back for his boots someone else had taken his place, expectantly waiting for their bag to appear.

"Excuse me please," he said to the lady.

She glanced round, turned up her nose and stared back at the rear of the x—ray machine.

Oh well, if you want to be like that, Nicholas thought as he pushed his way through.

The woman huffed. Nicholas didn't care. He grabbed the tray and carried it to the table.

It had taken a good few minutes to put his belt and boots back on, put the items back in his pocket and grab his bag. In that time he had seen people push, shove, lose their patience and their tempers. He looked back at the queues lining up to come through security, now much longer than they had been before — so many people.

Nicholas straightened the backpack on his back, exited security and went off to find where to go next.

He entered the 'Departures' area. He had no idea quite what he was expecting, but it certainly wasn't this. It was as though he'd walked into a shopping centre.

A huge duty free shop was in front of him and as he walked around he could see Nike, French Connection, Dixons, Virgin Megastore, even Boots and a Starbucks. The more he walked the more he saw, even to his surprise, a Harrods.

He stood and watched. There were people rushing around, people sitting, people buying. He had no idea where to go.

He noticed two girls walking towards him wearing bright red uniforms. They had bags with 'Virgin' on them. They were both beautiful and a little older than him, he suspected.

"Excuse me. It's my first time at this airport and I am not sure where to go, can you help me?"

They both smiled and the brunette reached out, "Can I see your ticket?"

"Yes, of course."

She looked down at the ticket, her eyes widened, "look at this!" she mouthed to her colleague.

She handed the ticket back to him, "You'll want the American Airlines first class lounge. Go that way, then look for the signs, you can't miss it."

"Thank you," he said.

They giggled as they walked away and looked back a couple of times.

He shrugged it off and walked in the direction they had suggested.

He realised he was thirsty, he'd get a drink.

The shop was bustling and there was a queue at the checkout but it seemed to be moving quickly enough.

He noticed a display stand with cakes neatly lined up behind a small glass front. There were scones, muffins, doughnuts and various other pastries. Then he spotted his favourite, a lemon Bear's Claw. There was only one left and that was the one he wanted.

As he was about to reach for it, a woman pushed in front and grabbed it with her hand. She didn't even use the tongs provided. She snatched a bag and dropped it inside. She sniffed loudly and tried to reach into her handbag. She began to juggle the cake and her bag, but before she could pull out a tissue, she sneezed explosively over the display stand.

She walked off towards the checkout, wiping her running nose with the back of her hand.

Nicholas definitely wouldn't be choosing anything else from the cake selection.

He was sure they'd serve drinks in the First Class Lounge so he walked out of the shop in the direction he'd been advised.

***

Nicholas sat down and looked around. He couldn't quite believe where he was.

He felt like a celebrity as he reclined into the leather sofa and reached for the tea cup on a small table to his side.

This was the life. This was his life — and he still struggled to get his head around it at times.

He spent a very pleasant hour or so relaxing in the lounge and, by the time the flight was ready to board, he didn't want to move. His lethargy was short–lived, however, as the excitement of actually being on board a plane spurred him into action.

Chapter 36

As Nicholas boarded the plane his stomach was churning over with both nerves and anticipation.

"Hello, sir," the beautiful stewardess said, smiling. "May I have your boarding pass?"

"Hello, certainly," Nicholas said, enjoying every moment of this experience.

"First class, this way sir," the stewardess said, taking his bag.

Nicholas smiled. *She called me sir!*

The first thing that surprised him about first class was how much space there was between the seats — each seat was more of a cubicle than just a seat. There was so much room — just as the adverts said there would be.

Another stewardess welcomed him on board and helped find his seat.

Nicholas looked at the console in front of him. He examined the buttons on the arm–rest and stretched out in the extra leg room provided.

"Comfortable, sir?" The stewardess bent over and smiled.

"Yes, very. Thank you."

"If you need anything in flight, just press this button here."

"I will. Thank you."

The stewardess walked off to greet the other arriving passengers.

A few were already seated.

A very smart woman with dark sunglasses and a black scarf.

A man with gold metal rimmed glasses and a suit that appeared to shimmer in the light.

An Arab man and his wife.

Nicholas turned and looked out of the window. He watched the ground crew loading the plane and rushing around underneath the aircraft. From the number of bags going into the hold there were obviously a lot of people on this flight.

He could hear people taking their seats in the cabin behind him but his eyes were firmly glued to what was happening outside.

After a few minutes there was an announcement from the captain saying the plane was on schedule to make an on-time departure and asking everyone to sit down and fasten their seatbelts ready for take—off.

He felt exhilarated — his first flight, flying first class — it was unreal.

Now everyone had taken their seats Nicholas turned round to see who else was sharing the first class cabin.

He did a double—take. He couldn't believe it — in the seat to his left was Angelina Jolie.

He looked again. Angelina turned her head, nodded and smiled.

Nicholas smiled and turned away. *Oh my God!*

Nicholas stared out of the window and watched the ground crew finish loading and completing final preparations.

Before he knew it, they were taxiing down the runway listening to the safety briefing.

Nicholas's nerves started to get the better of him.

Whilst this was all terribly exciting, it was terribly scary too.

As the plane accelerated down the runway, he was pushed back firmly into his seat.

The force took him by surprise — he was worried — *was this normal?*

His hands gripped the arm rests so tightly that his knuckles were white.

The aircraft rose sharply, he was almost unable to move.

The engines were making a loud roaring noise — he was scared — *should they make that sound?*

The aircraft suddenly banked to the right. He looked out of the window nervously. As the aircraft turned he was looking directly down at the ground. He felt as if he would fall out of the seat — he was terrified — *should this be happening?*

He glanced around the cabin. Everyone seemed to be taking it in their stride. No—one else seemed worried. *This must be normal*, he told himself.

The plane began to rise less sharply.

The sound of the engines changed and they didn't seem to be struggling quite so much.

He heard a noise like a ping and the stewardesses were up and about checking on everyone.

After a minute or two the plane levelled out and seemed to be cruising smoothly.

Thank goodness for that.

"First time?" a voice said from beside him.

The voice was strangely familiar. He looked round to see Angelina Jolie looking directly at him.

"Pardon?" Nicholas said wide–eyed.

"Is this your first time flying?"

"Yes. Yes, it is, how did you know?"

"You look petrified but don't be. Flying is still one of the safest ways to travel."

Nicholas smiled. He couldn't believe Angelina Jolie was reassuring him about air travel.

He let go of the arm rests. His knuckles ached. He rubbed the blood back into them.

"What do you do?" Angelina asked.

"I run a charity," Nicholas said. The shortness of his answer surprised himself a little but he was in awe of his travelling companion.

"What's it called?"

"Have you heard of Rapture?"

"Rapture? That's the charity that Leo DiCaprio helped get off the ground isn't it?"

"Yes, that's right. I couldn't have done it without Leo. He's been amazing — so supportive."

Angelina smiled a big smile. She seemed genuinely impressed.

"You'll never guess who this is," Angelina said turning to her male travelling companion.

He looked over.

"You remember that charity that Leo helped fund, well this is — Nic Savage — that's right isn't it?"

"Yes, I'm Nic," as if things couldn't get even more awesome — now a movie star had heard of him.

"We're really inspired by what you're doing. Well done," Angelina said.

"Yes, well done," the man said.

"Thank you. Thank you both of you, that means a lot."

Angelina reached into her bag and pulled out a card.

"If you need anything, or if I can help in anyway, give me a call."

Nicholas took the card, "Wow, thank you very much, I appreciate that."

A stewardess appeared, "Champagne sir?"

"Wow," Nicholas had never had Champagne.

"Yes, please."

She carefully poured a glass for Nicholas and then for Angelina.

"Your good health," Angelina said, raising her glass.

"Cheers," Nicholas replied and smiled.

Leo had insisted he upgrade to first class and fly American Airlines. He hadn't understood why, but now it made sense. He put Angelina's card into his pocket and sipped his drink.

Chapter 37

Nicholas had cleared customs.

If someone had told him six months ago that he would be arriving at the airport of Manaus in Brazil, he wouldn't have believed them in a million years.

Whilst most arrivals halls probably looked the same — everything else was different. The people, the clothing, the colour of their skin, the signs — even the air smelled different.

People dashed around and shoved him as they passed.

Up ahead, family members and taxi drivers were waiting for the arriving passengers. Some were holding cards — but he couldn't see Larry.

Another heavy shove from behind almost sent him flying. He stumbled but caught his balance.

He watched people rush by and listened to their voices chattering in a language he didn't understand.

The realisation hit him that he was many thousands of miles from home, all alone in a foreign land.

He missed his Mum. He felt worried and alone.

Part of him wanted to turn around and go home but, luckily at that moment, he noticed a man walk up to the line of waiting drivers and hold up a card with the name 'Nic Savage' written on it.

His worry turned to relief.

He walked up to the man.

He was big and tough — like a soldier.

"Hello, I'm Nic Savage."

"Hello Mr Savage. My name is Tyler Mills. I have a car outside."

"Where is Larry?"

"He is busy finalising arrangements for our trip. Come with me please."

"Our trip?" Nicholas asked.

"Yes, I'll be accompanying you."

The man turned and walked towards the exit.

He hadn't even offered to help him with his bag — *what kind of taxi driver was this?*

The man's stride was long. Nicholas hurried to keep up.

As they walked outside it was like a blanket of hot air had enveloped him.

He struggled to get his breath and sweat began to leak from every pore.

"My God, it's so hot," Nicholas said, breathless.

"You get used to it," Tyler said. "The car's this way."

Behind him a woman screamed in English.

"My bag! My bag!"

She was pointing at a man who was running in the other direction.

No–one helped and no–one seemed to care.

Nicholas watched. He felt a tap on his shoulder.

"Pick–pockets and bag–snatchers are common here. Tuck any valuables away and keep your bag over your shoulder at all times," Tyler warned.

Nicholas nodded.

The most valuable possessions on him were his phone and his wallet. He took the phone out of his pocket and wondered what to do with it. He shoved it down his pants, sideways on. He took his wallet from his back pocket and shoved it in his front pocket.

He wasn't sure where they were going until he realised they were walking towards a large black car covered in dust and mud. It looked like a military vehicle.

Tyler pressed a button on the remote, opened the drivers' door and jumped in.

Nicholas walked around the other side. The door was so high up he had to use a small step to reach it. As he opened the door he noticed a small puncture hole in the metal. He climbed up and got inside.

"Buckle up," Tyler said.

"Oh right," Nicholas said.

"Are we going far?"

"It's about an hour's drive to the airfield and then a three hour flight to the river."

"The river?"

"Yes, the Amazon river."

"We're going down the Amazon?"

"Of course."

The man seemed surprised that Nicholas didn't know where he was going.

He started the car and pulled away.

It was a very different world to the one Nicholas was used to.

He saw apartment blocks surrounded by fencing and

walls with barbed wire. Other buildings were vacant or in a severe state of disrepair. Rubble and rubbish littered the side of the road.

The car jostled and jolted on the unmaintained roads, which were full of cracks and potholes.

In some places it was like driving through a third–world country. Nicholas had only ever seen places like this on the news.

He desperately wanted to know answers to questions but clearly Tyler wasn't the talkative type. He hadn't said a word since they had left the airport.

The state of the roads got even worse until tarmac turned into dirt track. They seemed to leave civilisation behind. Nicholas was partly excited but also anxious at the thought of what was to come.

Nicholas was growing weary of the bumpy roads when Tyler began to slow down.

Ahead was an access track into a large clearing.

Nicholas hadn't known what to expect but when Tyler had said airfield, he had at least expected a building and a runway — it wasn't even that.

It was a small plane on a grass landing strip which had obviously been cleared out of the forest.

"Is this it?"

"Yes."

As they approached, Nicholas could see Larry with two other men.

The car came to a halt and they got out.

"Nicholas, so glad you made it okay," Larry said extending his hand.

"Not quite what you expected huh?" Larry observed Nicholas's expression.

"No, not at all."

"You're in the jungle now, kid." Larry laughed.

A man ran over to the plane and got in, obviously the pilot.

Another man high-fived Tyler and began to go through the bags and start handing Tyler various pieces of equipment.

What Nicholas saw next left him very shaken — guns.

"They're here for our protection. This jungle is full of bandits."

"Oh, right," Nicholas said, still alarmed.

"I've worked with Tyler and Rusty many times. I trust them with my life."

"Okay," Nicholas wasn't sure what else to say, this wasn't his world.

Nicholas watched them put pistols into holsters and sling machine guns over their shoulders. They attached various other items to webbing against their jackets and slotted spare magazines in pouches.

"Two minutes till departure," Larry shouted.

"Nicholas, we're nearly ready. Get in."

Nicholas nodded and walked over to the plane.

"Welcome aboard," The pilot said, gesturing to one of the seats in the back.

He climbed in.

This was very different to the previous flight into Manaus.

There were six seats in three rows. He sat in the middle seat on the left hand side as instructed.

There didn't appear to be any overhead lockers on this plane so he tucked his bag under the seat.

The seat was ripped and stuffing was coming out. The plane had certainly seen better days.

Down by his side he noticed a number of holes in the side of the plane, about the same size as the one he saw earlier in the door of the car.

Surely they can't be bullet holes?

The pilot started the engine and the plane began to vibrate.

Larry climbed in.

"Is this a problem?" Nicholas said, pointing at the holes in the side of the plane.

Larry sat in the seat opposite him. "Only if we get more of them," and laughed.

Tyler handed the bags to Rusty who dragged them to the rear of the aisle.

Rusty jumped in and slammed the door shut.

The next thing Nicholas knew, Rusty and Tyler grabbed each other, high fived and chanted something.

"It's a ritual. They do it before every take–off," Larry shouted over the noise of the engine which was now deafening as the plane lurched into take–off position.

Rusty sat down behind Nicholas.

Tyler approached the front of the aircraft and patted the pilot on the shoulder.

He sat down in the seat in front of Larry and turned.

Larry gripped his shoulders and squeezed tightly.

Tyler smiled, nodded and gave him a thumbs–up signal.

Tyler turned to glance over at Nicholas.

The smile quickly disappeared from his face.

There was something very odd about this whole experience and Nicholas was beginning to think that there was more to Larry Bell and his comrades than he had initially been led to believe.

Chapter 38

Nicholas's knuckles were white.

He'd lost the feeling in his hands half an hour ago from clinging onto the edge of the seat.

He felt like he was on some kind of roller coaster ride. He'd only been on one of those once, and that was enough to convince him that he would never go on one again.

He felt very queasy.

Larry had said something about it being perfectly safe, but there was little point in trying to talk as it was impossible to hear each other over the deafening roar of the engine.

He just wanted this whole experience to be over as quickly as possible.

He looked down at the holes in the side of the plane — Larry's words "Only if we get more of them" kept running through this mind.

Chapter 39

Nicholas was starting to lose the will to live.

His hands were still numb and now he'd lost the feeling in his arms as well.

His neck was stiff and he was desperately trying to stop himself being sick.

Larry leaned over and said something.

"What?" Nicholas shouted.

"We — are — coming — in — to — land," Larry shouted and slapped him on the forearm — he didn't feel a thing.

The plane dipped and started to angle downwards.

Nicholas felt his stomach rise into his chest.

Thank heavens.

The plane suddenly buffeted up and down and jerked to the right.

The pilot raised his arm, extended his fingers and formed a fist.

Larry slapped Tyler on the shoulder.

Nicholas felt a slap on his shoulder from Rusty behind.

Larry shouted something but he couldn't make out what it was.

Nicholas could sense tension in the air.

The plane banked from one side to the other and back again.

Nicholas heard a clanking noise over the sound of the engine and his seat started to vibrate.

The plane banked sharply to the left.

It pulled up, levelled out, angled down and wobbled from side to side.

There was a sudden sharp jerk as they landed — he was thrown upwards — his seatbelt cut into his stomach — he was thrown back into his seat with a jolt.

The plane twitched from left to right and then slowed and stopped with an almighty judder.

They had landed — *thank God for that.*

As soon as they had stopped, Tyler jumped out of his seat, opened the door and, with weapon at the ready, leapt out of the plane.

Rusty reacted quickly.

He dragged the bags from the rear of the plane, down the aisle and threw them out of the door.

"Let's go kid, hurry."

Nicholas wasn't sure what the rush was. Maybe they were late for the connection to catch the boat?

He let go of the seat arms. He could hardly move his fingers.

He stood up. His whole body was stiff.

With clawed hands he clutched the strap of his bag and pulled it from under the seat.

That's odd. I don't remember those holes in the floor under my seat as well?

Larry grabbed his shoulder, pulled him over to the door and almost threw him out of the plane.

Nicholas gulped for air.

It was hotter and more humid here than it had been in Manaus. Before he had just been sweaty, now he was almost drenched.

"Wow the air here is very different," Nicholas said looking around.

"You're in the jungle now kid — it's all very different down here," Larry said hurriedly, pushing Nicholas in the direction of the tree line.

"Quickly, head over to those trees. Over there!" Larry shouted.

This was all very odd. The plane hadn't shut down its engine. Tyler was constantly looking around with his gun raised and Rusty was unloading the plane like a demon.

Nicholas did as he was asked and ran over to the trees. He stood behind some long grass and watched as Larry signalled something to the plane. Tyler and Rusty picked up the bags, threw them over their shoulders and ran over towards him.

The plane burst into life. It turned awkwardly, accelerated and took off.

"Where's the plane going?"

"He's only dropping us off kid, he can't wait."

"Does he have other people to pick up?"

"Something like that, kid."

Larry spurred him on with a slap on the shoulder.

"And why are we rushing, are we late for the boat connection?"

"Yeah, something like that, something like that."

Why couldn't Larry ever answer a simple question with a simple answer.

"Now, come on, the boat is that way," Larry said pointing deep into the dense undergrowth.

Rusty brushed past and led them swiftly through the forest.

Chapter 40

"Is this it?" Nicholas asked.

"What were you expecting, kid?" Larry said.

"Erm, well, I am not sure really — something a little bigger?"

He hadn't thought to tell Larry he was scared of water.

What greeted him at the river did little to give him any confidence.

The boat was about twenty feet long and made out of wood with a single engine at the rear.

When he had been told they were going down the Amazon, he imagined a ferry or some kind of riverboat — this looked more like a large canoe.

"I'm not sure about this?" Nicholas said.

Larry wasn't listening.

He had done canoeing once at school. It had capsized and he had nearly drowned.

"I'm really not sure about this?"

Larry still wasn't listening.

He'd also thought there would be other passengers getting ready for a scheduled departure but there was no one around — just them — and no sign of anyone with the boat.

"Pablo!" Larry shouted.

A head appeared. He had been lying down.

"Who's that?" Nicholas asked.

"Remember the contact I told you about? Meet Pablo."

Nicholas was expecting to see a man in a suit, not a half–naked, dark skinned man having a snooze in the back of a boat.

"Did you wake him up?"

Larry laughed, "He's just keeping out of sight."

Out of sight? But why would ...

"Come on kid — hurry up — get on board."

As Larry rushed him towards the boat, Pablo said something in his own language.

Nicholas had no idea what they were talking about.

He handed his backpack to Pablo.

Pablo tossed it into the boat.

Pablo then reached out and grabbed his hand.

Nicholas hesitated.

Pablo wasn't having any of it and yanked him onto the boat.

It rocked furiously. Nicholas struggled to keep his balance.

Larry got in. The boat pitched from side to side.

Tyler and Rusty stood on the bank with their weapons raised, constantly looking around and scanning from side to side.

Every time someone moved, the boat rocked. Nicholas felt queasy.

Larry said something to Pablo.

Pablo rushed to the back of the boat and began to tug a cord attached to the engine. It choked and spluttered but didn't start. Pablo tried it again and again.

Nicholas watched.

Tyler and Rusty appeared to become agitated.

Larry said something to Pablo, he tried again and again. Pablo muttered something under his breath.

Nicholas watched. *Why hadn't they loaded the bags yet?*

"We need to get going," Tyler said with concern in his voice.

Larry said something to Pablo. His tone was very firm.

Pablo chattered back with a string of incomprehensible words.

Why are we rushing?

Tyler and Rusty crouched down.

"Got to go now!" Tyler whispered.

What was going on?

Rusty kept low, dragged a bag towards the boat and heaved it in. He went back for the other, dragged it across and lifted it over the side. He shoved it behind the other in the centre of the boat.

Tyler was now staring through the sights of the gun as though he was taking aim at something.

Larry snapped at Pablo who was still furiously yanking on the engine starter cord.

Rusty got into to boat and crawled towards the front.

Whilst Larry and Pablo traded insults in Portuguese, Nicholas took the time to look around and was taken aback by the view. He really was on the actual Amazon river in South America. He had only seen sights like this in pictures or on television. But he was here, in the flesh. What an amazing experience.

He watched a large bird glide down the river, its wingspan was enormous.

He turned to Larry to ask what it was called but he was too busy physically manhandling Pablo to try to get the engine started.

The engine finally coughed and burst into life.

Pablo said something. Larry snapped. They were clearly at odds with each other.

"Quick!" Rusty said and beckoned Tyler over.

Tyler climbed into the boat. It rocked from side to side. Nicholas was now alarmed at how low it sat in the water. Another tip like that and they could capsize.

Not only was he uncomfortable with water, he hadn't mentioned to Larry that he couldn't swim — and they didn't even have life jackets.

"Prisa — Prisa!" Larry shouted to Pablo.

The boat jolted forward and away from the bank.

Nicholas looked out towards the centre of the river and wondered if the big bird would come back.

The engine continued to cough and splutter but it had already got the boat up to a decent speed.

BANG! BANG!

The sudden noise startled him. It must have been the engine backfiring.

Tyler and Rusty kept low in the boat and trained their weapons on the riverbank. They looked at Larry who shook his head. They nodded and gave him an 'OK' signal.

As they pootled off down the river everyone seemed to become much more relaxed.

***

Nicholas looked up at the sky, the trees that lined the river bank and the Amazon river itself. It was like a scene from a film, or a wildlife documentary.

"This is great," Nicholas said turning to Larry.

"I'm glad you're enjoying it. I'm really impressed at your cool."

Nicholas wasn't quite with him.

"My cool?"

"How calm you were — with the bandits back there."

Nicholas sat bolt upright.

"Bandits!?"

"Yes, bandits. They spot the planes coming in to land and then try to rob or kidnap the people inside."

Nicholas could feel himself mouth the words, bandit — armed — rob — kidnap.

"That's why Tyler and Rusty are here."

Pablo said something and Larry laughed.

"What did he say?"

"He said you weren't calm, you were just oblivious."

Pablo said something else and pointed to his backpack.

Larry reached over and grabbed the bag.

"What did he say this time?"

"He said, it also looks like you had a lucky escape," Larry said, turning the bag to show Nicholas a hole.

"What's that?"

"It's a bullet–hole kid — a bullet–hole."

"Just like the ones in the side of the plane."

"It's the bandits. They take pot shots at the plane."

"I thought I felt a jolt under my seat when we were coming in to land."

"That'll be it — but the seats all have bulletproof pads under them — luckily for you."

Nicholas was well out of his comfort zone.

"Don't worry — we've got Tyler and Rusty with us."

They looked at each other and nodded.

Nicholas glanced around the boat and noticed two small holes in the side of the boat, exactly the same as the ones in the side of the plane and in his bag.

The engine obviously hadn't backfired!

Chapter 41

"You feeling better now, kid?"

"Yes, thank you," Nicholas replied. The gentle rocking motion of the boat and the calm of the environment had done wonders to curb his panic.

He even felt quite comfortable on the water — not at all like kayaking.

He'd also found out what that big bird was called. It was a Jabiru, a large stork. The name means 'swollen neck'.

Pablo said something to him.

Nicholas turned round and looked enquiringly.

"He asked if you could pass him a big hook from that box," Larry said pointing underneath his seat.

Nicholas looked down at a box he hadn't even noticed. He opened it up to see fishing tackle, a knife and an array of hooks in various sizes from small to terrifyingly large.

Nicholas reached into the box.

"Careful of your hands Nic, you don't want to cut yourself. Not down here."

Nicholas was alarmed once again. "What do you mean — not down here?"

"In this climate cuts don't heal too well which can cause infection."

Nicholas's hand hovered over the box.

"It can get very bad, very quickly."

"And, er, what happens if it gets very bad?"

"Amputation," Larry said menacingly.

Nicholas grabbed the hook very carefully and handed it to Pablo.

He gazed at the river, disturbed by the dangerous hook and Larry's tone.

Nicholas's thoughts were cast back to Great Uncle Winston who used to be a Spitfire pilot during the Second World War. He had been shot down over enemy territory and captured. He was very badly burned and the Nazi's had to amputate his hands. His body was horribly disfigured including his face. He remembered the first and only time he saw him, at a family gathering when he was about seven years old. He had been told that there was something different about Great Uncle Winston but that it was okay and he didn't need to worry about it.

That had already played on his mind — *different, how?*

He was intrigued and when the car arrived he rushed to the window. The car door opened and two people got out — his Dad who had gone to collect them, and Great Auntie Mary. They walked around the other side of the car, opened the door and the man, who he presumed was Great Uncle Winston, got out. His Dad walked down the path first, followed by Great Auntie Mary, and behind her, Great Uncle Winston. He couldn't see properly but his eyes were drawn to the ends of the man's sleeves — he couldn't see any hands.

He could hear the key in the door and voices in the hall.

Nicholas had jumped down off the sofa and stood in the living room waiting for the door to open.

He wasn't prepared for what happened next.

The door opened, Nicholas looked up and saw a face unlike any other looking down at him.

At first he thought it was a prank and perhaps Great Uncle Winston was wearing a mask but as he leaned over towards him, he could clearly see that it wasn't a mask. His skin was wrinkled and taut as though it had been melted and then stretched tight. One eye was slightly higher than the other. He looked down at him with a chilling stare and didn't blink. His mouth didn't move properly and a deep croaky voice muttered the words, "Pleased to meet you, Nicholas."

Nicholas took a step back in horror. He had never seen anything like it before. He didn't know what to say. This was Great Uncle Winston, the war hero that he had been told about. His Dad had said he was different and that there was nothing to worry about — but he was worried, he didn't look normal.

Then, Great Uncle Winston raised his arm. Nicholas watched the sleeve rise and something pale and gnarled emerge from within, but it wasn't a hand — it was a stump.

The other sleeve raised and another stump.

Nicholas recoiled in terror and fell backwards. Great Uncle Winston shuffled forward, that strange stare fixed on him, his disfigured mouth repeating the words, "Pleased to meet you Nicholas," and handless stumps reaching out to him.

Nicholas never saw him again, but the nightmares continued for months afterwards.

Pablo said something but he didn't understand.

"He said, can you pass the knife," Larry translated. "And be careful, it's sharp."

"Yes, sure," Nicholas said and cautiously picked up the old and dangerously sharp knife.

He handed it to Larry, who handed it to Pablo who kept a firm hold of the engine with his other hand.

Pablo said something and chuckled. Larry laughed.

"What did he say?"

"He said, if you do cut yourself, don't get the blood in the water."

Nicholas became even more alarmed?

"Er, Why not?"

"Cocodrilo!" Pablo said.

"Crocodile — they can smell the blood," Larry translated.

"Or Anaconda," Larry added, "they're a serious predator down here. They grow to up to seventeen feet — almost as long as this boat."

Pablo laughed and contributed another, "Piraña."

"You don't need to translate that one," Nicholas said anxiously.

"Don't worry kid, you'll be fine," Larry said.

His words offered little comfort.

"As long as you don't cut yourself and you stay in the boat," Larry laughed. Pablo laughed.

"What does he need that great big hook for anyway?" Nicholas asked.

"Dinner," Larry replied.

"Dinner? He's fishing for dinner with a hook like that?"

"You're in the Amazon now. Big fish. Plus we need to feed five of us. It's a long ride."

"I forgot to ask — how long?"

"Sixteen hours."

"Sixteen hours? Oh my God. I had no idea we would be on the boat that long."

"You're in the Amazon now. We've got a long way to go."

Nicholas did his best to process the information he'd just been given. Sixteen hours, in a small wobbly boat, cruising along a river infested with crocodile, anaconda and piranha — this was going to be a very long journey.

A worrying thought came into his head.

"What do I do if I need to go to the toilet?"

"You go over the side. We can't stop — it's not safe."

It's not safe? — Nicholas wondered — *what from? The animals or the bandits?*

He crossed his legs and tried to take his mind off it all by looking for another stork.

Chapter 42

"Es hora!" Pablo shouted from behind as he struggled with a fishing line.

"This looks like dinner, kid," Larry said.

Whatever it was, the way Pablo was tugging at the line suggested that it was something big.

Tyler and Rusty kept watch at the front of the boat. They were obviously very disciplined. They had hardly said a word the entire time.

Nicholas yawned.

"Tired?" Larry said.

"Yes. It's been a very long journey."

"Probably best to get your head down after dinner."

"You mean we're not stopping?"

"No, like I said earlier, kid, no stopping, we go the whole way — sixteen hours straight."

Pablo gave a huge tug on the line. The fish at the end was at least two feet long. It landed heavily in the boat and flapped its tail wildly, gasping and thrashing its body.

Pablo reached to his side, grabbed the knife and stabbed the fish in the head. It thrashed even more wildly so he stabbed it again in the eye.

Nicholas looked away.

This is why he didn't eat meat.

Now he'd seen one more thing that he would struggle to ever get out of his mind.

"You don't fish?" Larry asked.

"I'm a vegetarian."

"You're in the Amazon now, kid — vegetarians don't last long down here."

Nicholas caught a glimpse of Pablo's frantic fish gutting exercise and looked away.

Larry reached forward and fumbled in a bag.

He tossed over a type of bread that looked like a baguette.

He reached in again and pulled out a banana, "Enjoy."

Nicholas heard a splash in the water and looked around.

"What's he doing?"

"Throwing the fish guts into the water."

"But I thought you said you shouldn't get blood in the water."

"Yeah, but it's not our blood."

"Wouldn't it be safer to keep it in the boat?"

"You don't want rotting fish guts in the boat — predators!"

"I thought we were safe in the boat?"

"You're in the Amazon now kid — you're never safe. If a crocodile were to smell fish guts in the boat it could turn us over just like that," Larry said with a loud snap of his finger and thumb.

Great — something else to worry about.

Nicholas took a bite from his bread. It was tough but he was so hungry, he'd eat just about anything right now — except fish.

"How are you going to cook it anyway?"

"We ain't gonna cook it kid, we eat it raw," Larry said breaking the bread ready to mate it with the fish that Pablo was slicing.

"I think I am going to throw up!"

"You never heard of Sushi, kid?"

Nicholas lost his appetite. He dropped the bread into his lap and tried his best not to think about it.

Chapter 43

Nicholas's appetite had finally returned.

He'd finished the bread and took the final bite of his banana.

"It's about time you got some kip, kid," Larry said.

"What do I do with this?" he asked, guessing what Larry was going to say.

"Over the side."

As he suspected — Nicholas tossed the skin into the river.

"Next to the bags is probably the most comfortable place," Larry said, as if pre–empting the next question.

Nicholas moved carefully so as not to rock the boat and lay down next to the bags.

He used one of the bags as a pillow. There was something hard inside. He remembered the guns and ammunition and had an uneasy feeling about what his head might be resting on.

"It's getting very dark, don't we put any lights on?"

"No lights kid, it's not safe."

"Does it alert the predators?"

"Not the predators kid, the bandits."

"But I thought we were safe once we were on the river?"

"This is the Amazon, kid — here you're never safe!"

Great, he definitely wasn't going to get any sleep now.

Chapter 44

Nicholas awoke.

"Good morning," Larry said.

"Morning," Nicholas replied and rubbed his eyes.

He stretched his stiff body. It was an uncomfortable sleep but he obviously needed it, the journey had caught up with him.

He'd had a strange dream that he was on holiday on a tropical island. He was lying in a hammock between two palm trees on the beach just watching the world go by. The locals were talking in their native language but now and again he could hear the odd English word spoken by others. He remembered that the same scene kept repeating itself, almost like it was on rewind, and he could recall certain words like, 'asesinato', 'matar', 'cadáver', 'rio' and 'bandido' but didn't really know what they meant. The odd thing was that the voice saying those words sounded just like Larry's.

As he pulled himself back into his seat, he thought he'd ask Larry.

"Larry, what does ..." At that moment, a phone rang in Larry's pocket.

He pulled it out, "Sat–phone, hold on — Hello, yes?"

Larry obviously knew the person on the other end of the line. He smiled and chatted away in Portuguese.

Tyler and Rusty seemingly hadn't moved as they were in exactly the same positions as before he'd gone to sleep.

Pablo called out from behind, "Comida aquí" and tossed him another small loaf and a banana.

Nicholas nodded.

He took a bite of the bread. It didn't taste right — it had started to go off.

He imagined what Larry would say, *You're in the Amazon now, everything goes off quickly down here.*

At least the banana was okay.

***

Despite the uncomfortable sleep and the worries and stress of the journey he felt surprisingly relaxed this morning.

Rusty and Tyler were obviously tough and it did make him feel safe that they were there to protect them.

Pablo seemed very experienced. He was dedicated and clearly knew how to handle the boat.

Larry seemed to have everything under control and was concerned for his welfare.

As he watched the world go by he could, for just a moment, mistakenly feel that he was on holiday.

He had watched other types of birds fly overhead, even parrots, to his amazement and delight.

He had wanted to mention it to Larry who seemed something of an expert on birds but he was still on the phone. He had heard him say the word 'rio' which appeared in his dream last night, but, as was often the way with dreams, he couldn't remember the other words he had heard.

Never mind, it was only a dream.

Larry hung up and said something to Pablo.

"Sí, sí," he replied.

"About half an hour now," Larry said.

Nicholas was overjoyed.

"What does rio mean?"

"It means river," Larry replied. "El río Amazonas — The River Amazon."

Pablo said something.

"He said Rio Grande, the Great River. That's what it used to be called until the Portuguese conquered and renamed it."

Nicholas nodded and returned to his own little world. If only he could remember what those other words were.

Chapter 45

A sudden flurry of activity stirred Nicholas from his trance.

Tyler and Rusty were alert. Larry was talking to Pablo who rapidly replied in his native tongue.

For a moment he thought he heard one of the words from his dream, 'cadáver' which was very similar to the word cadaver which he was sure meant a dead body. He guessed many words sounded like others in different languages.

Pablo pointed over towards the bank where there appeared to be a sandy beach.

Nicholas grabbed his bag.

He had a strange feeling in his stomach, like a feeling of dread.

He cast it aside. He was hot, anxious and hadn't eaten properly, no wonder his stomach didn't feel right.

"Two minutes," Larry shouted ahead.

Tyler and Rusty raised their fists in acknowledgement but kept their eyes fixed firmly ahead.

Pablo steered the boat towards the shore line. As they got closer, Nicholas could see it wasn't sand but more like a mixture of earth and mud.

Larry and Pablo sounded as though there were having another argument as their voices were raised and Pablo kept repeating the words, "No matar en el barco."

'Matar', it was one of those words from his dream again. *What does it mean?*

The boat came to a stop and Nicholas looked at the muddy shore. He could make out small bird footprints in the mud and then animal prints. He also noticed troughs, as though something heavy had been pulled up the bank. It reminded him of when he'd been kayaking and the shape the boat made in the sand. *This must be a popular place for people to come ashore.*

Nicholas stood up uneasily, "You want me to get out? Here?"

"You're in the Amazon now, you're not afraid of a bit of mud are you?"

"Well, I'd rather not get dirty if I can help it."

Larry laughed, "Out of the boat."

That was odd, Nicholas thought. There was something about Larry's tone. Perhaps the argument with Pablo had put him in a bad mood or something.

Nicholas looked around, "But where are we going?"

"For fucks sake, kid, get out of the boat!" Larry snapped.

"Why are you talking to me like that? You're supposed to be helping me?"

"Of course I am not trying to help you, you stupid, naïve, dumb little fucker. I can't have you or your organisation meddling in other people's business."

Nicholas was gobsmacked.

"You talk about the rainforests, the delicate eco–system and balance and harmony, well that is what we've got down here, kid. Twenty years I've worked my ass off to make sure we have balance. Sure there are drugs, sure people get killed and sure trees get cut down — but, as long as the people at the top are happy, we get paid, that's all I care about — now — get out of the fucking boat!"

Then the words from his dream popped into his head. He said them aloud, "Asesinato, matar, cadáver, rio and bandido."

"So — you heard us talking in the night did you. Well, that's right kid, we are going to kill you and throw your body in the river and make it look like the bandits did it," Larry said.

Tyler and Larry turned their weapons on Nicholas. Larry took a step back, the boat wobbled. Pablo tried his best to keep the boat stable with the engine still running but the propeller caused them to move away from the bank.

"Pablo!" Larry shouted and ranted something in Portuguese.

Pablo replied with obvious frustration in his voice.

"No matar en el barco" he kept shouting.

The boat wobbled again. Nicholas struggled to keep his balance. He looked at Tyler and Rusty with their weapons now pointing at him, waiting for the instruction to shoot.

Larry was even more angry and agitated. He waved his fist. Pablo waved his fist back.

Nicholas heard the engine backfire, then again.

No, this was different.

Then he heard a whistling sound and a crack.

The boat jolted violently. Nicholas stumbled.

As he fought to regain his balance it seemed like everything began to happen in slow motion.

Tyler and Rusty had once again turned to face the front of the boat. Larry had his hands raised to his head as if he was worried or anxious about something. Pablo had dropped to his knees and was cowering beside the engine.

The boat was now heading away from the river bank.

Another loud crack and a whizzing sound. Nicholas looked down at the side of the boat. Where there were two holes, now there were five. It was then he realised what was happening — bandits!

Time sped up and normalised.

He heard the rat–a–tat–tat of automatic gun fire. Bullets whizzed by, crashing through the side of the boat and peppering the water around them.

Tyler and Rusty began to fire back.

The noise was deafening. He tried to cover his ears, manhandling the backpack over his shoulder.

There was a loud popping sound. Tyler and Rusty stopped firing. Larry fell to the deck. There was complete pandemonium — BOOM!

An enormous plume of water erupted beside the boat.

A tremendous shockwave hit him and before he knew what had happened, he was in the water.

He panicked. He went under. He flung his arms from side to side and managed to get his head above water.

The rat–a–tat–tat of gunfire continued.

He took a deep gulp of air. He felt a searing hot pain in the back of his right hand. He heard another popping sound and the gunfire stopped. He went under again. He thrashed his arms and broke through the surface.

Why was this happening to me?

How did I get myself into this situation?

He could feel himself drifting, his vision fading. He could feel himself blacking out.

BOOM!

A huge wave covered his head and he went back under.

Through the murky water he could just make out their boat. In that instant, it was blown to smithereens.

Chapter 46

Visions passed through Nicholas's mind.

He was in the water. He was swimming, unaided, he felt alive.

He could hear someone call his name. He turned. It was his Father standing with his Mother at the side of the local swimming pool. They were both smiling and cheering him on.

The pictures in his mind changed, now he had swapped places. It was his Father in the water and Nicholas was watching. His Dad appeared to be struggling. Nicholas shouted but words would not come out. He screamed louder and louder but there was no sound.

Then he could see his Mother in the kitchen, sobbing.

Then he could see his Gran, dressed in black.

It was as though a page had been turned in his mind.

He saw his Dad, painting the walls of his bedroom. He was finishing the picture of the dolphin. He turned and smiled.

He saw his Mum, rummaging in her handbag trying to find something. She seemed excited. She smiled. She laughed.

He saw his Gran, pouring water into a teapot.

She smiled. She laughed.

He saw the faces of his team. They were sitting around the board room table. They smiled. They laughed.

He saw the face of Leo. He wasn't smiling. He was angry and shaking his fist.

He saw animals in distress.

He saw rubbish in the oceans.

He saw huge areas of rainforest that had been cleared.

He saw Larry's face.

He saw a gun pointing at him.

He saw darkness.

Chapter 47

Nicholas lay looking up at the blue sky.

The sun was shining.

The face of a large cat appeared above him.

It licked its lips.

"Hello," Nicholas said and smiled.

The cat didn't reply.

Was this another strange dream?

The cats face disappeared from his eye line but he could hear it breathing right next to him.

He felt a rough scratching sensation on the back of his right hand.

It stung at first but then was actually quite pleasant, soothing almost.

He wondered whether he would be able to sit up in his dream and take a look.

He sat up.

It wasn't a dream.

He was lying on a muddy river bank.

His clothes had partly dried in the heat of the midday sun.

The jaguar was to his side, licking the bloody wound on the back of his hand.

It growled.

Nicholas looked at the back of his hand.

He looked at the jaguar, its head low, its teeth exposed — snarling.

Now he remembered where he was.

Somehow he had survived the boat, Larry and his crew and the bandits — only to be eaten — hand first — by a large wild jungle cat.

The jaguar raised its haunches as if it were about to strike then all of a sudden he heard a familiar sound — CRACK.

Something hit the ground with great force beside the cat, it growled again.

Then, almost before he could register the sound, the cat's head exploded.

It dropped to the ground beside him. A bloody mess of mangled fur, bone and blood.

In that moment, Nicholas had gone back to hell.

He turned his head to see a large grey boat heading in his direction.

There were many men on board all pointing their guns in his direction.

He tried to get up, but he couldn't. He was sore, his lungs hurt and the cut on the back of his hand felt as if it were on fire.

He lay there and watched as the boat pulled up against the bank and five dark skinned men in green military clothing jumped off. He had a feeling this trip was going to end very soon but he wasn't sure how, or when.

The men spoke rapidly in Portuguese. They pointed with their rifles and laughed. He had no idea what they were saying or what their intentions were.

One of the men approached and kicked him in the leg.

Nicholas recoiled and pulled his leg away. The man laughed and did it again.

The men circled him. He didn't know what to do — or say.

"Hello, my name is Nic, I mean you no harm."

They looked at each other wondering what he'd said. The man kicked his leg again.

Two of them seemed more interested in the cat they had just killed beside him.

One man grabbed the carcass by its back legs, another by its front. They carried it back to the boat, leaving a bloody trail down the bank.

Nicholas did his best not to look, it made him feel sick.

Then one of the men took an interest in the back of his hand. Nicholas brought his arm close to his chest. He felt a powerful grip from behind and an arm around his throat. Another crouched by his side and grabbed his wrist. The man was strong. Nicholas was no match.

He appeared to be saying something about the wound on the back of his hand.

Nicholas looked at it properly. There was a piece of wood stuck in it.

The man prodded and poked with his finger. The pain was excruciating. Nicholas screamed.

The men laughed.

Nicholas felt a searing pain and screamed again.

The man held a large splinter in front of his face.

He said something in Portuguese and smiled.

"Thank you," Nicholas said — *perhaps these men didn't mean him any harm at all?*

The man stopped smiling and was suddenly deadly serious.

They chattered amongst themselves.

He wasn't sure what was going on.

The man reached to his side grabbed Nicholas's wrist and held his arm outstretched.

He called another man over and said something in Portuguese.

The man behind tightened his grip around his neck.

The man walked over and pulled a huge machete from a sheath hanging from his waist.

Nicholas was now petrified. He had a dreadful suspicion he knew what was about to happen.

The man with the machete got into position, lowered the blade towards his wrist and lined it up.

He said something and all three of them laughed.

His whole body went rigid.

He didn't want to lose his hand.

He couldn't lose his hand.

He'd rather be dead than lose his hand.

In that moment his mind was transported back to Great Uncle Winston, he could see him clearly in his mind, his ruined face, his mangled stumps, reaching out, trying to grab him.

The man raised the blade, the men laughed loudly, but Nicholas couldn't cope with it all any more — everything went black again.

Chapter 48

Nicholas awoke to a hard slap around the face.

"Wake up," the man said, crouching in front of him.

He was alive, but dazed. He wasn't sure where he was, but it was dark. The flickery golden glow of a large fire illuminated the surrounding trees and wooden buildings.

The memory of recent events came back to him — his hand, or rather probable lack of it.

He was sitting upright, cross–legged, tied to a large wooden pole with his arms around his back.

The rope was so tight he could hardly feel his fingers let alone work out if he still had his hand.

It felt as though it was still there, but he remembered what doctors referred to as 'phantom limb' where the amputee could still feel the part of his body that had been removed.

The crouched man simply stared at him as if trying to work something out.

Nicholas finally twisted his wrist. At first he thought he could feel a stump where his hand had been but it wasn't a stump, it was his wrist. There was some sort of bandage around his hand.

The man continued to crouch and stare.

Nicholas smiled, pleased they had taken care of his hand. "Thank you, thank you."

The man looked confused, "Why you thank me?"

"Because I am still alive and because I've still got my hand."

The man laughed and poked a finger firmly into his chest.

"You worth money to us."

"You ransom. They pay, very much."

"I don't think so — I'm not worth anything, to anyone."

The man pulled Nicholas's wallet from his jacket pocket and held it in front of his face.

"We know who you are, you worth money to us," the man stood up and walked off. He heard voices in the distance and he could make out the shapes of people sitting near the fire.

Did they really know who he was, or did they just think anyone from the UK was worth money?

Maybe they really did know, maybe they'd tracked his name back to the charity and back to Leo?

Why did everyone talk in riddles, why couldn't people just be honest?

Nicholas remembered his phone. He'd obviously lost his bag and his wallet but he really hoped he hadn't lost his phone. His whole life was on it, although he wasn't sure what state it would be in after being immersed in the Amazon river.

He tried to move his hips but he couldn't feel whether his phone was still in his pants where he'd left it for safekeeping.

He looked at the men sitting around the fire.

They were eating something they were cooking on the flames. When one of the men moved, he could see — the remains of the big cat.

They seemed to be in a deep and heated discussion and kept looking over and pointing. They were obviously talking about him but as usual he had no idea what was going to happen next.

He was obviously in their camp. There were two wooden huts, a bit larger than garden sheds, poorly constructed with old planks and some polythene sheeting draped over the top as a makeshift roof. There was a clearing where the fire was, with a number of men sat around in a half circle, most with their backs to him. The jungle loomed above him, dark, dense and foreboding.

He tried to move his arms again, but the rope was tight. He tried to move his hands and was reminded that he still had them both, which was the only good news he'd had in quite a while.

He swivelled his wrists and could feel how his hands were tied and what type of knot it was. He could feel the rope loosen slightly the more he moved his wrists. This in turn enabled him to free his hand a bit more and he was able to loosen the rope again.

For an exciting moment he had the thought he could set himself free and escape back to civilisation, but that moment was short lived. He was deep in the jungle, thousands of miles from anywhere, in a bandit camp with men sitting nearby with automatic rifles — any hope of escape was probably futile.

As he sat there, his senses started to come back to him.

His hand throbbed. His chest was tight. His head hurt and he felt bruised almost everywhere on his body.

He could do little but accept his fate.

The flicker of the fire made him sleepy.

Chapter 49

Nicholas awoke.

It was still dark.

He was surrounded by sounds. They filled the air all around him.

Scuffling, scratching, tweeting, hooting, howling, hissing, whistling and rustling — from all directions.

He watched the flickering patterns from the light of the fire illuminating the trees.

It was eerily both relaxing and quite disturbing at the same time.

It was then he realised, he couldn't hear any voices.

The only noises he could hear were from the jungle itself.

He looked over at the fire and noticed the silhouette of a man sitting, watching.

The man had something in his lap — a rifle.

There was no sign of the others. He guessed they had gone to bed, presumably in the wooden shacks.

Nicholas looked at the man. He saw a flash of white teeth — the man was grinning.

The man raised his hand in the shape of a gun, pointed his finger and made a clicking sound.

Nicholas looked down.

No hope of escape.

He went back to sleep.

Chapter 50

Nicholas opened his eyes.

He wasn't sure how long he had slept but it didn't feel that long.

The man was still there, sitting in front of the fire.

Nicholas struggled to see through the darkness and the light of the fire — it looked as though he was asleep.

This could be my chance.

Nicholas swivelled his wrists and felt for the knot with his fingers. The rope was already looser which allowed him to move his hands more. He probed around, found the knot and pulled and twisted. He felt the rope loosen further.

He had to use quite a bit of force on the rope. The exertion and his bruised lungs caused him to cough.

The man moved.

Nicholas stopped dead still and watched.

If they caught him trying to escape, what would they do to him?

What were they planning to do to him anyway?

He waited a moment.

The man was still asleep.

Nicholas carried on, being extremely careful not to make a sound.

He moved his wrists back and forth, back and forth, the rope loosening a little every time but still not quite enough to free his hands.

He had no idea what time it was. The man by the fire or the others in the huts could wake up at any moment. He had to hurry, he must escape.

He wriggled his wrist again and used his thumb and fingers to try to get in between the knot — at last — one hand became free, then the other — he was loose.

He rubbed his wrists behind his back and looked carefully at the man in front of him to make sure he was definitely asleep.

He was. This was it, he could make his escape.

He thought for a moment about grabbing the man's gun from his lap but that might wake him up. He wouldn't know what to do with it anyway. He hated guns. Guns meant death. He thought of the poor jaguar that lost its life earlier. He felt a jolt of pain through his hand — poor animal.

That thought alone gave Nicholas enough motivation to get out of the place, fast.

He didn't know which direction to go in but decided that behind him was probably the easiest — he wouldn't have to walk past the fire or the huts.

Nicholas started to get up, very carefully and quietly. He got to his knees and then onto his feet. All the time he kept a watchful gaze on the man in front of him. He stepped slowly backwards so that he could keep his eyes on him.

SNAP

Nicholas's body stiffened.

He'd trodden on a twig.

The man in front of the fire coughed and spluttered, he opened his eyes and took a moment to register what was happening. Nicholas felt like a rabbit in the headlights of a car, the man looked at him, he looked at the man. The main raised his gun. Nicholas darted into the jungle.

A loud crack erupted from behind him, then another and another. He could hear the whizzing sound of bullets flying past him. The shooting stopped and the man started shouting.

Nicholas crashed through the undergrowth. He couldn't see where he was going. Everything was trying to trip him up. He held his arms in front of him to try to protect himself from the leaves and branches that were tearing at his face and body as he ran.

He could hear the man behind him shouting the same thing over and over, "escape del muchacho." Then he shouted something else, "Él viene en tu dirección."

Nicholas presumed that he was rousing the troops from their slumber to give chase.

He kept going as quickly as he dared through the treacherous undergrowth.

At first he thought he was imagining it but he saw what looked like lights up ahead — civilisation.

He had assumed he was miles from anywhere but now he was sure he could see lights twinkling through the trees. He rushed towards them.

As he got closer it looked like the lights were moving from side to side and also closer to him. He stopped, they were definitely moving and in his direction.

But who ...

There was a single loud crack and a thump into the tree beside him.

"No escape. You worth money to us," shouted the voice.

Oh no ... Nicholas thought, the men weren't asleep in their huts, they were obviously out on patrol and he was heading straight for them.

Another crack — and a whizzing sound directly overhead.

He heard the man shout something from behind him then more shouts from the men in front.

He couldn't go back and he couldn't go forward — he'd go to the side.

He turned to his left and dashed.

The undergrowth was thicker and it was making it difficult to move forward.

He could hear loud laughing.

It was obvious which way he was going, he was making such a racket they'd be able to hear him for sure.

Another crack from behind and the whizzing of another bullet overhead.

Whilst they probably didn't want to hurt him, a stray bullet could easily hit him by mistake.

Another burst of fire — something whistled past his ear — that one too close for comfort.

He tried to quicken his pace, all the more difficult when he couldn't see a thing.

The undergrowth started to get even more dense. It was like trying to fight his way through a thick bush.

More shouting — much closer now.

They were gaining and he was hardly moving at all.

For a moment he was tempted to just accept his fate.

But then he remembered the big cat, it probably wasn't going to eat him, then those bastards had to shoot it — the anger he felt spurred him on.

He fought on with determination, pushing the undergrowth aside, barging through with vigour.

If it slowed him down, it would slow them down too.

He dragged himself through the dense foliage which eventually began to clear. It was now much less overgrown.

He thought he could make out a clearing ahead and then what looked like a darker patch of ground.

He ran forward, through the clearing and towards the dark area. To his surprise, as he reached it, the ground seemed to give way and he suddenly felt himself falling through the darkness.

Chapter 51

"Hello, what's your name?"

Nicholas opened his eyes. His head ached and his vision was blurred, but he could see that right in front of him sat a monkey.

"My name is Paul."

A monkey called Paul?

He'd had such a roller coaster of a journey so far, he happily accepted being greeted by a talking monkey.

"It's Nicholas — or Nic for short."

His head ached. He'd obviously banged it quite badly — he felt queasy.

"Where are you from — Nic for short?"

"Just Nic."

He tried to move, but he couldn't. He was tied again, just like before.

"Nic for short — from just Nic?"

Nicholas shook his head — it throbbed.

"No, you don't understand, just call me Nic, it is the short version of my full name Nicholas. I am from England in the UK."

"Nic from England, in the UK," the monkey repeated.

"Yes, that's right."

The monkey was well spoken but with a strange accent.

"How did you get to speak English so well?" Nicholas asked.

"I learned so that we could communicate with outsiders."

"Like me?"

"Yes, like you."

Nicholas winced. The pain in his head was getting worse.

"You have a very nasty cut on the side of your head. I am going to take a look at it. Is that okay?"

Nicholas looked directly at the monkey.

"Are you qualified?"

"Of course, I studied medicine as well as English."

"Okay, then go ahead," Nicholas said, hoping the monkey could do something to stop the discomfort he was in.

Nicholas closed his eyes. He could feel hands cradle his head and move it from side to side.

This monkey's got very big hands.

Nicholas opened his eyes. The monkey was still sitting in front of him with its arms by its side. He blinked and looked again. The monkey was still in front of him but there was definitely a pair of hands around his head.

Nicholas turned.

There was someone sitting to his side.

It was like a ghostly apparition of a man.

The face was a deathly white colour with big dark brown eyes. On his head he wore a crown of very bright bird's feathers. Through his nose was a small bone.

The ghost smiled — a friendly welcoming smile.

"You will be fine. We'll get the cut on your head and your hand attended to."

"Paul?" Nicholas said, looking at the ghost.

"Yes?"

"But, if you are Paul, what's the monkey's name?"

Paul laughed.

Nicholas wondered what was so funny.

"It's a monkey — it doesn't have a name."

Nicholas tried to move — he couldn't.

He realised his hands were tied around his back and he sat cross legged on the floor.

"You are tied," Paul said.

"Can you untie me, please," Nicholas said.

Paul shooed the monkey away and sat directly in front of him.

"Before I do, Nic, there are two very important questions that I must ask you."

Nicholas nodded, which reminded him his head ached.

"Yes, of course, what are they?" He winced.

"Why are you here?"

"I run a charitable organisation to help save the animals and the planet and our top priority is to try to protect the rain forests of South America."

Paul stared hard at Nicholas's face as he spoke, looking for any tell–tale sign of a lie.

"And, do you mean us any harm?"

"What? No, of course not. Paul, I've had the most horrible time. I've been with people who wanted to kill me, I've been shot at and held prisoner by bandits. For once, I actually feel safe and hopefully you don't mean me any harm!" Nicholas blurted out.

Paul stared for a moment and then smiled, "I believe you."

He reached around Nicholas's back and untied the knots in the rope.

Nicholas was free.

He blinked and blinked again.

His vision was slowly returning.

He looked around.

He was at the far end of a camp, in fact it was more than a camp — it was a village.

Paul stood up.

Nicholas could see that it wasn't just his face that was ghostly but his whole body as well.

Paul turned to the camp and shouted something in a language Nicholas had never heard before.

Hoots and shouts erupted from all around. More ghosts began to emerge from the grass roofed huts. There were many ghosts of all different sizes, some short, some tall, male and female — all with the same pale grey faces and bodies, all rushing towards him.

When he had first awoken he'd thought it was all a dream. Then he'd thought he was in heaven. Now, perhaps this really was heaven and these were the spirits of people who had passed on.

He felt fearful.

He watched the ghost–people rush closer.

The fear turned to panic — he screamed.

In the next instant all the ghosts screamed in reply.

Nicholas was perplexed. Without thinking what he was saying, he blurted out an involuntary "What?"

The ghosts replied with "What?"

Nicholas turned to Paul.

"These are my people, they are here to say hello."

Nicholas looked at the ghosts in front of him, looked at Paul and back at the ghosts.

"Hello," Nicholas said.

"Hello," all of the ghosts said in unison.

As they moved closer, Nicholas could see that they were not ghosts — they were people — Paul's people. They were naked apart from a simple garment to cover their modesty and their entire bodies from head to foot were painted in some kind of light grey paint which gave them their ghostly appearance. There were children pointing, teenagers standing confidently and adults muttering and whispering amongst themselves.

"I will help you stand," Paul said, grabbing Nicholas's arm and helping him to his feet.

As he tried to stand, he almost passed out due to the pain in his head. He still felt dizzy and nauseous.

"I don't feel very well, Paul," Nicholas said, stumbling.

"We will get your wounds cleaned up and your head seen to."

Paul said something to the crowd around him and before Nicholas knew what was happening, others helped take his weight and led him towards one of the huts.

Chapter 52

Nicholas kept passing in and out of consciousness.

He was lying on a straw bed propped up by a large straw pillow.

There were two women at his side.

He felt jolts of pain from his hand. He tried to pull it away but they were too strong. They smeared something on the back of his hand. It was followed by a cool soothing feeling.

They were chattering between themselves.

His head still ached.

Another woman held a wet rag and was wiping the dried mud from his head, arms and feet.

Paul crouched nearby and smiled sympathetically.

He called a woman over who appeared at Nicholas's side and said something.

She held a wooden cup to his mouth and pressed it against his lips.

"Drink. Drink," Paul said.

"What is it?" Nicholas asked.

"You drink. It's good for you," Paul replied.

Nicholas was hesitant.

Paul smiled, nodded and gestured towards the cup.

The woman holding the cup said something.

"Drink," Paul said.

Nicholas opened his mouth and drank the liquid from the cup. It was thicker than water, but runnier than yoghurt, a consistency somewhere in between. It had an odd taste, not unpleasant but not quite nice either and like nothing he'd ever tasted before. It was earthy but also fruity with an edge of sharpness, like lime.

Nicholas licked his lips.

After a moment, he began to feel peculiar.

Random thoughts and visions began to flash through his mind. He could picture Tyler, Rusty and Larry and especially the expression on Larry's face when they were going to kill him. He had seemed so kind at first. Paul and the tribe seemed helpful too, but was he mistaken about them as well?

He'd heard stories about many different tribes of people in the South American jungle and how they lived in isolation from outside influence. They had their own customs, practices and beliefs, some more brutal than others, and this is how they had lived for hundreds or even thousands of years.

He felt sleepy.

In his mind he could picture what little he had seen of the village.

He thought of the journey walking to the hut.

He remembered a fire in the centre of the village and a huge pot above it.

More thoughts flashed through his mind. Bones, he saw piles of bones near the fire, but what type of bones? Were they — human?

He'd read somewhere that some tribes still practiced cannibalism — they were cannibals!

That explained the bones. That explained why they were taking care of him. They were cleaning him up — they were preparing him as their main course for dinner!

They didn't care about his welfare — they just wanted to eat him.

He could hardly keep his eyes open.

The drink, they'd put something in the drink.

He just hoped he wouldn't be awake when they ate him.

His eyes closed.

Chapter 53

Nicholas was running along a wide dirt track that had been laid in the middle of the jungle.

The sun was out and it was hot, but he wasn't sweating and the running was effortless.

As he looked around he could see that trees had been cut down on both sides and the forest decimated.

He stopped running and listened — nothing — what was left of the jungle didn't make the same cacophony of sounds as it did when he last heard it.

He started running again. He looked around and stopped. He wasn't moving. He was running on the spot and not getting anywhere. He was in the same place in the same decimated forest.

He turned around.

Behind him all this time was Larry, holding something in his hand.

Beside him stood a rhino, a monkey, a tiger and a dolphin.

Larry opened his hand — a coin.

"Heads or tails?" Larry said.

"Tails," Nicholas said.

Larry flipped the coin into the air and it landed back in his hand.

"Heads."

The rhino vanished.

"Heads or tails?"

"Tails," Nicholas said hesitantly.

Larry flipped the coin again.

"Heads."

The tiger vanished.

"Heads or tails?"

"Tails," Nicholas said reluctantly.

Larry flipped it again.

"Heads."

The monkey vanished.

"Heads or tails?"

"I don't like this game," Nicholas said in desperation.

"Heads or tails?" Larry demanded.

Surely the coin can't be heads every time.

"Tails."

Larry flipped.

Nicholas watched the coin rise into the air and back into the man's hand.

Please not the dolphin. Not the dolphin.

"Heads."

The dolphin vanished.

Larry handed the coin to him.

Nicholas looked at it and turned it over — it had heads on both sides.

Nicholas opened his eyes.

He knew immediately where he was — he was in the hut — lying on the same straw mattress, propped up by the same straw pillow.

He didn't feel at all queasy or sick and his mind felt alert — very alert.

He sat up.

The back of his hand felt itchy. He remembered his cut.

He looked down and was horrified by what he saw — his hand — discoloured and inflamed.

He looked away. He remembered watching a film once with his Dad. The lead character had damaged his hand. He was nowhere near medical attention and after a little while it had developed gangrene. It had got so bad that they had to cut it off.

Images of Great Uncle Winston started to flood his mind — leaning forward with outstretched stumps — repeating the words 'Pleased to meet you, Nicholas'.

He heard the character in the film saying that the wounded hand smelt bad.

He sniffed his own, but it didn't smell bad at all. It smelled like mown grass.

It wasn't gangrene — it was some sort of paste they had smeared over his cut, it was green coloured and applied so thickly it made his hand look larger than it actually was.

He moved his fingers and clenched his fist. No pain and no discomfort.

He was alive and, so it seemed, very well cared for.

Whoever these people were, he owed them his life — and his hand.

Nicholas lay back and sighed.

He felt well rested and very relaxed.

As he lay there he began to tune in to the world around him.

He could hear voices outside — adults talking in their native tongue and children playing.

He turned his head. He could see shapes rush past the hut through the gaps in the straw.

The hut was about the size of his bedroom back at home. It was simple, straw walls and a straw roof with main timber uprights and roof joists. The door was made of woven grass.

At that moment, the door opened.

A head appeared.

"Hello," Paul said.

"Hello," Nicholas replied.

"Are you okay?"

"Yes, I feel great."

"Good," Paul said and crouched down beside him.

"Where am I?"

"You are here yet you do not know where you are?"

"I know I am in South America, I presume in Brazil, but I don't know where."

"Then how did you get here?"

"By plane to America, then a flight to Manaus, then another flight down an airstrip and then a boat down the Amazon for sixteen hours."

"You are deep in the jungle now," Paul said. "You said something about nearly getting shot?"

"Yes, by the men who were helping me."

Paul was confused, "Men helping you tried to shoot you?"

"Well, they weren't really helping me," Nicholas replied. "They were going to shoot me. But then bandits came along and I fell in the river. They caught me and then held me hostage. I managed to escape and then I fell down some kind of slope — that's where you must have found me."

"Yes, a hunting party found you at the bottom of a large ravine."

Paul appeared worried by something.

"If bandits chase you to the ravine then that means they are close. This is not good. I will tell my people. They are dangerous. They will kill us."

"But why would they kill you? You seem to be peaceful people."

"We are peaceful people. But they do not care. They kill because they can. If they are lucky, they might even get a reward from the loggers or the farmers."

"Are the loggers cutting down the trees for the farmers?"

"The loggers cut down trees for wood to sell, but also for farmers so they can grow large crops — crops for your people."

"My people?"

"The food is grown here to be sent to your country, to feed your people. There are too many people — the world cannot cope."

It brought back the memory of the conversation he'd had with his Gran on the same subject.

Paul was clearly emotional about what was happening around him.

"The land cannot continue to be carved up. It is ruining the habitat for the animals who live here: orangutans slaughtered or displaced, birds who nest on the ground and in the trees, all suffering the effects. Last week one of my people was attacked by a jaguar. It should not have been here but its habitat has been destroyed by loggers nearby."

"Nearby? They are close to here?"

"Oh yes, just a mile or so in that direction," Paul said, pointing.

"Can't you move?" Nicholas asked.

"Move? But this is our home and has been for many generations of my family."

"But, what will happen if you don't move?"

"We may be killed."

"But ..." Nicholas was shocked. He was lost for words.

"If that is the will of the gods then we will accept that."

"But that's not right — that's not fair!"

Nicholas felt enraged. These kind folk had saved his life and yet there are those others who are destroying the forest, ruining the habitat and killing poor defenceless people like Paul and his tribe.

In that moment he was glad he had come to South America.

The information he had read online, in magazines and in newspapers had given him an idea of things here, but hadn't quite prepared him for the stark reality of what was actually happening. It was especially hard–hitting to hear it directly from the inhabitants who had lived there peacefully for centuries.

"Paul, I will do something about this — you have my word — I will do something about this!"

Paul looked at the face of the young man who sat in front of him. He saw the fire in his eyes and sensed the passion in his heart — he knew he meant every word.

Chapter 54

"Come on," Paul said.

"Where are we going?" Nicholas asked as they went outside.

There were children running around and everyone seemed busy.

"Now you are better, we are going to see the village elder."

"Okay," Nicholas said, nervous that he was going to meet someone so important.

At the far end of the village there was a hut, open on one side, where a man sat on what looked like a throne. He was obviously quite old and elaborately adorned in coloured beads and feathers.

There were two men standing either side of him, their bodies covered in paint, with knives and spears to protect their leader.

"There are some things that must be observed, okay?" Paul said as they approached.

"Yes, what are they?"

"Do not stare, it is rude to stare."

"Oh, okay, and?"

"Do not sit down until he tells you."

"Okay."

"Do not look at him unless he has asked you a question and you are addressing your response to him."

"Okay, anything else?"

"Do not raise your arms whilst you are in front of him. Keep your arms at your side."

"Right — don't stare, don't look at him unless he has asked me to speak, don't sit down until he says and keep my arms at my side."

"Yes, this is very important, otherwise you may be asked to leave the village."

"Okay, Paul, thank you for looking after me."

Paul smiled and laughed. "Paul has a new friend," and placed his hand on Nicholas's shoulder.

Nicholas was anxious as he approached. Instinctively he wanted to look up, but had been told not to.

Paul said something in his native tongue.

The leader of the tribe spoke.

Nicholas stood with his head lowered. He didn't know whether the man was addressing him or not and he didn't dare look in case he wasn't. Nicholas waited.

"The chief asks how you are."

Nicholas raised his head and looked directly at the chief.

It is the first time he saw him properly. He sat majestically with a straw crown embellished with feathers. He had a bone through his nose and paint on his cheeks.

"I am very well. Thank you for taking me in and looking after me," Nicholas said and lowered his head again.

Paul relayed his answer back to the chief.

The chief replied.

"The chief says that you are welcome to stay here as long as is necessary."

Nicholas looked up. "Thank you for your generosity," he said and looked down again.

Paul translated Nicholas's words and the chief spoke again.

"He said that I will look after you."

Nicholas raised his eyes, "Thank you".

"We go now," Paul said.

"Okay, thank you." Nicholas said, with his head bowed low, he walked backwards.

"You can look up now, turn and we walk away."

"Wow, that was nerve–racking," Nicholas said.

Paul looked bemused, "Does that mean you were nervous?"

"Yes, it does."

"It is okay, the chief is a generous and kind man."

As they walked away, Nicholas was intrigued.

"Paul, if you don't mind me asking — how old is the chief?"

"He has been alive for one thousand and one hundred and nine moons," Paul said.

"Moons?"

"Yes, we follow the passage of time by the moon, its rise, when it is full and when it falls."

"Is that each full moon then — that you are counting?"

"Yes, that is right."

"Wow, that means the chief is — ninety two years of age — and one month," Nicholas replied in a flash.

"Yes, that is right — in sun years."

"How old are you Paul?"

"I am 275 moons."

Nicholas did some quick mental arithmetic. "Almost twenty in sun years then," Nicholas replied.

"Yes. It is the celebration of the day of my birth in three days ..."

"That'll be nice," Nicholas said.

"... when I will take over from my Grandfather," Paul continued

"Your Grandfather?"

"Yes, the chief is my Grandfather."

"Oh I see — sorry, I didn't realise," Nicholas was taken aback by the importance of what he had just been told. "Wow, you're the next in line to be chief."

"But, what about your Father, shouldn't he be next in line?"

"My Father was killed by those that threaten our lands."

"Oh, I'm sorry, Paul."

He wasn't sure how to act after this revelation. He had been speaking to Paul like an equal but now he wondered if he should be observing the same strict protocol as he did with his Grandfather. What should he do?

Paul observed his confusion, "It is okay, until I am chief, I am a normal Ashai."

"A what, sorry?"

"Ashai, we are the Ashai people."

"Wow, sorry Paul, so much has happened I am just trying to keep up with it all. I presume then that Paul is not your real name?"

"No, my name is Asheatamai," Paul said.

"Ash–ee–yat–a–mai," Nicholas said slowly.

Paul smiled, "Yes, very good."

"Does it mean anything, your name?"

"Yes, it means, the son of the man who is leader of his people."

Nicholas nodded, "But that won't be relevant when you are the leader of your people?"

"That is right — then I will take my Grandfather's name, Ashamai."

"Ash–a–mai," Nicholas said. "The man who is leader of his people."

Paul laughed, "That is right — we make an Ashai out of you yet."

Nicholas smiled.

"The chief — your Grandfather — is very with it."

"With it? I do not understand what you mean?"

"Erm ..." Nicholas was unsure how to put it, "Quick witted. He has all his faculties."

Paul looked confused.

"His brain is very agile — he has the mind of a younger man."

"Ahhh ... " Paul said finally understanding him, "It is the 'Sisa Qhali Kay Uma'"

"Sorry — the what?" There was no way that Nicholas was going to try to pronounce that first go.

"Sisa," Paul said.

"See–sa," Nicholas replied.

"Qhali," Paul said.

"Khal–lee," Nicholas repeated slowly.

"Kay."

"Kay," Nicholas said at the easier one.

"Uma."

"Oo–mah," Nicholas replied.

"See–sa — khal–lee — kay — oo–mah," Nicholas said proudly.

"Yes — that is right. Good," Paul placed his hands together and nodded in appreciation.

Nicholas smiled.

"What does it mean?"

"It means — the flower that gives health to the head."

"It's a flower?"

"Yes, the seeds of the flower. Very powerful — great care taken — affect my people."

Nicholas wasn't sure what he meant.

"It is what we gave you."

Nicholas looked confused.

"In the drink — with Hampiy Punuy."

"hamp–ee–aye — pun–ewey," Nicholas attempted.

"Yes, it means healthy sleep."

"Oh right, so you gave me a drink which gives a healthy head and healthy sleep."

Paul thought for a moment, "Yes, that is right."

Nicholas smiled.

"Well it must be amazing stuff if I can feel so much better the very next day."

"What do you mean — the very next day?" Paul said.

"The drink I had last night," Nicholas said matter–of–factly.

"No, you not understand. You sleep for six nights. Today is the seventh day you have been here."

Nicholas said the words out loud — "Six nights, seven days"

"The drink very powerful, but heal quickly."

Nicholas shook his head. He couldn't believe it. He'd been away for six nights and seven days. Surely someone must know he's missing by now. He had said he would check in regularly using Larry's satellite phone, so if no-one had heard from him, surely they would have done something — but what? The Amazon was massive, they could have been looking for days, where would they even begin to look.

Nicholas suddenly felt homesick and sad.

He thought about his Mum, he missed her.

"What is the matter?"

"I am homesick."

"I am not sure what that means."

"I miss my home. I miss my Mother. I feel sad."

"I understand. It was the same for me when I left the village."

Nicholas raised his head, "When you went away to learn English?"

"Yes, that is right. Eighteen moons. I was sad too. I was happy to be home."

Nicholas nodded.

"Would you like to be alone?"

"Yes, Paul. I think I would."

"You can go back to the hut. I'll be around here if you want me."

"Thank you Paul — thank you for everything."

"You are welcome. My friend."

Chapter 55

Nicholas was standing on the edge of the platform in an underground station in London.

A constant flow of people brushed past him in a desperate hurry to get to wherever they were going.

"Nic Savage?" a voice called out from behind.

"Yes?" Nicholas replied, but when he turned all he saw were people barging and shoving their way past.

"Nic Savage?" the voice called out over the station public announcement system.

"Nic Savage?"

This time the voice seemed to come from his side.

"Nic Savage?"

He turned again — just crowds of people in a rush.

"Nic Savage?"

He didn't know where else to look.

"Nic Savage?"

The voice got louder and louder.

He felt an almighty shove from behind. He lost his balance and fell forward.

He woke up.

"Nic Savage?"

Nicholas was confused.

As he came to, he could hear his name being called again. The voice sounded amplified and distorted.

Paul rushed in.

"Nic, Nic — wake up!"

"Paul, what is it?"

"It is men in the sky. They are looking for you," Paul said, pulling at his arm and trying to drag him outside.

He could hear the voice again, over a loudspeaker with the distinct noise of rotor blades in the background.

"It's a helicopter. They're looking for me."

"NIC SAVAGE. NIC SAVAGE. IF YOU CAN HEAR US, MAKE YOUR PRESENCE KNOWN."

Paul shrugged his shoulders, "The trees, difficult for them to see, or to land."

"I've got to do something otherwise they'll go and leave me here," Nicholas said panicking as he could hear the helicopter was now overhead.

"The fire!" Nicholas said.

Nicholas remembered the fire in the middle of the village.

He rushed through the village and past the villagers who were confused and frightened, standing and pointing at the helicopter hovering above the tree top.

There was a pile of leaves that were still quite green next to the fire. He scooped up an armful and tossed them on the fire. A woman rushed forward and tried to stop him. Paul intervened and waved her away. A plume of thick smoke wafted upwards.

Nicholas bent down, scooped up another armful of leaves and threw them on, and again, and again.

Confused villagers gathered, chattering and waving their arms.

More leaves, more smoke, belching upwards into the tree canopy above.

He could see the dark shape of the helicopter pass overhead and disappear from sight.

He was almost out of leaves.

Paul did his best to calm his fellow villagers who were now crowded around him obviously worried about what was going on.

Nicholas looked at Paul and threw his arms wide in desperation.

The helicopter was flying away.

Paul looked up, smiled and pointed. "It's coming back!"

Nicholas turned as the sound of the helicopter began to get louder.

"NIC SAVAGE. IF THAT IS YOU, SEND ANOTHER PUFF OF SMOKE."

Nicholas leapt forward, grabbed the last remaining armful of leaves and tossed them on the fire.

One final large plume of dark grey smoke belched upwards.

He watched the smoke rise up through the canopy and waited desperately.

"ROGER. NIC SAVAGE. LOCATION CONFIRMED. THERE IS NOWHERE TO LAND. TWO MILES DUE WEST IS THE RIVER. PICK YOU UP AT TWELVE MIDDAY."

Nicholas couldn't believe it. He began to jump up and down for joy.

Paul said something to the villagers.

The mood changed and they too began to jump up and down.

"REPEAT. RIVER TWO MILES DUE WEST. PICK UP AT TWELVE MIDDAY."

The helicopter turned around and flew off at speed.

"Wow, they found me!" Nicholas said running up to Paul.

"Yes, that is good."

"I've got two problems though."

"What problems?" Paul said with concern.

"Which way is due west — and — how do I know when midday is?"

Chapter 56

Nicholas was all smiles as he followed Paul through the well–trodden path towards the river.

When he asked Paul which way was West he simply pointed and said 'that way' as though it was obvious.

With such a thick canopy over the village he hadn't seen the sun for ages. But now it was breaking through the trees in shafts of light. He could feel the warmth from its rays.

He chuckled to himself as he remembered Paul's explanation of how to tell when it was midday.

Paul had led him to a clearing in the forest. There was a large pole staked into the ground and around it were stones placed at equal intervals in a giant circle. It was called 'Pacha Tupuq'

When Nicholas had asked him what it meant, he simply replied, 'Clock'.

They had left the village with plenty of time and he couldn't believe that very soon he would be rescued.

"What was that commotion in the village last night, Paul?"

"Do you mean the screaming sounds?"

"Yes."

"It was a family of Capuchin."

"Capuchin?"

"Yes, monkey. The forest clearing drives them out of their home. They flee and run into us. They get scared and cause noise."

"Does that happen often?"

"Yes," Was Paul's shockingly simple reply.

Nicholas lowered his head.

They walked in silence for quite some time, when Nicholas noticed a plant at the side of the path.

The stems were narrow and long, rising up to an elaborate arrangement of bright red leaves and what looked to be a large seed pod.

The moment he saw it, Nicholas felt his stomach turn over.

"Paul, what's this?" he asked.

Paul stopped and turned round.

"That is Sisa Qhali Kay Uma — the one I told you about. Beautiful isn't it."

"Yes, it is. I've never seen a plant like it."

"It is the seeds inside the pod, here," Paul said pointing.

"They are removed, ground and mixed with water to make a drink. Good for the head," Paul tapped his temples. "It is very powerful though. Very powerful."

"You said yesterday about it affecting your people — in what way?"

"This plant is said to be quariwarmi."

"Quarry — Warmy," Nicholas repeated.

"Two — Spirits", Paul translated. "Small amounts make a very healthy head, like you said, quick–witted or brain agile, but too much and it bad."

"Bad how?"

"It no longer possible to make children."

Nicholas looked at the plant and then back at Paul.

"This is what my people found when we moved here. They took too much. No more children for some. Thankfully we not all affected, so our people live on."

"Wow, that's incredible — but also rather sad."

"Only here it grows. Only here."

Paul turned and continued walking along the path.

Nicholas looked at the plant.

There was that feeling in his stomach again. He felt an urge, a driving force and before he knew what he was doing, he reached out, ripped the seed pod from the stalk and shoved it in his pocket.

He hurried his pace to catch up with Paul.

Chapter 57

"It is now I leave you," Paul said with a hint of sadness.

Nicholas smiled. He too felt a little sad.

"Thank you so much for your help. I'd be dead if it were not for you."

"You are welcome — my friend."

Nicholas held out his hand, Paul took it and they shook.

"I hope you and your people will be okay."

"Thank you. And you and your family."

"Oh, and all the best with becoming chief, I hope it goes well."

"Thank you — my friend."

Paul smiled, turned and walked away.

Nicholas watched him disappear into the tree line and out of sight.

Nicholas felt a tear trickle down his cheek. He wiped it away. He wasn't sure if he was sad to leave this remarkable place or whether it was the sheer joy of being able to go home.

He looked out at the river. It was at least half a mile wide at this point and he was amazed at the sheer scale of it.

The bank was steep with a drop of about six feet down into the murky river that was flowing past.

Up ahead he could see what looked like a muddy rocky beach.

A large log had been washed up. He walked over and sat on it.

His mind was still struggling to cope with the reality of the experience in the jungle. It had seemed to be just a few days but was actually over a week. And what a week it had been.

He went through all the recent events in his head. From Burger Ville employee to Charity Chairman — from being almost killed by a government fixer and his henchmen to being almost eaten by a large wild cat — from being held hostage by bandits to being rescued by a local tribe.

He smiled and shook his head in disbelief. If this was a story in a book no–one would ever believe it and yet here he was, living it for real. He felt overwhelmed and emotional.

His Gran had said, 'Put yourself in situations to develop your experience' and what situations these were.

He couldn't wait to tell her what he had been through.

He just hoped she would be able to take it all in.

He put his hand in his pocket and pulled out the seed pod. He tried to remember what it was called, but he could only remember that it began with Sisa and ended in Uma — *that'll do* — Sisa Uma, or Sisa for short. He clenched it tightly and put it back in his pocket.

He pulled out his mobile phone. He couldn't believe he still had it. Thank heavens he'd put it down his pants other-wise he'd have either lost it in the river or the bandits would have taken it like they had everything else.

He tried turning it on again. It was still dead.

He wondered if it would ever work again.

He put it back in his pocket.

He sighed.

He stood up and picked up a large stone.

He tossed it into the river.

It splashed and sent ripples extending outwards.

As he watched the ripples a deeply painful memory came into his mind.

He sat back down.

He thought of his Father and cried.

Chapter 58

"Oh my gosh, it must have been terrifying." Summer said as they sat around the table in the meeting room.

"To be honest I was mostly caught up in the heat of the moment. I dealt with each thing as it happened. I guess I was in survival mode. I just did what I needed to get through it."

"Thank heavens for Paul and his village though."

"I know. If it hadn't been for their kindness, I don't think I'd be here now."

"Amazing. Simply Amazing," Romain said.

"Anyway, I am back now. Was everything okay while I was away?"

"Yes, fine," Summer said. "We held the fort. Of course, you've got a message list as long as your arm."

"And just about every newspaper wants to talk to you about your story," Pierre said.

"And every TV channel as well," Alex added.

Nicholas nodded, "Well, it will certainly help to promote what we're doing, especially the deforestation in South America and how it is affecting the indigenous people."

Nicholas contemplated for a moment and looked around the table, "Thank you so very much. You're a fantastic team and I am really grateful and proud of you all."

"We're just pleased to have you back safe and sound. Rapture wouldn't be Rapture without you at the helm," Alex said.

Nicholas blushed, "You're very kind."

"Megan, can you find me the number of a company called BioMedSyn please."

"Bio — Med — is that S I N?"

"No, S Y N as in synthetic," Nicholas replied.

Megan wrote it down, "Okay, will do."

"What's that for?" Summer asked.

"Oh, it's just something that I came across in the jungle. It might work out to be nothing but I just wanted to check it out with an expert first."

Chapter 59

It had been a whirlwind week.

Interview after interview for TV, radio and newspapers — everyone wanted to find out about his incredible journey and how he'd made it out alive. Some reporters came to Nicholas's offices and, for other interviews, he travelled to theirs. He went to radio stations in London and even went to Manchester to appear on BBC Breakfast.

Sitting at the boardroom table in the BioMedSyn offices was a stark contrast to the last few hectic days. It was silent, apart from the hum of the air conditioning. He looked around the room. They had incredible state of the art technology, including tablet screens in every position, overhead projector, television, voice communications and webcams. They clearly had money.

He looked at the clock.

He was purposely early.

He liked to be punctual.

He was waiting for the CEO, Rufus Fitzwilliam and the head of development, Hugo Wentworth.

As the hand struck the hour, the door opened and a formidable man stormed into the room.

Nicholas stood and smiled.

"Nic, sorry to have kept you waiting," Rufus said and offered his hand.

Nicholas shook it and silently winced at the strength of the grip.

Hugo followed closely behind. His grip was weak and clammy.

Thank you for seeing me so soon."

"Not at all, it's the least we could do for Nic Savage the Chairman of Rapture," Rufus said inviting Nicholas to sit down.

"We heard about your recent ordeal on the news and we are so pleased that you made it through okay."

"Thanks," Nicholas replied.

"It must have been terrifying."

"It is the life experiences that help shape us," Nicholas said and waved the comment away.

It surprised Rufus to hear that reply from such a young man.

"Now, what can BioMedSyn do for Nic Savage?"

"You seem to be the leading bio–medical company in the field of developing synthetic drugs."

"We are indeed," Rufus said proudly.

"You also have a charitable arm, BioMedLife that provides drugs and essential medical supplies to areas rife with famine and poverty."

"Yes, we invest millions, every year."

"Well, I'd like your help."

"What type of help, Nic?" Rufus asked.

"The tribe I met in the Amazon rainforest have a drug that can help stimulate the brain. I believe that it could be a cure for Alzheimer's and Dementia as well as an aid to improving cognitive function."

Rufus and Hugo shared a look of amazement and interest.

"How do you know this?" Rufus asked.

"Because they told me what it does and I saw its effects on the chief and other older people in the village. Whilst their bodies were frail for their age, their brains were just so — so with it."

"It could just be good genes," Hugo said. "There is nothing to suggest it's the result of taking the drug."

"Oh it is."

"How do you know?"

"Because they gave it to me — it was incredible. I was aware and alert. It was like my brain was firing on all cylinders."

"Really? And is it still like that now?"

"No, it wore off throughout the day. That is why I believe it could be used to improve short term function, say for an exam or when learning — but — it can obviously work on a longer scale too because all the old people in the village were so cognitively active."

Rufus rubbed his chin and pondered.

"A drug?" Rufus asked. "Is this already refined?"

"Sorry, excuse my terminology. I say drug. It's a plant. They extract the seeds, grind them up and put them in a drink."

Hugo was clearly sceptical.

"It's probably just a form of indigenous South American herbal tea."

"I don't think so," Nicholas said firmly. "This is a tribe that has been around a very long time and they said that these plants only grow in that area and nowhere else."

Rufus sighed.

"Tantalising as this is, Nic, I don't think I could convince the board to agree to a mission to South America to find seed pods. We are a leading biomedical synthetic drug company with medical assets valued in the trillions — but we don't go on wild goose chases to find plants with magical properties."

"But, you don't have to," Nicholas said excitedly, "I already have one."

Rufus looked at Hugo.

Hugo looked at Rufus.

They nodded to each other knowingly.

Rufus leaned forward over the table.

"If this drug can do what you say it can, what would you like us to do with it?"

"I'd like you to synthetically reproduce the active ingredient so that we can manufacture tablets to supply the world."

Hugo rubbed his hands together, "This could be worth billions!"

Rufus smiled in agreement.

Nicholas stepped in, "No you don't understand, I don't want to charge anything — I want to give them away. I want to help the planet."

"Give them away, but you can't be serious — this could be worth a fortune."

"I thought you would understand. Your division —

BioMedLife — we can do something wonderful together," Nicholas said in frustration and disappointment.

"Yes, but we use that division as ..." Hugo said and was cut off by Rufus's outstretched hand.

"Nic, that is a very noble gesture and I fully understand where you are coming from."

Rufus leaned forward.

"Tell you what, Nic. If you can let us have the seed pod, we'll run some tests and get back to you."

Nicholas placed his hand in his pocket and gripped the seed pod that he'd had with him all along.

His stomach turned over.

There was something in the way Rufus spoke — a glint in his eye that just didn't feel right.

"Thank you, I appreciate it, but I think we need to get some paperwork drawn up first, like a non–disclosure agreement, or something like that."

Rufus bit his lip and sat back in his chair. He seemed impatient.

"Yes Nic, that is very wise. If you leave your address and contact details with my PA on the way out, we'll get something in the post to you."

"Okay, great," Nicholas said standing up. "Thank you for seeing me, I appreciate the time."

"Where do you have the seed pod by the way?" Rufus asked.

"Erm ... it's ... " Nicholas didn't know how to reply.

"It's just that the best place to put it is somewhere cold — to help preserve it."

"Somewhere cold?"

"Yes, like the fridge. Keep it in the fridge — as soon as possible."

"Oh, okay, thank you."

"Good to see you, Nic, we'll talk soon," Rufus said. He grabbed Nicholas's hand and squeezed tightly again.

"Thank you for coming, Nic, see you soon." Hugo said and shook his hand too.

As they watched Nicholas leave the room, Rufus turned to Hugo.

"Are you thinking what I am thinking?"

"Yes," Hugo replied.

"Okay, make it happen," Rufus ordered.

Chapter 60

As Nicholas headed home, he had mixed feelings about the meeting. On the one hand, he knew he needed a company like BioMedSyn to help him, but on the other, he was worried that they just wanted to take control and do things their way for their own gain.

Leo had told him to 'keep control' and this was one of those situations, where he knew he had to stay on top.

He didn't like the way Hugo and Rufus spoke. Their behaviour and the way they suddenly became so animated when they talked of the 'billions' they could make, made him feel uneasy. He was convinced they just saw pound signs.

His Gran popped into his thoughts and he changed his mind. Rather than going straight home, he'd go and see her.

He hadn't seen her since flying back and a visit was definitely overdue.

Chapter 61

"Hello?"

"Hi Gran, it's me."

"Not today, thank you," she said slamming the door.

We've been here before, Nicholas thought to himself.

He rang the bell. The door opened again.

"Gran, its Nicholas Savage, your Grandson."

There was a hesitant pause, the chain was removed and the door opened.

He hadn't been away that long but the face in front of him seemed to have aged.

He felt sad.

Perhaps the body lives so closely in tandem with the mind that a decline in one can affect the other.

"Hello Gran. May I come in?"

His Gran seemed to stare right through him with no recognition at all.

Then suddenly there was a slight glimmer in her eye, followed by a smile on her face. It was as though someone had flicked a switch and she had come to life.

"Don't stand there all day — come on in."

Nicholas walked in, not sure what to expect.

He walked into the living room and everything was

where it has always been — no shoe on the mantelpiece and nothing out of place.

"Would you like a cup of tea ..." She seemed about to say something else but the word didn't come to her.

Nicholas's heart sank — I think she's forgotten my name.

"Don't worry Gran, you sit down and I'll make the tea."

"Okay, thank you dear."

Nicholas walked into the kitchen, again, hesitant about what he might find but thankfully everything seemed to be in the right place.

He filled the kettle with water, turned it on and got two cups and saucers from the cupboard.

He grabbed a box of tea bags from another cupboard, lifted the lid off the tea pot, and checked inside to make sure that there was nothing there that shouldn't be. He tossed the tea bags into the pot, repeating what Gran had said so many times.

"One — two — and one for the pot."

What else did he need — *milk*.

He opened the fridge — *the fridge!*

He remembered what Rufus had told him about putting the seed pod in the fridge.

He certainly didn't want it to go off and Rufus did say to do it as soon as possible.

He reached into his pocket and pulled out the pod.

Its bright colour was beginning to fade and was looking a little brown in places — he hoped it would still be okay.

He pulled open the vegetable drawer at the bottom and tucked it behind a bag of carrots.

He grabbed the milk and closed the door.

"Here you are Gran," Nicholas said handing her a cup.

Nicholas sat opposite on the sofa.

"Did Mum tell you what happened to me?"

She sat there looking at him but seeming not to hear.

"Gran? Did Mum tell you what happened when I was in South America?" — no reaction, nothing, she just stared.

Nicholas felt so helpless. The deterioration seemed to be so rapid and so severe.

They sat silently in each other's company until Nicholas had drunk his tea.

He made his excuses and left, much sooner than intended, the whole experience was too upsetting.

He wondered what his Mum thought of the situation.

He made his way home to find out.

Chapter 62

As Nicholas walked through the front door, he noticed his Mum's shoes and coat — she was home already.

It was only quarter to five — he hoped everything was okay with her new job.

He walked into the kitchen.

"Hi Nic, you're home early."

"I had a meeting and then came home. Is everything okay?" Nicholas asked.

His Mum seemed engrossed in some kind of paperwork.

"Yes — everything is fine," she replied and put the papers down.

"I have to say, my new boss is a delight to work for."

Nicholas sat down to listen.

"He wants me to review this contract and he told me to go home and read it as it would be a quieter environment and I would be able to concentrate without the distractions of work."

"That's really nice."

"I think it's the best thing that's happened. I feel so at home, everyone is lovely and I'm trusted with important company documents like this," she said pointing at the contract. "It's great."

"So everything has worked out for the best then," Nicholas said.

"Yes, it has. They say everything happens for a reason."

The condition of Nicholas's Gran was playing on his mind. He really wanted to discuss it with his Mum but didn't want to interrupt when she was so busy.

"Sorry, do you want me to come back later or can I talk to you now?"

"No, of course you can. What is it?"

"I went to see Gran."

His Mum put the contract down and gave him her full attention.

"How was she?"

"I'm worried about her, she's getting worse."

"I know. I went round the day before yesterday and she just wasn't at all with it. I found a shoe on the mantelpiece."

"I know, that happened one of the last times I went round too."

"But, then, I spoke to her last night on the phone and she seemed really perky. It's like she's better in the evenings than she is during the day."

"What do we do?"

"There isn't a lot we can do unfortunately. It happened to her Mum, my Gran. She went downhill so quickly and she couldn't cope. Mum and Dad took her in but it got to the point where she didn't recognise them anymore. She was aggressive too and always worried and panicky."

"Then what happened?"

"Well, the end was very quick, and though it seems awful to say, we were grateful for that."

"You mean — she died?"

"Yes. It was a rapid downturn and then she just died. I was only young at the time but I remember it well, towards the end. She used to stare right through me with dead eyes. It was horrible."

Nicholas was about to say that was just how Gran had looked at him earlier, but it was an upsetting subject in itself and he didn't want to make it worse.

The thought of his own Gran slipping away like that could well prove to be a blessing, but he'd become so close to her again and, with everything that had happened since, he had a hell of a lot to thank her for.

"Sorry, Mum. I've interrupted you. I'll let you carry on."

"What are you plans?"

"Oh, I've got about a thousand emails to go through. I need to catch up on everything that's been happening while I was away."

"Okay. I'll do dinner for seven."

"Thanks," Nicholas said and left his Mum to it.

Chapter 63

Nicholas reflected on the odd dreams he'd had last night while he was getting ready the next morning.

It had been a very strange night and quite disturbing. He had put it down to the experience with his Gran and then reading through emails that discussed graphically the state of the planet, the threat to the environment and the horrors that were happening everywhere.

He'd also finally been able to watch Leo's documentary about climate change called 'Before the Flood'. Watching that and thinking of what he had learned from being involved with Rapture didn't help him get a good night's sleep either.

He walked into the kitchen and rubbed his eyes.

"You look tired," his Mum said.

"Yes, didn't sleep well."

"Nightmares?"

"No, just odd dreams."

"Well, you've been through a lot."

It hadn't even been a week since he'd left Paul at the edge of the river, but, after the journey home and then all the interviews and attention he'd received, it felt like weeks since he'd been back.

"Breakfast?"

"Not hungry really."

"Okay."

"Oh, I spoke to your Gran last night. She sounded so well."

"Oh that's good. Mind you, you did say that she sounded better in the evenings."

"No, this was more than that, she sounded so well, so — so with it."

There was something about the words that his Mum used that struck a chord, he felt like he was aware of something without knowing what it was.

"You should go and see her today if you can."

"Yes," Nicholas said. "I will."

Chapter 64

Nicholas rang the bell.

In no time at all, it opened, the chain was on.

"Hi Gran, it's me."

"Hello Nicholas, nice to see you. Come on in," She said as she unchained the door and opened it.

The lady in front of him was a changed person. Her eyes were brighter and she had more colour in her cheeks.

"I'll get the kettle on. You go and make yourself comfortable and I'll be right in. Would you like anything to eat?"

"No thanks Gran, I had lunch at work. I popped round to see how you are."

"Oh I couldn't be better thank you. I feel great. Take a seat. I'll be back in a jiffy."

Nicholas stepped into the living room and looked around. Everything was in order, just as it was the previous day, but now everything looked a bit cleaner. Even the brass ornaments in front of the fireplace seemed shinier.

He sat down and pulled out his phone. He checked his email.

His Gran came back with the cups. She seemed so sprightly — she almost jumped into her chair.

"So, how did you get on in your trip to South America?"

Nicholas was taken aback. "Didn't Mum tell you what happened?"

"No," his Gran said, looking concerned, "Why, what happened?"

"Oh ..." Nicholas said, quickly thinking what to say so as not to worry her, "It was certainly a very interesting experience and I learned a lot."

"Oh that's good, you got me worried there for a moment — I thought something bad had happened."

Nicholas shook his head. He wondered if she couldn't remember or if she just hadn't taken in what his Mum had told her.

"How's Leo?"

Nicholas laughed. "He's fine thank you," still not quite used to the fact that they were all referring to the international superstar by first name.

"He's been so good to you, helping you get this project off the ground."

"Yes, he has."

Nicholas couldn't believe how 'with it' she was and then he remembered, that was what his Mum had said and he still couldn't place why it sounded so familiar to him.

"So, how are you?"

"Oh I am fine thank you."

"You certainly seem to be well."

"Well, it's funny, but I feel twenty years younger."

"It's almost like I haven't been feeling myself recently but today I feel great again."

"If I had to put it down to something, I'd put it down to the peculiar strawberry."

Nicholas had a worrying thought.

"Er, what peculiar strawberry?"

"Last night, I was going through the fridge. Your Mum had been shopping for me and stocked it up and there, behind the carrots, was a peculiar looking strawberry."

Nicholas almost fell off the sofa.

"You ate the Sisa Uma?"

"The what?"

"The Sisa — the peculiar looking strawberry that was in the fridge — you ate it?"

"Is that what it was called? Yes, yes, I did."

Nicholas couldn't believe it. He'd only brought the one pod back and he couldn't very well pop back for another. Could this be the end of his hopes — all the plans he had?

He looked at his Gran. He didn't know how long the effects would last, even if they only lasted a few days, at least he would have his Gran back for a little while. She looked great and she obviously felt great and so, if that was the one good thing to come out of this then perhaps it had all been worthwhile.

"Is everything okay?"

"Yes Gran, sorry."

"Shouldn't I have eaten it?"

"No, it's fine. It was meant to be a surprise that's all. It was a very exotic fruit that I brought back from South America."

He had an idea.

"I just remembered something I need to check on my phone."

"Okay dear, I'll just pop the telly on, I do like to watch the one o'clock news, I'll turn the sound down and put the subtitles on though."

"Okay, Gran."

Nicholas secretly turned his phone onto record and surreptitiously pointed it at her so she wouldn't notice she was being filmed.

Even if his plans were dashed, he could at least record the evidence that the effects of the Sisa had worked on his Gran.

Nicholas looked at the TV screen. They were talking about the Southern Rail strikes and how it was affecting passengers.

"This reminds me of the story you told me about Grandfather and the unions."

"Oh its terrible isn't it," his Gran said, he zoomed in a little to capture the brightness in her eyes and the speed at which see seemed to be processing everything.

"All those poor people, trying to get to work, live their lives, it's so disruptive. From what I hear, the company have guaranteed their jobs and pay and yet they still strike. It's like they're doing it just to cause trouble."

"Apparently they're doing it because they're worried about passenger safety."

"Nonsense, there are other trains where the drivers are responsible for closing the doors. Mark my words, I see it in their eyes, just as I did in the eyes of the workers in your Grandfather's factory, they're relishing the power and they're doing it to cause trouble. They're probably just enjoying their days off and not caring a jot for the disruption they're causing."

"Maybe", Nicholas said, not wanting to trigger a deep discussion. "Oh, by the way, I thought more about that castle you were talking about."

Within a flash she replied.

"Tynmouth Priory and Castle in South Shields? Oh do go, it's a magical place. And, it sounds like you deserve the break. Also, remember to go to Sandhaven beach — the sandy beach stretches for miles!"

She began recounting stories and memories, including the flavour of ice cream that they had on the beach. She could even remember the number plate of the car they'd used to drive there.

Nicholas was amazed. Whatever the Sisa Uma had done, it had worked magic. As she related story after story he imagined all the cells in her brain, presumably being reconnected by whatever it was in that special little seed pod.

Suddenly Gran stopped talking. She appeared to be mesmerised. One moment she had been so bright and alert and now she was just staring at the TV.

"What is it, Gran?"

"It's you," Gran said.

"Er, yes, it is me, I'm here."

"No, I mean it's you — on the telly," Gran said turning up the volume.

Nicholas turned his head towards the screen. It was the interview that he'd given the day before to the BBC. It had already started but he assumed his Gran had got the gist of it by reading the subtitles.

His Gran watched and listened, Nicholas stopped recording and lowered the phone.

The news moved onto the next story.

She muted the TV and turned to him.

"Why didn't you tell me you almost died?"

"I didn't want to worry you," Nicholas replied.

"It said that you were almost shot and taken hostage?"

"Well, they're exaggerating a little — it is the news. In actual fact, I fell overboard and I was found by some local bandits who hoped that they might be able to hold me to ransom. But, I escaped, found a lovely tribe of people and they looked after me till I was rescued."

His Gran looked at him with an expression which suggested she thought there was more to it.

"But you're definitely okay?"

"I am fine — look!" he said raising his arms to prove it.

"Well, it's good to have you back in one piece."

"Carry on watching the news," Nicholas said and turned back to his phone.

He tried to check his email but in reality he was terribly disappointed.

He had had such an opportunity with the Sisa and now it was gone.

His Gran turned off the TV, the news had finished, just as Nicholas finished his tea.

"I suppose I'd better get back to work," Nicholas said.

"Okay, dear. Nice to see you, thank you for coming."

"I am at least glad you enjoyed the Sisa Uma?" Nicholas said.

"Oh I didn't enjoy it, it tasted horrible. I threw the rest of it away."

Nicholas couldn't believe his ears.

"You did what?"

"It didn't taste right, not like a normal strawberry, so I threw it away — in the bin."

"The bin!"

Nicholas rushed into the kitchen and pulled the top off the bin. He pulled out the bin liner, plopped it on the floor and began to rummage through it.

Food scraps, dirty kitchen roll, soggy tea bags, no Sisa Uma — *come on* — *come on, it must be here.*

Nicholas willed it to be there as he continued to rummage, then he spotted what he was looking for.

He grabbed it — it was the remains of the Sisa Uma, with a bite taken out of it. Thankfully there was about two thirds of it left and although the flesh had started to brown a little all the seeds still seemed intact.

He put the bin liner back in the bin and washed his hands.

He looked through the cupboards to find some cling film and carefully wrapped the Sisa Uma.

If the seeds needed to be ground, he could only assume that his Gran had bitten into them and crushed them in her mouth — she'd obviously had enough to cause such a dramatic effect.

He heard his Gran call out so he rushed back to the living room.

"Got it!" Nicholas said.

"You're welcome to it."

"I have high hopes for this Gran and you've just helped get things back on track."

"I have?" his Gran said with a perplexed smile.

"I have to go. I'll see you soon."

Before his Gran could reply, he'd gone.

Chapter 65

Nicholas rushed home, but as he walked up the stairs, something didn't feel right.

He turned the corner. The front door to the flat was open. This was odd, they never left the front door open. As he got nearer he realised that the door frame was broken, as if the door had been kicked in.

He saw figures inside, moving around. They wore dark clothes. He approached quietly and cautiously. Whoever they were, they were still inside. He saw one of the figures. He had something written on his back. He saw it again — Police. He pushed the door wide open and was confronted by a police officer.

"And you are?"

"Nic, I live here with my Mum."

The police officer gestured to the kitchen, Nicholas rushed in. His Mum was talking to another officer and had obviously been crying.

"Oh Nic, Nic, we've been burgled," she said, sobbing again.

"But who would want to burgle us Mum, we don't have anything of value."

"Opportunists," the police officer said, looking up from

scribbling notes in his little black book. "Probably checking out the whole block for flats with poor security."

"Oh, I see," Nicholas said.

"You've only got the one lock on your door you see. It makes you an easy target. A swift kick and it opens right up. You really need to get another lock on that door."

Nicholas had no idea what the other rooms were like but they'd even trashed the kitchen. All the drawers and cupboards had been emptied. He looked around. He noticed that they'd even been through the fridge.

"The fridge!" Nicholas said aloud.

"Yes," the office said. "You'd be surprised how many people put their valuables in the fridge. It's an obvious place to look."

Nicholas wasn't so sure. There was something very fishy going on.

"Okay Mrs Savage, we're about done here. If you call this number they'll give you a crime reference number for insurance purposes."

His Mum reached out and took the card.

"If you feel you need any help in dealing with this, call victim support and they will be happy to assist. And you'll need to get a locksmith round to fix that lock pronto and make sure you get a second lock fitted as well."

His Mum nodded and saw them out.

Nicholas stared at the fridge.

"Are you okay, Nic?" his Mum asked as she came back in.

"I am angry and disappointed that this has happened."

"I know. There are some nasty people around these days."

"Yes," Nicholas said. "Unscrupulous and devious people."

"Nic?" his Mother said, concerned.

"I'll help you clean up in a moment Mum. There is one thing I need to do."

Chapter 66

Nicholas sat at the kitchen table with his Mum.

Neither of them had much of an appetite.

They had spent the remainder of the afternoon and the early evening tidying up.

Thankfully nothing had been broken. Things had mostly just been tossed aside as though the burglars had been looking for something particular. They'd even left his laptop and his Mum's tablet computer.

They sat in silence. Nicholas considered the situation — he had to say something.

"Mum?"

She looked up.

"I've got something to tell you."

"Oh, this sounds ominous."

"No, not ominous — good actually."

He reached into this pocket and pulled out the Sisa Uma, tightly wrapped in cling film and put it on the table.

"It's a very rare seed pod from a plant in South America. The Ashai tribe use it — the ones who looked after me."

"Use it, how?"

"They grind the seeds and make it into a drink. It has amazing healing powers for the brain and it seems to reverse dementia and Alzheimer's."

His Mother looked amazed.

"Oh wouldn't it be wonderful if that were true. Imagine what it could do for your Gran."

"No Mum, you don't understand, it is true."

She looked at him intrigued.

"It's Gran."

"What do you mean, it's Gran — what's happened?"

Nicholas told her the whole story about his plans, BioMedSyn, the fridge and Gran taking a bite of the Sisa Uma and, most of all, the remarkable effect it had had on her.

His phone rang.

"Hold on Mum, let me get this."

His Mum watched her son on the phone. His expression changed. His smile disappeared. He seemed worried and concerned. The tone of his voice changed. He hung up.

"Nic, what is it?"

"There's been a break in at the office. I need to go in."

"A break–in? At the office?"

Nicholas nodded.

"The same day we have a break–in here?"

Nicholas nodded.

"Nic, I don't like this. Is someone after you? Or do you think they're after that seed pod?"

"I think they're after the seed pod."

Chapter 67

Nicholas thanked the police for coming and saw them into the lift.

The office had been ransacked, just like his home, but again they didn't appear to have taken anything.

Apparently the security guard saw nothing but the police said they'd check the CCTV cameras to see if they could find anything out. There wasn't much more he could do.

He looked at the time. It was quarter past eleven but he felt wide awake, his body clock probably still on South America time.

He turned off the lights, locked the door and got the lift down to the ground floor.

The security guard waved and said goodbye.

Nicholas was still intrigued as to how anyone could have got past him without being seen.

He walked out into car park. The night was dark and the air was cold, a stark contrast from the warm, humid heat of the Amazon. He shivered, a reminder he hadn't put enough layers on.

He'd already phoned his Mum to say that he was on the way home.

He began to walk across the car park.

There was a flash of headlights. A dark black car raced towards him. He couldn't see anything in the glare of the headlights. He didn't know what to do. There was nothing he could do. He was frozen to the spot, unable to move. The car pulled up alongside. It had dark tinted windows and he couldn't see inside. The door opened. A big man in a balaclava appeared. He was grabbed and a hood was pulled over his face. He was manhandled, dragged and thrown in the car. The door slammed. He was bent forward in the seat. He felt a sharp blow to the back of his head.

Chapter 68

Nicholas came to, but everything was dark.

He groaned.

He heard a voice.

He could feel the hood still over his head.

"He's awake," another voice said.

There was a light in front of him. He could see it through the material of the hood.

He tried to see what was going on but he couldn't really make anything out.

He heard whispering from behind him.

A figure moved in front of the light — then another.

That suggested there were at least three people in the room, two in front and the man whispering from behind.

One of the men approached and whipped the hood off his head.

The light was shining directly at his face. He blinked and tried to see. It hurt his eyes.

"What's going on?"

"We ask the questions," a hand slapped him hard around the face.

Nicholas was disorientated for a moment, squinting into the light trying to make sense of what the hell was going on.

"Where is it?"

"Where is what?"

Another slap.

"Will you stop hitting me — I don't know what you want."

The man who had slapped him stepped forward with a clenched fist.

He was about to strike when he heard a loud clap behind him.

The man stepped back.

"Where is the seed pod that you brought back from South America?"

"Ahh, so that is what this is all about," Nicholas said.

"Rufus? Is that you standing behind me?"

No answer.

"It's either Rufus or Hugo but considering what's at stake, I am guessing Rufus — and by the way you're too late!"

The man beside him was about to punch him.

"Wait!" the man said from behind.

As Nicholas suspected, it was Rufus's voice.

"What do you mean, we're too late?"

"Where is my phone?"

Nicholas was sure that the man standing in front of him was receiving visual cues from Rufus behind.

The man pulled it out of his pocket.

"Is it on?" Nicholas asked.

The man touched the screen, it lit up.

"Draw a square," Nicholas said.

The man drew a square to unlock the phone.

"Press Youtube."

The man once again looked at Rufus for instruction. He pressed Youtube.

"Press the top one," Nicholas said.

The man hesitated for a second and then pressed it — the video played.

It was the video that he'd recorded earlier in his room. He explained all about his experience in South America, the Sisa Uma and how he was working with the world–leading BioMedSyn and their charitable arm BioMedLife in collaboration, with the aim of eradicating Dementia and Alzheimer's from the world.

The video finished.

The lights came on.

Rufus walked in front of him and tore off the hood.

"You ..." Rufus began.

"Rufus! I can't believe you've done this," Nicholas snapped, his adrenalin surging.

"I can understand you wanting to make money, but you're already a multi–trillion pound company and you've got cash reserves larger than the GDP of some countries."

"I came to you because you have a charitable arm and, even if you use that as a way of cutting your tax bill — I don't care — because regardless of the money, you actually do some good for the world."

"Millions of people are better off because of your medicines and I wanted you to help me. I wanted us — together — to make a difference. This could help carry BioMedSyn's name to the furthest reaches of the world, it could open up new opportunities and carry the names of both our organisations into the history books for making a massive difference to the planet."

Rufus stood with folded arms and stared.

He'd seen Nic's passionate talks on TV and knew that he had made a reputation for himself as someone that talks from the heart.

"How many views has that video had?" Rufus asked.

The man looked at the phone. "Over nine hundred and eighty thousand," the man replied.

"And," Nicholas said, "I only posted it this afternoon. Wait until the word really gets out — then it will be millions, not to mention the media picking up on it — I've already emailed my contact list."

Rufus took the phone and pondered his options.

He knew there were none.

"Untie him."

One of the men reached around Nicholas's back and untied him.

As Nicholas rubbed his wrists it sent a shudder down his spine. It stirred up very recent and uncomfortable memories.

Rufus handed Nicholas his phone, "What do you want?"

"I want you to help me mass produce a pill made out of the seeds from the Sisa Uma. You take care of manufacture and I'll take care of the distribution."

Rufus grinned, "You realise there is a little more to it than that."

"I'll hold up my side of the bargain — you hold up yours."

"Nic, but what about this?" Rufus said, gesturing to the room and the situation they had put him in.

"I need your help. I am happy to brush this aside and forget it ever happened."

Nicholas held out his hand, "Do we have a deal?"

"Yes, Nicholas, we have a deal."

Rufus shook his hand, firmly.

"Oh and one more thing — I would appreciate it if you could compensate my Mum for the damage you caused to her flat."

"Okay, Nicholas. I'll sort it out."

Nicholas nodded.

"Come into the office at eleven in the morning. We'll start the ball rolling," Rufus said.

"11am — will do."

Rufus clicked his fingers and pointed to the door.

"Take him home."

As Nicholas followed one of the men out of the room a well–known phrase popped into his head:

Keep your friends close — keep your enemies closer.

Chapter 69

Nicholas had been at work since 8am.

He was getting prepared for the meeting at 11am.

He opened his briefcase. Inside was half of the remaining Sisa Uma.

He wasn't going to make the same mistake again.

The phone rang. It was Leo.

They'd had the opportunity for a quick chat after he'd got back from the Amazon. Nicholas had told Leo he had some exciting news but nothing specific.

"Hi Leo, how are you?"

"I've just seen the video — what's going on?"

"It's the big thing I told you about when I got back from South America — the seeds of the plant which help reverse the effects of dementia and Alzheimer's."

"But you didn't say you were going to move this fast."

"Sorry Leo, an opportunity presented itself and I had to act quickly. The company BioMedSyn have arranged a meeting for 11am today. They say they can fast–track the project."

"Have you done any background research?"

"Oh yes, lots — as soon as I got back. They're very well connected, have a charitable arm and invest millions each year in producing medicines for people all across the world."

Nicholas could tell Leo was worried.

"Don't worry, our core strategy is the same and all the other projects are on track. Consider this a side venture but my goal has never changed — it's still to help save the planet."

"Okay, Nic. It's late, I'm tired, we've just wrapped up filming and it's been a very long day."

"Thank you for calling Leo, you have a good night."

"'Nite, Kid," Leo hung up.

He put the phone down. He knew that he had to sell this to everyone and the next stage was to tell the team in their meeting at 9.30.

***

"Surely this is a departure from our true aims?" Romaine said.

"I don't see it that way," Nicholas said as he stood in front of the map on the wall. "This is our world and, if we have an opportunity to improve it in any way, then we should."

"This isn't the planet we're talking about though, it's people — and as we know from this list –" Alexandra said highlighting the issues in front of her, "– people are the cause of the problems."

"I know, but that is why I have a plan. You just need to trust me."

"But this is the plan," Alexandra said throwing the list onto the table.

Nicholas sighed. He had been trying to make his point for the last twenty minutes.

"Do any of you have ageing relatives?"

Everyone nodded.

"Me too — my Gran."

"She's always been there. She helped look after me when I was a baby and she was supportive to my Mum and me when Dad died. She's been like this immovable, unflappable, wiser linchpin in our family throughout all of our lives. But now, that wise old sage is putting her shoes on the mantelpiece, she can't remember what day it is — and — most upsetting of all — the other day she forgot my name. I can still see those dead eyes, staring right through me not knowing who I was. It was so devastating."

The whole team knew what he meant.

"She ate some of the Sisa Uma. It was completely by accident, I left it in the fridge to help preserve it and she thought it was a strawberry, but I am not kidding, the transformation in her was staggering. She was like a new person — I'd got my Gran back."

"We're not talking about making people live forever or making them immortal, we're just talking about helping those older people that we care about in all of our families — so that they have a better quality of life in their twilight years."

"And — who knows — if those older people can have some influence on the youth of today, maybe they will encourage them to take better care of our planet — this planet we all call home."

Summer tossed her pen on the table, "Well — I'm sold."

"Yes, me too," said Alex.

"Meg?"

"Oh sorry, I am just taking minutes."

"Yes, but are you on board with this?"

"Oh yes, of course. My Grandad is in a home and he doesn't know who I am anymore. He's only in his sixties."

Romaine sat unconvinced.

"Romaine?"

"I thought the rainforests were our priority?"

"And, they are. This is not to distract any of you from your roles here. This is something that I feel I need to do personally."

"But will it distract you from your role here?"

"No, because once BioMedSyn go into production, other groups will take over distribution."

"Let me put it like this — consider me the catalyst and, once I have set the balls in motion, I will have done my bit and the rest of it will be ..."

Nicholas couldn't think of the word.

"Destiny," Romaine suggested.

"Yes," Nicholas said. "Destiny."

Chapter 70

"Thank you all for coming, Nic, please take a seat."

"I'd like to introduce you to everyone," Rufus said, gesturing to the table.

"Craig Buchanan, one of our Medical Synthesists. His role is to identify how the plant extract works and synthesise it so that we can reproduce it."

"Harriett Bunce is from our legal team. A necessary presence due to the strict controls that relate to drugs and medicines."

"Professor Michael DaSilva from University College London who specialises in the brain."

"And — Myla Newbury from the Medicines Regulatory Authority, the part of the government that overseas all medical trials and approval of new medicines."

"Nice to meet you all," Nicholas said.

"And of course, you know Hugo."

"Hello again."

"Thank you for coming, especially at such short notice, but what Nic Savage has brought to us is really rather, well, quite frankly, extraordinary."

"Whilst on his recent trip to South America, which we have all read about, he came across the seeds of a plant that he claims has a remarkable effect on the brain."

"Yes, that's right."

"And you have seen for yourself, Nic, the effects of this seed pod on the local indigenous people, who you say grind the seeds down, mix them with water and then drink it for its beneficial effects."

"That is correct, yes."

"And, you also say that you had this drink yourself."

"Yes."

"And how did you feel?" Myla asked jumping in.

"I felt — alert, 'with it', capable of processing information much more quickly, as though my brain was firing on all cylinders."

"But it wore off?"

"Yes, it did."

"And you were able to see the effects of long–term use on the villagers?" Michael asked.

"Oh yes, all of them. The chief was over 90 and, although frail in his body, his mind was very alert. It was the same with all the other older people in the village."

"The one point I am keen to make though is that this doesn't extend life, it just seems to make the brain keep functioning properly — probably right up to the end of life."

"What do you think, Michael?"

"Well, as you know many of our medicines have evolved from a variety of plant sources, not to mention drugs derived from plant extracts — we are just getting our head around Marijuana and its medicinal benefits on the brain — so yes, there could very well be something in this."

"Wow — imagine — a cure for Alzheimer's and dementia," Myla said. "This is one of our biggest concerns at the moment. It's a huge drain on our medical services in a lot of different ways."

"Out of interest, how long will it take?" Nicholas asked.

Hugo sat forward, "To get the drug to market?"

"Yes," replied Nicholas.

Hugo pondered the question, "Ten to fifteen?"

"Sorry — ten to fifteen what — weeks?"

Everyone laughed

"Months?"

"No Nic. Years!" Hugo replied.

"What? Ten to fifteen years?!" Nicholas was flabbergasted.

First we need to get approval from the board that they are willing to invest company time, money and resources into this project. Craig will spend time analysing and synthesizing the product, then there will be somewhere between three to six separate medical trials, each of which probably spanning one to two years. Then there is the government approval process. Licensing ... "

"Okay, you've made your point," Nicholas said, disappointed.

"The important thing we need to find out, Nic, is does it actually work," Myla said.

"Yes, it works."

"I know you say you've seen it, Nic, but that's not enough. We need clear medical evidence."

Nicholas was getting impatient.

"But, I've got evidence — it works!"

"But how can you be so certain?"

"Can you bring up a browser on that screen?" Nic said pointing at a screen on the wall.

Craig reached across to the centre of the table, picked up a remote control and turned on the TV.

He shoved a keyboard across the table in front of Nic.

He brought up Youtube, went to the charity's channel, selected the latest video and pressed play.

***

"Oh Nic, what have you done!" Myla said.

The room was reeling from the footage they had seen.

"This is a serious breach of medical ethics," Harriet added.

"I didn't give it to her. I was told to put it in the fridge, which I did. My Gran mistook it for some fruit. She only had a bite but it was really transformative as you saw."

"It's still not enough," Myla said. "Your own personal trial is not the same as ensuring that documented medical evidence is in place to support that it works — plus any side effects or adverse effects when mixed with other medicines have to be carefully monitored and noted."

"And how many more lives will be ruined while we delay?" Nicholas said.

"But, this is how things are Nic," Michael replied.

"How many more billions will we spend on healthcare and the health service when it could all be preventable. By getting this to market sooner, how many trillions could be saved across the world."

"These are the rules, Nic," Myla said.

"Then change the rules."

"You can't change the rules on the basis of some private video that you've uploaded to the internet," Myla replied.

"Er, hang on," said Craig. "This video isn't private, it's public!"

"Oh my God — Nic!"

Craig scrolled down.

"Is that millions?" Myla asked.

"No," Craig said, "It is two billion, seven hundred and seventy million, four hundred and thirty one thousand nine hundred and fifty nine views — exactly."

"What have you done?" Harriett groaned.

"You shouldn't have said we were going into production straight away Nic. And you certainly shouldn't have mentioned BioMedSyn's name," Rufus said.

"Perhaps, but I bet it gets things moving."

"I wonder how long until the media find out?" Myla sighed.

Nic turned over his phone, looked at the display and showed the room.

"Thirty six missed calls. I suspect they have found out already," Nic said.

"It's out there and I can't stop it."

Chapter 71

"Well, look at this!" his Mum said, holding the newspaper in front of his face.

"Stop it Mum, it's embarrassing."

"It's a nice photo. Was it taken outside the office?"

"Yes, yesterday after the meeting at BioMedSyn."

"You wouldn't know it. With the trees in the background, looks nice."

She shook her head in disbelief.

"My son — 'the saviour' they call you here. They say you're fighting the government to get them to fast–track the drug to market and that it would improve people's lives and save trillions for health care across the world."

"I'm just — just so ..."

She started crying.

"Oh Mum, don't cry."

"I am so proud of you."

"Thank you."

"And I am so impressed at how you seem to be taking it all in your stride."

"I am just taking each step at a time. I believe what I'm doing is right and I'm just going with the flow. It's almost as if it was what I was put on this planet for."

"It's your ..." his Mum tried to find the word, "Destiny," she said.

There was that word again.

Nicholas noticed an unopened envelope on the table.

"What's that?"

"I don't know, I haven't opened it yet."

"Well, open it then," he said — anything to change the subject.

Nicholas watched as she ripped open the envelope.

It was all very mysterious.

"What have we here?" his Mum said examining the contents. "Congratulations, you have been selected in our draw. Please find your prize enclosed?"

Inside there were five postal orders. She counted them out.

"Oh my! It makes a total of one thousand two hundred and fifty pounds."

She looked at him quizzically, "But who is it from?"

"Who knows, but those postal orders are as good as cash so it can't be a con."

"I guess not," she said, trying to find more information in the envelope.

"Congratulations, Mum"

She shook her head and put the postal orders on the table. She seemed confused.

"What is it, Mum?"

"There are some odd things happening at the moment, Nic."

"There sure are Mum, there sure are."

Chapter 72

Craig Buchanan led Nicholas through the various levels of the BioMedSyn synthetics division.

Nicholas was gobsmacked at the security measures that were in place.

All the doors had coded keylocks which required special cards that hung around the employees' necks.

There were palm readers granting access to some areas and even the door to the main facility required retinal eye scans.

"It's so secure," Nicholas said.

"It has to be. This is a cut–throat business and our competitors would do anything to get their hands on our research and technologies."

They turned a corner and walked up to a white door.

"This is me," Craig said presenting his key card to the lock.

The door beeped and a light turned green. Craig pushed.

All the offices in the corridor were like pods with floor to ceiling windows and the glass to each was opaque, so whatever was going on inside was obscured from view.

"The door will close on its own," Craig said as they walked inside.

The room was compact. In one corner there was a workplace with a desk and two screens. To the side of the desk was a machine that looked like a large laser printer. There was also a small meeting table and three chairs. In the other corner was a fridge with a kettle on top.

Craig sat down at the desk.

"Bring one of the chairs over."

Nicholas grabbed a chair and sat down next to him.

Craig placed his identity card into a reader on the desk and the screen came to life.

He typed in his login and a separate password and his desktop appeared. It had a background of a high resolution picture of a cell structure and the BioMedSyn logo.

Craig spun on his chair to face Nicholas.

"We've never had a product fast–tracked like this before. It's almost unheard of for our company. I think it's probably fair to say it's unheard of in the medical profession as a whole. You must have some powerful friends, Nic."

"I'd prefer to call them supporters. To me it just seems nonsensical to have to wait 15 years for something that could be delivering results straight away, both in terms of cost saving and improving people's quality of life," Nic replied.

"Oh, Nic, I completely agree. I'm with you — but I'm only a product synthesist."

Nicholas smiled.

"Something else, Nic — I've never known an outsider get involved at this stage, or be allowed into such a secretive area of our company."

"It's probably because I insisted."

"Well, you must have a lot of clout with the men up-stairs."

That's one way of looking at it. Nicholas thought to himself and changed the subject.

"I am really looking forward to finding out more about this process," Nicholas said.

"Do you have it?" Craig asked.

"The Sisa Uma?"

Craig nodded.

"I do indeed," Nicholas said as he reached into his pocket and pulled out a metallic container. Rufus had given it to him to help protect the seed pod. It used the warm air from the surrounding environment to cause a reaction which cooled the air of the container inside.

Craig opened it and removed the pod. He took out a slide and a sharp knife. He carefully extracted one of the seeds from the pod, cut it open and squashed it on the slide. He got up, positioned the slide in the analyser on the other desk, pressed a button and sat back down.

"So that's not a laser printer?"

"No it's an analyser. It's incredible the technology we have at our disposal these days. We can do in minutes using a compact machine what it would have taken days to do years ago — and we would have needed a room full of machines."

"What's it doing?"

"This machine measures the chemical composition of the material put inside, in this case, one of the seeds. In a moment we should start to see the results on screen of all the elements of the seed so that we can work out what chemicals are present and in what quantities."

"So, it's as though you have a cake, already made, and you're using your machine to identify what ingredients originally went into it?"

"Yes, that's it. Although this amazing machine can take that one step further. You can take the original cake ingredients and then work out what chemicals they themselves are made of."

"That's amazing. It's a shame we didn't have these machines at school, I would have been so much more interested in science."

"Most schools don't have the budget for a machine like this."

Nicholas looked at the machine and dreaded to think how much it must cost.

Information began to appear on the monitor in the form of a graph.

Craig watched the screen. Nicholas looked, but didn't really understand it.

"Wow, this is amazing," Craig said. His eyes widened and he smiled.

"I specialise in neurodegenerative disorders and there is a chemical that we're studying at the moment that is — actually, sorry, do you want me to keep it simple?"

"Yes, it's probably best," Nicholas said.

"We've had quite a few breakthroughs in recent years in relation to Dementia and Alzheimer's, mainly in relation to making the connections between brain cells more resilient and more resistant to plaque."

"Plaque? Like with teeth?"

"Similar but not quite," Craig demonstrated with his hands, fingers outstretched.

Imagine my hands are brain cells. My fingers are the synapses that connect all the brain cells together. Plaque, like in teeth, can build up and form between the brain cells

"There is a protein in the brain called beta–amyloid. It's what you'd call 'sticky' and when this clumps together it forms the plaques, which in turn block the cells from being able to send signals through the synapses."

"So, the brain is like a computer and the wiring between all the bits in the memory is being disabled by the plaque which then reduces the capability of the memory."

"Yes, I can tell you did computers instead of biology."

"Yes, I did."

"Well, it gets a little more complicated as we believe the immune system then kicks in, causes inflammation and even begins to devour the damaged brain cells, thereby effectively destroying the brain over time. That's kind of it, in a nutshell."

"And you said you've had a breakthrough?"

"Yes. What we've been able to do is to prepare the brain for the potential of this plaque build–up and make the body better at dealing with it. And that is why this bit is interesting — here," Craig said, pointing at the screen. "This is the chemical we're currently looking at."

He pressed a few keys on his keyboard and more information appeared.

"What's that?"

"This is our knowledgebase. Virtually everything we know, all the company's intelligence, is in Holly."

"Holly?"

"Yes, Holly," Craig laughed. "Our technical bods are big Red Dwarf fans."

Nicholas wasn't with him.

"Holly was the name of the computer in the TV series, Red Dwarf," Craig said.

"I've never seen it," Nicholas replied.

"They could have had JARVIS from Iron Man — or HAL from 2001 Space Odyssey was another one on the list," Craig said.

"Oh, I don't know that one either," Nicholas admitted.

"Anyhow — we have a colossal database of information relating to lots of chemicals, which is what I am going through now. So I am able to look up any particular chemical direct in the database. We also have a cutting–edge biochemical modelling tool that is able to look at how that chemical could behave under certain conditions or when combined with other chemicals."

"Like a bio–medical sandbox," Nicholas added.

"That is exactly what it is, yes," Craig confirmed. "This chemical here is the one we've been looking at in our research. What makes this incredibly interesting though are these other chemicals," Craig pointed at the screen, hardly able to contain his excitement.

"If I had to summarise, I would say that, not only can this enable the chemical we know to prepare the brain to cope better with beta–amyloid, but also — and this is the remarkable bit — to actually reverse the effects of the plaque, revive the brain cells and make them work more efficiently by strengthening the synapses."

"Like a mixture of oil and antifreeze — it keeps the brain lubricated and running properly whilst preventing it from clogging up later in life," Nicholas said.

"Yes. Just like that. I am going to have to start using your analogies in my work," Craig smiled.

"But if you've got this amazing computer called Holly and all this knowledge, how come you haven't come up with something already?"

"Well, it's like saying if you have a thousand ingredients and an almost infinite number of ways to mix them, how come you haven't made this particular recipe yet. People are coming up with new recipes all the time. But they all have to be tested meticulously, before we can say they work."

Craig pointed at the screen.

"So that's what we do. We mix, we experiment, we model and hypothesise, but, whilst our database helps, it isn't possible to know what combination of chemicals will have what exact effect on the body. This is why the process takes years. But, the more we know, the more it can help, and with the technology we have today what would have taken ten years, now takes six months — but it still takes time."

"So what now?"

"I just need to work out the active ingredient and then which chemicals to include and in what quantities to make sure that we have a printable template ready to go into production."

"Printable template?"

"Yes. When we've got the template finalised, basically to start the production, we call it 'Printing' — literally someone presses a button and the machines go into action."

"So you don't have people mix it by hand?"

"Oh no, this is the 21st century. We have a computer–controlled chemical containment room which has all the chemicals we can use. Robot arms select the chemicals, mix the required quantities and blend them all together to match the exact template we've asked the computer to make," Craig explained.

"That's amazing. Thank you for showing it all to me."

"You're welcome. Now I just need to work on this template."

"Ok — er — can I use your toilet please?"

"Yes, of course," Craig said, "It's just down the corridor at the far end. Tap on the glass and I'll let you back in."

Nicholas left the room and walked down the pristinely clean white corridor which resembled a hospital or a scene out of a science fiction film. On the left were offices, just like Craig's, with opaque glass. He could just see that the lights were on but nothing else.

On the other side was a smooth white wall. Up ahead was a door. As he got closer he could see a sign on the door which said 'Bio Synthesis Meeting Room A'.

The door opened.

It made Nicholas jump and he froze on the spot.

A hand appeared holding the door open.

"Wait — I don't care how you do it ..."

Nicholas recognised the voice immediately, it was Rufus.

"... reduce the active ingredient so that it doesn't work. He'll be a laughing stock and we'll jump in with one that really does work. Except we'll charge for ours and people will pay."

Nicholas knew if he continued to walk past the door, whoever was holding it open would see him. He also knew that whoever was about to walk out of that room would have known he'd heard them talking. He froze on the spot.

"In fact, come back in and close the door."

The door closed.

Nicholas let out a huge sigh of relief and rushed back to the office.

"That was quick, did you find it okay?" Craig said as he opened the door.

"Yes thanks — anyway you were saying the next stage was to work on the printable template?"

"Er, yes, I was just working on it, come take a look."

Nicholas sat down and did his best to ignore his bladder.

Craig explained exactly what he was doing. He showed him how each chemical had been assigned a letter and that the amount of that chemical was reflected in the peak on the chart on the screen.

"So is column H the active ingredient?"

"Yes, that's it," Craig said with surprise. "You seem to be picking this up more quickly than some trainees."

Nicholas smiled and concentrated on the screen.

"There are three working in tandem with one another, H, K and P — like the oil, antifreeze and er ..."

"Water?" Nicholas suggested.

"Yes, that'll do, oil, antifreeze and water — H, K and P."

"And how do you know what level they should be at?"

"Ahh, that's remarkably easy and that comes down to the trials we're already running at the moment with H, here," Craig said, pulling up another template on the screen.

"As you can see, we've got it set to this level, so if we go back to our template, I can set H to here."

"So you're specifying the level based on what you know already works."

"Yes."

"What if you increased it?"

"Well, what we found is that, once you increase it beyond this amount, the body doesn't do anything more with it. It's like it only needs a certain level and anything else will be discarded."

"And if mixed with other chemicals as a compound?"

"Well, that's the thing, as soon as you increase the amount overall, the body is then getting more of the other chemicals in the mix as well. At this dosage they probably don't do anything but at a higher dose they could have other effects on the person."

Nicholas was tempted to ask about the other effects but quickly decided not to.

"And what would happen if you decreased it?"

"Then nothing would happen. It would be like eating a sugar–pill, or a placebo, it would have no effect whatsoever."

Nicholas stared at the screen and studied the shape of the curve and the levels of the Sisa Uma template — "Amazing!"

"So, what next?" Nicholas asked.

"I just need to get this signed off and then we print it."

"When does that happen?"

"You'll need to give us a bit of time on that one. This needs to be signed off by the powers that be. Normally months, sometimes weeks, but, at the pace this is running, I think it will probably be days."

Chapter 73

Nicholas sat in the reception of BioMedSyn and waited.

A man appeared. He walked over.

"Oh, hello, my name is Dominic. I'll be overseeing the printing of the template for the new SISA medicine.

"Sisa Uma," Nicholas replied.

"Er — they decided SISA was shorter and punchier than your original name — so they changed it — come with me please."

I wonder how many other things they intend to change, Nicholas thought to himself.

Nicholas followed Dominic through to a different part of the facility, one that he had never been to before — one that appeared to be even more secure.

"I haven't been this way before," Nicholas said.

"Outsiders don't get to come here. You must be very privileged," Dominic said as he lowered his eye to a lens and waited for the door to open.

"One more door and we'll be there."

They turned a corner into another corridor and approached a door.

Dominic inserted his key card and the door opened.

They walked into a large laboratory.

Inside were three technicians focussed intently on various pieces of equipment and referring to tablet computers they were all carrying.

"This is what we call the 'print room', basically where we set the template that Craig has been working on to make it ready for printing."

"These are my three technicians, Ryan, Juliet and Emma."

They didn't look up.

Dominic continued to explain as he led him through the maze of equipment and benches towards a desk with one of the technicians sitting at it.

"It's obviously gone through all the red tape so now it's just a case of printing the template."

Nicholas nodded and looked around. There was an office at the other end of the room with a large window. There didn't seem to be anyone inside.

"Okay, Nic. This is the main console."

Nicholas looked at the large display screen.

"As you can see, one of our technicians has already brought the SISA template up on screen. Thank you Ryan, I'll take it from here."

Ryan nodded and stood up. He handed the tablet computer he was holding to Dominic and walked away.

Dominic looked at the screen. "Oh, hang on, Ryan. You've got the MERIAN–K up next, I thought this was delayed?"

Ryan shrugged, "I haven't been informed of any delay."

"Sorry, excuse me a moment please, Nic," Dominic said as he chased after him.

Nicholas glanced around the room.

The other two technicians looked over briefly, but soon returned their attention to their machines.

Nicholas took a step closer to the screen. The console was effectively a computer, with one display and a keyboard with a mouse attached. He could see that there was a card reader connected with someone's card inside it, obviously not Dominic's as it was still around his neck, presumably Ryan's.

On the screen was the Sisa Uma template — or SISA as it now seemed to be called — he recognised it immediately from the distinctive shape of the curve — but something was different.

Nicholas sat down in the chair.

He looked around once more.

One of the technicians looked up and watched as though he was checking to make sure Nicholas didn't touch anything. Nicholas smiled and nodded. The technician's expression didn't change. He eventually looked back down at the machine in front of him.

Nicholas looked at the screen again. Something was wrong. The shape of the template was still correct but the levels were different.

The bastards had meddled with it. The levels were too low.

He closed his eyes. He could see the display in Craig's office distinctly in his mind and the peak at which columns H, K and P should be, but they were lower, just where Craig had said they would have no effect.

What could he do?

He quickly glanced around again.

No–one was looking.

He felt a compelling urge to reach out and adjust the levels.

He knew if he didn't do something, the whole project would fail and, as he had heard Rufus say, he'd be a laughing stock. It would ruin his life and BioMedSyn would rush in with another medicine with the correct levels and make billions out of it.

I can't let that happen.

I have to do something.

He hesitated.

"Sorry to keep you waiting, Nic."

Nicholas almost jumped out of the chair.

"We get this sometimes. We have templates scheduled for printing and then issues arise. This particular one had complications during the last drug trial that have only just come to light, er — well, actually I can't talk about it — legal stuff and all that."

Nicholas stood up — his heart pounding.

"Now, where was I? Oh yes, we need to print this template," Dominic said referring to the tablet computer left on the desk..

Oh no, it's going to be a disaster and I can't do anything about it.

"You okay?"

"Yes, fine," Nicholas said. "Just excited, it's been an incredible journey to get to this point."

Dominic smiled and turned his attention to the screen.

He grabbed the mouse and dragged the cursor across the screen.

"It really is very straightforward. As I said, this is your template as prepared by Craig. To print the template, we press this big button that simply says print."

Nicholas watched Dominic move the mouse pointer closer and closer to the big red button that said PRINT.

It was as if everything was happening in slow motion.

Nicholas was silently willing Dominic to not proceed.

"By this stage a drug would have gone through all of the necessary red tape and trials, so we click print — "

The mouse click was amplified a dozen times in Nicholas's brain — 'CLICK'.

Just as he was about to admit defeat, another button appeared that asked 'Are you sure?'.

Please, please, please, not now, don't let it fall through now.

"Then it comes up with the confirmation screen and we confirm by clicking, yes."

Dominic hovered the mouse over the Yes button.

What is he waiting for?

"Hang on, this can't be right?"

"What's that?" Nicholas asked.

Dominic glanced at the screen. He referred to the tablet computer on the desk and then looked back at the screen.

"This drug hasn't been through any trials."

Nicholas was about to explain it was because their other medicine with the same active ingredient had been through the trials already, which is why it could be fast–tracked but something inside told him not to mention it.

"Hmmm, sorry Nic, I really must check this out. Just wait here a moment."

Nicholas looked at the screen and had an idea.

"Dominic, shall I say No?"

Dominic wasn't sure what he was referring to at first. "Oh yes, probably best, I want to make sure that we're ready to actually print it."

Nicholas nodded, grabbed the mouse and clicked the No button.

The SISA template reappeared on screen.

Dominic walked off towards the office.

I have another chance.

"All done, Dominic," Nicholas said aloud to ensure the technicians heard.

All three technicians looked over casually and then focussed back on what they were doing.

Nicholas glanced towards the end of the room and could see that Dominic had picked up the phone. He appeared to be waiting for someone to answer. Dominic looked over at him and raised his hand to apologise for the wait.

Nicholas watched intently.

Someone had obviously answered. Dominic started talking and turned his back.

This is my chance.

He was about to grab the mouse when Ryan suddenly glanced over at him.

Nicholas smiled and nodded.

Nicholas tried to read his expression. Was he just one of those sullen scientists who never smiled, or did he suspect what he was up to. Surely Ryan couldn't think that he would meddle with his own drug. After all, they were working together on this. And then he realised, they weren't working together. BioMedSyn were working against him and he was indeed intending to meddle.

A voice called over from the office. It was Dominic. Ryan turned, nodded, looked at Nicholas one more time and then walked over to the office.

Nicholas glanced at the other two technicians. One was engrossed with whatever was on a screen, the other one looked over.

Nicholas smiled and nodded — this was getting stressful.

Nicholas sighed loudly enough for the technician to hear and slumped over the desk as if bored. The technician watched for a moment and then looked away.

Nicholas casually glanced towards the office. Both Dominic and Ryan had their backs to him, deep in discussion.

The other technician looked up from her display and walked over, staring at him as she approached.

They know what I am up to. I won't be able to do it.

The technician walked right up to him and looked him directly in the eye.

It's over.

Nicholas could see her lips move and then the words reached his ears.

"I just need to borrow this tablet to check the rest of the day's schedule," the technician said.

"Of course, here you go," Nicholas said and handed her the tablet computer.

Nicholas swallowed hard and smiled.

As the technician walked off, her back was towards him. Dominic and Ryan were still deep in discussion and the other technician appeared to be very deep in thought.

371

This is it, this is my moment.

Nicholas grabbed the mouse.

He formed a mental picture in his mind of where the levels should be. He could see the letters H, K and P and visualised the optimal point of potent efficiency that Craig had shown him and the shape of the curve.

He clicked on the sliders and dragged them upwards.

He swallowed hard.

His heart was pounding.

He looked around.

Still no–one was looking.

He increased them further.

He clicked the Save button.

He was about to sigh with relief when he heard a voice from the other side of the room.

"What are you doing?" Dominic called out.

Oh no, I've been caught.

His heart almost stopped.

He looked round.

Dominic wasn't talking to him — Dominic was talking to Ryan.

"I am going back to my station," Ryan replied.

"No, Ryan, get it done now," Dominic said sternly.

"Okay, Okay," Ryan said and walked off to the other end of the room and out of the main door.

Dominic approached the desk.

Nicholas could see him look at the screen.

"Hang on a second!"

Nicholas looked at the screen. It was then he noticed with horror that the revision had changed.

Instead of being SISA–D it now read SISA–E — changing the levels and saving the template meant that the revision number had also been changed to the next one in the sequence, so it no longer corresponded to what they were about to print.

"Where is the tablet computer?"

Nicholas couldn't believe it. He hadn't noticed the revision change. He'd only noticed the tablet computer was missing.

Nicholas pointed at the technician who had taken it.

Dominic stormed off towards the technician.

He could hear them talking.

Dominic walked back over with the tablet computer and sighed.

"Everything okay?" Nicholas asked.

"Oh yes, everything's fine. Apparently part of the drug has already been through the necessary trials which meant this drug could be fast–tracked through without repeating the trials."

"Oh that's good."

"Now — where was I?" Dominic said, sitting down.

"You just need to press the Print button," Nicholas urged.

"Oh yes, that's right."

Dominic looked at the screen.

He paused.

Nicholas didn't dare breathe — he couldn't breathe. He just watched Dominic stare at the screen.

"Hmmmm," Dominic said as he cross–referenced the template on screen and the display on the tablet computer.

"Is there a problem?"

"Well the screen says the template is SISA–E but the printing schedule on my tablet says SISA–D — it's like a double–check failsafe system to ensure the correct template version gets printed."

Nicholas's heart sank.

He began to panic.

Was he going to get caught?

And then what?

He had already seen first–hand what Rufus was willing to do to get hold of the Sisa Uma, what would he do if he caught him meddling.

Nicholas leant over and looked at the tablet computer in Dominic's hand.

He noticed a refresh button.

"When I was with Craig he produced a number of revisions to get what he called the optimal potency, could it be that you don't have the latest one — what if you press Refresh?"

Dominic considered what Nicholas had said and pressed the Refresh button.

The display refreshed and showed the next print job as SISA–E.

"Yes, you're right," Dominic said in disbelief. "You seem to know our systems quite well."

"Craig did say that I learned more quickly than some of your trainees."

Dominic hesitated and re–checked the displays.

"So is it now just a simple case of clicking Print again?"

"Yes, that's it," Dominic said as he reached for the mouse and clicked Print.

The 'Are you sure?' message appeared and he hesitated. Nicholas willed him to press the button.

Dominic checked his tablet, checked the screen and clicked the Yes button.

He'd done it.

"Right — that's it. We can't see it, but the computers will now be setup and scheduled to begin production of the first batch."

"How many in the first batch?"

Dominic consulted his tablet computer.

"Now let me see — here we are — two point four million," he said.

"Oh ..." Nicholas replied.

"Where you expecting a different figure?"

"Well, yes. We've arranged for worldwide distribution, I was expecting many more times that."

"No, you don't understand. That is — per day!"

"You'll be producing two point four million tablets — per day?"

"That's right. The machines work around the clock. They can produce around one hundred thousand per hour for this line and we have many different lines in production at any one time."

"And, that's only this facility. We also have printing lines in Germany, America, Australia and China who will be printing as well — it's a lot of tablets."

"Wow — now that's more like it."

Chapter 74

SISA Production Day One

Nicholas sat on the red sofa in the hot BBC Breakfast studio.

Hosts Dan Walker and Naga Munchetty were reading various notes and scripts.

Crew were rushing around getting everything set up whilst an outside broadcast played live on the monitors.

He sat with the Independent newspaper on his lap with the headline 'New Wonder Drug SISA in Production' with the sub–headling 'One Man's Meteoric Plan to Save the World'.

He swallowed hard. He'd been to the toilet three times and couldn't really be excused to go again.

He'd done many interviews now but this was quite different. The creation of Rapture was one thing, the launch of Clarion was another, his experience in South America another still, but this, distributing a drug to people all over the world, was something else.

"Hello Nicholas," a familiar voice said.

It was Hugo.

"Hi Hugo. I thought Rufus was coming."

Hugo sat down next to him whilst a member of the crew fitted a microphone to his lapel.

"Unfortunately something came up so Rufus sent me instead."

A member of the crew signalled thirty seconds until they were live.

"Nervous?" Hugo asked.

"A little," Nicholas admitted.

"I am not surprised. A man, your age, about to change the world, I would be too."

Nicholas thought about his words — 'change the world'.

Twenty seconds.

Crew members disappeared behind the scenes.

"Okay guys?" Dan asked

Nicholas nodded.

Hugo nodded.

Ten seconds.

Nicholas counted down as the studio quietened.

A red light appeared on a camera pointing directly at them.

"Welcome back to BBC Breakfast with me Dan Walker."

"And me, Naga Munchetty."

The camera focussed on Dan and pulled back.

"Joining us today we have the young man who keeps making the headlines, Nic Savage and joining him today is a representative of BioMedSyn, Hugo Wentworth — welcome gentlemen."

"Nic, you've done so much in such a short time and now with what the headlines are calling a Wonder Drug called SISA, can you tell us about it?"

"It is something I came across whilst I was in South America. It is a plant whose seedpod contains a special mix of chemicals that can reverse the effects of Dementia and Alzheimer's," Nicholas said.

"It sounds incredible," Dan replied. "And BioMedSyn are producing this?"

"That's correct," Hugo replied. "In conjunction with our charity BioMedLife, we are working with Nic and Rapture to ensure that everyone in the world gets the opportunity to benefit from the SISA drug."

"So Nic," Naga said. "Is it the case that if someone is diagnosed with either Dementia or Alzheimer's they can start taking the drug?"

"In part, yes. Anyone with an existing condition can take the drug and it will reverse it, but it is also capable of programming the brain before the condition arises to prevent the onset of Dementia or Alzheimer's in the future."

"Hang on, are you saying that it is almost like an inoculation?" Dan asked.

"Yes, exactly. It will prevent diseases like that from arising in the future for anyone who takes the drug."

Dan and Naga looked at each other in disbelief.

"But, that's amazing. I know someone who has Dementia and this will be able to help them," Naga said.

Nic nodded.

"It's the same for my Gran," Dan said.

"And my Father," said Hugo. "I think what Nicholas has come up with will change everyone's life in one way or another all around the globe."

Dan began to sift through the papers and read the headlines.

"The breakthrough of the century. Wonderdrug. Life–changing ..."

Nicholas began to drift off.

There was headline after headline about the positive effects the drug would bring, but then he heard Naga's voice reading out something in a different tone.

His attention was brought back to the present.

"Possible prison for man who wanted to save the world," Naga said. "What do you say about that, Nic?"

"I haven't done anything wrong."

"But they say that you gave your Grandmother SISA which effectively constitutes carrying out your own human drug trials without the appropriate approval, licencing, legal authority — the list goes on."

"The fact is, I didn't give her the drug. I put the original SISA pod in the fridge to help preserve it. My Gran went through the fridge, thought it was fruit and tried to eat it. She only had a bit of it but the effects on her mental ability afterwards were incredible and so, quite by chance, that was proof that it worked."

"And that is the only trial that has been done, your Gran eating some of it — is it really safe for people to start taking?" Naga probed.

The interview was taking an unexpected turn.

Hugo jumped in.

"I can assure you and the viewers that the drug has been properly tested. It corresponds with a drug that we've been working on for some time, which has been through all the correct procedures including appropriate human trials."

"So, it's not a new drug?"

"Not quite ..."

Nicholas interrupted.

"Think of it like a cake — all of the ingredients have been

properly approved but the recipe is slightly different. It's a new recipe."

Hugo nodded and smiled.

"So, what next for SISA?"

"Manufacturing is underway and we're working together with Rapture and its partners to distribute the drug to as many countries as are willing to take it," Hugo said.

"And is it correct that you're giving the drug away free?"

Nicholas looked at Hugo.

He could tell by his expression that this was a sore subject.

"Effectively, yes, it is Nic's vision to change the world."

Nicholas noted with interest the reference to it being his vision.

"Obviously we have costs so we are asking for governments to contribute to those where possible, but we are doing as much as we can through our charitable arm, BioMedLife. Rapture and the charities it is associated with are also doing their bit."

Naga received an instruction through her ear piece.

"Well thank you Nic Savage and Hugo Fitzwilliam, we wish you the greatest success with your venture and look forward to seeing a positive outcome worldwide."

The camera focussed on Dan and Naga.

A crew member appeared and ushered Nicholas and Hugo out of the studio.

"That went well," Hugo said.

"It's a shame they mentioned the prison headline."

"Well, to be honest Nic, I don't think you realise just how much trouble you're in."

Nicholas looked at Hugo. He wasn't sure if he was referring to the impending court case or the fact that he thought
the drug wasn't going to work.

You'll see — Nic thought to himself — *just you wait.*

Chapter 75

Day Eight

Nicholas sat at his desk.

His head was reeling — it had been one hell of a week.

The phone rang.

"Yes, Megan?"

"Nic, I have Jane from the World Health Organisation."

"Thanks. Put her through."

"Hi Jane, how are you?"

"Hi Nic, I'm good thanks, you?"

"It's been a whirlwind week but all is good, thanks."

"Well done on everything you're doing. We are really impressed with your efforts."

"Thank you."

"You'll go down in history for what you have achieved. It will probably be one of the greatest contributions to the welfare of the older generation since — well, probably penicillin."

"Oh I don't know about that, Jane."

"You're too modest. But that's a good thing," Jane replied.

"Are the shipments into Africa arriving okay?" Nicholas asked.

"Yes, absolutely fine. We're really keen to ensure that everyone has the opportunity to benefit from the SISA drug and African communities are so often overlooked — as you well know."

"Indeed I do."

"I was phoning as we're having difficulty getting approval for distribution into Libya and Egypt."

"There are a number of countries which aren't accepting shipments yet, including Andorra, Iceland, Finland, Switzerland and, er — Denmark," Nicholas recalled from the top of his head.

"Is that because they don't trust it?"

"Basically, yes. They are refusing to allow the use of the drug until the widespread benefit has been proven, plus they want to carry out their own research and trials."

"Okay, well I am sure they will change their minds in due course. Until then we'll concentrate on the countries who do want it and where we can help most."

"Hopefully, yes."

"By the way, is there any particular reason you chose to partner with BioMedSyn. I presume you are aware of their reputation?"

"Oh yes. I did extensive research. The fact is they provided a service I needed. Their head office is in the UK and I felt this was an opportunity for them to redeem themselves."

"Okay, fair enough," Jane replied.

"Great. Well, if you need anything, you know where I am."

"Thanks Nic. Good bye," Jane said and hung up.

The phone rang.

Nicholas sighed.

"Yes, Megan?"

"I have the US President on the phone for you."

"Okay, I'll take it."

Chapter 76

Day Thirty Seven

Nicholas sat at his desk.

He scrolled through the BBC website under the Health section.

There were dozens of stories from all around the world about the amazing results that SISA was having:

— how older people showed dramatic signs of recovery
— how it was bringing families back together again
— how it was giving Dementia sufferers a new lease of life

The phone rang.

"Yes, Megan?"

"I have Clare from the New Scientist on the line for you."

"Okay, thank you, put her through."

"Hi Clare."

"Hi Nic, thank you for taking my call," Clare said.

"How can I help?"

"We're just doing an update on the progress of the SISA drug. There are remarkable results globally — it really works."

"Indeed it does. I never doubted it."

"I understand it's being distributed on a priority basis?"

"Yes, that's correct. I think all countries are prioritising the distribution, based firstly on those who are suffering from Dementia and then age. Those in their nineties, eighties, seventies, etc."

"And drug production is continuing?"

"Yes. BioMedSyn ramped up production to produce even more tablets to keep up with demand."

"And they're doing this for free?"

"Well, technically yes, but as I understand it they're accepting payments to cover certain costs such as distribution, but don't quote me on that. The good thing is, they're not charging for the tablets — that's most important."

"I have also heard that the drug is available on the black market?"

"I heard that too. I guess it is the same with anything that is in demand. However there is really no need. SISA is something we want to make available to everyone, so people just need to wait."

"So — what next for Rapture?" Clare asked.

"Well, we have the Clarion system in use which is helping charities across the world work more efficiently than ever before. Rapture continues to help bring attention to major issues across the globe. SISA is a complementary project which I was keen to pursue."

"And how is your Gran by the way?"

"She's doing great, thank you for asking."

"Well, I am pleased to hear it, Nic. Keep up the great work and I'll catch up in a few weeks if that's okay."

"Sure, any time. Good bye."

Nic put the phone down.

He'd read an article previously in the New Scientist about naysayer scientists who didn't believe that SISA was going to work. However, a more recent update stated that they had been forced to change their tune when they were shown the evidence that had come in.

Chapter 77

"What the hell is going on?" Rufus demanded and slammed his fist onto the desk.

Hugo, Craig and Dominic sat around the table, looked at each other and shrugged.

"I don't know," Hugo said, speaking for everyone.

"It was meant to have no effect — but look!" Rufus threw a copy of the Daily Telegraph across the table with the headline 'Revolutionary SISA Drug Helps Millions'.

"It must be the placebo effect," Craig suggested.

Rufus stared in disbelief.

"We all know that the placebo effect works to an extent, but not with this success rate. I want answers and I want answers now!"

Chapter 78

Day Thirty Eight

"Well?" Rufus asked.

Hugo, Craig and Dominic sat in the same positions as the day before.

"The template had changed," Craig replied.

"What do you mean the template had changed?" Rufus demanded.

"The last version of the template I worked on was SISA–D but the version printed was SISA–E." Craig admitted.

"And ... how did this happen?" Rufus asked.

Craig looked at Dominic.

"Someone changed it."

"Someone — who?"

"Well, the key card in the machine at the time of the change was — er — Ryan."

"And why would Ryan want to change the template prior to printing?"

"Well, I don't think he did. It was — er — Nic Savage."

"What?"

"Nic Savage changed the template."

Rufus was incredulous.

"What was Nic Savage doing in the print room?"

Dominic looked at Craig. Craig looked at Dominic.

"He said he had been given approval to watch the drug go to print."

"And who gave approval?" Rufus seethed.

"Er, you did," Craig replied.

"No I bloody well didn't," Rufus screamed. "I said he could sit with you, supervised, to watch how we prepare the template, I said nothing about him going into the print room."

"He said you did," Craig replied sheepishly.

Rufus cast a glare in his direction that could split stone.

"And — what was the difference in the template?" Rufus asked

"The levels had changed."

Rufus face was red — it looked like steam was about to come out of his ears.

The rest of the team kept quiet.

They had never seen him so angry.

"The clever little bastard must have noticed that we'd reduced the levels so he put them back to where they should be."

"Well, actually ..." Craig was cut off.

"Stop production — Now!" Rufus demanded.

"Well, I don't think that is such a good idea," Hugo piped up.

"Why?" Rufus asked.

"Because it's too late — the drug is out there, people are taking it — it's a success," Hugo replied.

Rufus threw another steely glance.

"If I may just elaborate," Hugo said whilst referring to some notes. "We've produced the drug, albeit with Nic's help, to help change people's lives. Our social media hits and influence is through the roof. Our website hits are up 800%. Our share price is up 43%, and we have an influx of product development enquiries, the likes of which we've not seen before — the share price increase alone has added billions onto our value — and all because of SISA."

Rufus sighed.

He knew Hugo was right.

Deep down he just didn't want to admit he'd let Nic get one up on him.

His pride was dented and he was consumed with anger.

"Sir, can I just mention something ..." Craig said solemnly.

Rufus cut him off again.

"And as for you two — we have security in this place for a reason and you both violated it."

"But ..." Dominic replied.

"I don't want to hear it — collect your things — you're both sacked."

"That's ..." Craig was cut off yet again.

"Gross negligence in a high security environment — Hugo — see them out."

Craig had something very important to say to Rufus but suddenly he couldn't be bothered — *He'll find out soon enough.*

Chapter 79

Day Sixty Nine

Nicholas was nervous and scared.

He sat at a table in front of the Health Authority Ethics Committee.

There were four very serious people preparing their papers and looking at him with severe expressions.

The hearing date had been arranged some time ago. He'd been mentally counting down the days until it arrived — and now it was here.

The room was full and every seat was occupied.

A hundred voices whispered and murmured.

The scrape of chair legs on the wooden floor echoed off the high ceiling.

It was mostly journalists from numerous countries around the world and scientists, research authority personnel and, as he noticed a moment ago, Hugo from BioMedSyn as well. His Mother was also somewhere in the audience.

Nicholas looked at the clock on the wall behind the committee — twenty seconds to go.

One of the committee members looked at the clock and with one final shuffle of papers he spoke.

"Thank you. Thank you. Can we have order please."

The noise quickly died down.

"Nicholas Savage. You have been called here in front of the Health Authority Ethics Committee. You understand this is not a trial. We seek answers to questions but any answers you provide are given under oath that they will be the truth and nothing but the truth — do you understand."

Nicholas leant forward and spoke into the microphone, "Yes."

"You will speak only when spoken to, do you understand?"

"Yes."

"Then we shall begin," said Dr Frederick Palmer.

Nicholas read the name tag on the desk.

"Nicholas," Dr Margaret Reilly addressed him. "You are brought in front of us today because you are accused of experimenting on your Grandmother with the SISA drug without the appropriate approval or licencing for human drug trials. What do you say to this?"

"It is not true."

"But it is true, is it not, that your Grandmother did take the SISA drug."

"Yes it is, but I did not give it to her."

"Then how did she take it?"

"She took it herself."

One of the other men, Dr Jonathan Donnelly spoke, "Can I put it to you Nicholas, that you put the SISA drug in a place ..." he consulted his notes, "... the fridge, where you knew your Grandmother would take it — therefore, whilst you did not give it to her yourself, you gave it to her indirectly."

"That is not true. I put it in the fridge to help preserve it."

Finally, Dr Louise Ormrod spoke, "Why did you not put it in your fridge at home?"

"I was going to but I decided to visit my Gran on the way back from work. I had been told to put it in the fridge straight away to help preserve it and I didn't want it to spoil."

"But surely another hour or so wouldn't make much of a difference?" Jonathan said.

"Possibly, but I didn't know that. I was just doing what I had been told," Nicholas replied.

"Told by who?" Louise asked.

"Rufus at BioMedSyn."

The committee consulted their notes.

"That is Rufus Fitzwilliam, CEO of BioMedSyn," Frederick clarified.

Louise consulted her notes, "We refer to it as the SISA drug but in fact at that time it was a seed pod that you had brought back from South America, is that correct?"

"Yes, that is correct."

She continued, "It had travelled with you all the way from South America and there was a period of time between you arriving back in the UK and seeing BioMedSyn where you were given the advice to put it in the fridge." She consulted her notes, "You could have gone home, but instead went to see your Grandmother. You could have taken it home and put it in the fridge and yet you put it in the fridge at your Grandmother's."

Louise looked at him.

"Yes, to preserve it."

She continued, "You were clearly worried about your Grandmother's health and you put the seed pod in a place where she could find it ..."

"But it wasn't like that," Nicholas interrupted.

Frederick threw a fiery glance in his direction for speaking out of turn.

"You even filmed before and after footage which you then posted to the internet and, if I am correct in understanding, you showed this footage to BioMedSyn as evidence that it worked."

Nicholas sat on the edge of the chair.

He felt like he was going to explode.

But it wasn't like that.

Frederick leant forward and spoke, "Personally, I am convinced that we have enough to go to trial, does everyone agree?"

Nicholas's heart sank as he watched the entire committee agree with one another.

"Is there anything you would like to say?" Frederick asked.

"Yes, there is, actually. A year ago I worked in a burger restaurant earning minimum wage ..."

Jonathan leant forward, "I am not sure this is relevant?"

Frederick jumped in, "Please continue."

Nicholas nodded.

"But I was worried about what was happening to our planet and I wanted to do something about it. It's been a difficult journey but I finally have. I couldn't have done it without people's help and support, but together we've made a real difference."

"Yes, I did film my Gran but initially that was to show my Mum how bad she was getting as Mum doesn't always get to see her when she is at her worst."

"In South America, an opportunity presented itself and

I felt the urge to grab it. It is so rare to be given opportunities that can help change the world, but there it was, right in front of me and I had to take it."

"Call me naïve but the CEO of BioMedSyn told me to do something to preserve the seed pod and I took it literally. I didn't want it to spoil as that would mean the whole project would be a failure. I hid the seed pod in the back of Gran's fridge because it was convenient. I didn't expect her to find it, let alone try to eat it."

"But, she did and the results were remarkable. It seemed obvious that I should record the difference in her behaviour on my phone as I had done before."

Nicholas studied the committee. Their stern expressions hadn't changed. He didn't feel he was getting through to them.

"Sometimes you act in a way that you believe is right at the time and everything that has happened since was because I felt it was the right thing to do. I feel truly honoured that I have had the opportunities I've had that have helped me make a real difference. I don't want fame or fortune, but I do want to know I have done everything I can to help save the world."

Jonathan leaned forward and spoke, "Nicholas, what you're referring to here is the SISA drug which is intended to save people, why do you keep referring to saving the world?

"People are part of our world," Nicholas said.

The committee members looked at each other and nodded in agreement.

"This case will go to trial — we'll let you know the date.

We'll be in touch," Frederick said. "We'll take a break of thirty minutes and then hear the next case — dismissed."

Chapter 80

Day Seventy Six

"Do you want me to open it?" his Mother asked

"No, I'll do it," Nicholas said ripping open the envelope that had just arrived.

"Well, what does it say?"

"It says that the case will go to trial."

"When?"

Nicholas did some quick mental arithmetic, "Eight months' time."

"Wow, they really plan in advance don't they," his Mother replied.

She could see he was worried.

"Don't worry. I am sure it will be okay."

"But you saw how the committee were. They didn't care about what I am trying to do."

"Yes, but it won't be the committee who hear the case. They were looking at facts in their own particular way. The case will be heard by a judge and a jury."

"Yes, but it will be the same facts."

"Yes, the same facts but the jury will be real people, people like you and me."

"I don't know."

"You wait and see, I am sure it will be fine. It is just a formality."

"I hope so Mum, I don't want to go to prison," Nicholas said. He lowered his head and stared at the letter.

A tear appeared in the corner of her eye. She quickly brushed it away before her son noticed.

She had a worrying feeling that something serious was about to happen.

Chapter 81

Day One Hundred and Six

"And welcome back to Radio Five Live with Anna Foster. In the studio today we have Nic Savage who is here to give us an update on the remarkable SISA medicine that has helped millions of people across the world from the debilitating effects of dementia — Hello Nic."

"Hello, Anna. How are you?"

"I am very well, thank you, Nic. So, it's been six months since SISA went into production with distribution across the globe, not to mention the work you've done with Rapture — how does it feel to change the world?"

Nicholas shrugged the comment off, "I just saw an opportunity to help and I took advantage of it."

"I understand that nearly every country has now accepted the SISA drug?"

"Most yes, there are still a few countries that have SISA going through their own trials which take longer due to their own national procedures and processes."

"Well, I have to say thank you on behalf of Dorothy."

"Dorothy?"

"Yes, my Mother. She was diagnosed with Alzheimer's when she was only sixty — but now I've got my Mum back — thanks to you."

"Well, not just me. Thanks to everyone at BioMedSyn for making the drug and to everyone helping to distribute it."

"You're too modest, Nic," Anna replied. "On line one we have Rebecca from Tunbridge Wells who would like to say something — Hello Rebecca."

"Hello Anna."

"I understand that SISA has helped your Father?"

"Yes Anna. My Father started to get Alzheimer's and he was only fifty two. He took SISA and he's like his old self again, it's just ..." Rebecca started to get emotional. "It's amazing, Nic, I can't thank you enough, it's a miracle — you are a miracle."

Nic didn't know how to reply.

Anna smiled and nodded.

"Thank you Rebecca, it's wonderful to hear your Father is doing so well."

"On line two, we have Derek — hello Derek."

"Hello Anna. I just wanted to say thank you to Nic personally. I am seventy two years old now but I've always felt very young for my age. Dementia put me in a very dark place. It was getting so bad that I was about to take my own life," Derek voice was wobbling.

Anna poised her finger over a button. Suicide was a taboo subject on the BBC.

"But, I heard on the radio about this new drug called SISA and how it could prevent and reverse Dementia. I went to doctor and he gave me a prescription before it was available to everyone else and it worked. One course of tablets and here I am, back to my old self — Nic, you've saved my life and for that I will be eternally grateful — thank you."

"Thank you for calling Derek. On line three we have Marion ..."

The calls continued and Nic sat there, soaking up the praise and the kind comments.

He was making a difference and the impact of his efforts was becoming known.

"Well thank you to everyone who phoned in and to Nic Savage himself for joining us in the studio today. Is there anything you would like to say, Nic?"

"Just thank you to everyone who phoned. You've all been so very kind, thank you."

"Well, keep up the great work," Anna said. "And now the news ..."

The studio relaxed.

Nicholas took off his headphones.

"Thanks for coming, Nic. That was great."

"Thanks for having me."

A door opened and Damian, one of the assistants, beckoned him out of the studio.

Nicholas was going to say good bye to Anna but she had picked up her phone and was making a call.

As he exited the studio he heard an extract of the news over the speakers.

"In Birmingham, GPs are concerned about a decrease in fertility rates ..."

The door to the studio closed.

Damian handed Nicholas his coat, "Here you are, Nic. You know the way out don't you?"

"Yes Damian, thanks."

Nicholas turned and left.

Chapter 82

Day One Hundred and Nine

"Don't tell me this is coincidence," Rufus demanded.

Hugo looked at Anthony — Craig's replacement.

"It isn't," Anthony said. "It appears that the SISA–E levels are considerably higher than they should be."

"Higher?" Hugo asked.

"Yes," Anthony replied. He grabbed the keyboard and showed a picture on the monitor.

They all watched the screen.

"This is the original SISA–C template, which has the optimum amount of active ingredient, which is clear from the level of H together with K and P."

He pressed a button.

"Then we have the SISA–D template, which according to the log is the version that was intended to be printed. The odd thing here though is that, according to my re–modelling, the active ingredient isn't enough to have any effect, so I am not sure why this would be set to print ..."

Rufus coughed, "It was a mistake."

"That would explain why the levels were increased. But rather than restoring the SISA–C template, they appear to have been increased way beyond the original levels and, as you can see, are now much too high, especially in this concentration of H, K and P together."

Rufus said. "Have you modelled what effect this would have on the body?"

"Yes, I have."

"And?" Rufus snapped.

"It would have an effect on the reproductive organs."

"Causing?" Rufus was getting both irritated and concerned.

Anthony hesitated, "Infertility."

"And — how?" Rufus growled. "Detail please."

"Well you know from the work we've done with the male contraception pill that we're trying to disable the enzyme ABHD2 to make the sperm inactive so they can't fertilize the egg. Well, ABHD2 is also in the brain, as well as in other parts of the body. It seems that SISA has in some way increased the levels of ABHD2 in the brain which has then overflowed into the male reproductive system thereby rendering sperm lazy and inactive. They just don't have the energy to get to the egg."

Rufus pondered for a moment, "Okay, so we'll turn this into a positive. We'll invest in a drug that counteracts the effects for men."

"Er, not just men, sir."

"What?" Rufus said.

"There is something there that will affect women too. We know that there is a receptor protein called FOLR4 that attracts the sperm to the egg. It seems that SISA also inhibits this protein and without it there is no attraction — the sperm simply can't latch on to fertilise the egg."

Rufus disappeared into thought again, "Okay, I repeat, we'll turn this in to a positive. We'll invest more into IVF, so in order for anyone to get pregnant we have to be involved, we'll charge ..."

Anthony interrupted, "Sorry, there is one more thing."

"Yes?" Rufus said, losing patience with this whole fiasco.

"In the modelling scenarios I have run I also believe it will activate gene expression during attempted fertilisation and destroy the sperm."

"What?" Hugo replied.

"It's a bit like if you tried to fertilise an egg from a different species. It will effectively trigger the immune system to destroy the sperm because it knows it isn't compatible."

Rufus buried his face in his hands.

Hugo and Anthony watched and didn't say a word.

Rufus pulled his hands from his face and sighed.

"In which case, we're well and truly fucked and so is the world by the look of it ..." Rufus said. He stopped short. There was that word again — 'world' — *Nic was always talking about saving the world.*

"What I want to know is did Nic know what he was doing when he increased the levels?"

Anthony looked at Hugo.

Hugo looked at Rufus.

"Hugo — arrange for our friends to pay a little visit to Nic Savage's offices tomorrow."

Hugo nodded.

"Oh, and Hugo — share all our findings with everyone."

"Everyone? Including the press?"

"Especially the press!"

Chapter 83

Day One Hundred and Ten

Nicholas sat at his desk.
The phone rang.
He ignored it.
He scrolled through the news headlines on his computer

Fertility Rates Decimated
The Double–Edged Sword that is the SISA drug
Brain Saving Drug Leads to Infertility
Arrest Warrant Issued for Nic Savage

Nicholas sighed and closed the browser.
He stood up and walked over to the window.
The phone continued to ring.
He looked out across London.
He smiled.

***

A black van pulled into the car park.
Inside were two men.
The driver waited with the engine idling.
The passenger made a call.

"Sorry boss, the police got here first."

"Okay, yes boss. We'll wait for instruction."

***

The lift door opened.

Police Constables Sahid and Miller walked up the hall-way to the desk at the far end.

"Where is Nicholas Savage?"

"He's in his office," Megan replied.

PC Miller grabbed the handle and stormed in.

The office was empty.

"He's not here?" PC Miller said.

Megan shrugged her shoulders.

"But you said he was in his office. Where is he?"

"He was. He must have left."

"But you sit right outside his office. Didn't you see him come out?"

"I was in the toilet," Megan replied. "I've only just got back to my desk."

PC Miller groaned.

PC Sahid pressed a button on his radio and waited for instruction.

"We're to try his home next," PC Sahid said.

"If you see him, please tell him that we need to speak to him urgently and to phone us on this number," PC Miller handed Megan a card.

"Okay," Megan replied and watched them walk in the di-rection of the lift.

***

Nicholas stood on the edge of the roof looking across the city.

He'd seen the police car pull into the car park and bolted from his office to avoid arrest.

It was a lovely day. The sun was warm.

He closed his eyes and in that moment he was back in his dream.

He was standing on top of the sand dune in the heat of the sun. All the animals that surrounded the dune were looking up at him.

He pictured his bedroom and the animals on the wall.

He thought of his Father and smiled.

His mobile phone rang.

"Hello?"

"Hello Nic," said the voice.

"Hello Rufus," Nicholas sighed.

"I hope you are proud of yourself, Nic. We know what you did," Rufus said.

"It was only a matter of time."

"The only thing I am curious about is did you know what you were doing?"

"I adjusted the levels high enough to have the desired effect."

"The effect of making everyone who took the drug infertile?"

Nicholas didn't reply.

"Well, it won't be long now till your trial. You had a hard time in front of the Ethics Commission — thanks to some good friends of mine on the panel."

Rufus waited for a response but didn't get one.

"You're a clever boy but that is what you are — a boy — you're out of your depth. Your name will be tarnished and you'll go to prison and that's where you will spend the rest of your life."

"I saw your share price this morning. It's taken a bit of a tumble," Nicholas said.

"We may be a little bruised, but we'll come out of this fine."

"I doubt it," Nicholas replied.

"What makes you so sure?" Rufus asked.

"Have you checked your email recently?"

Rufus sat down at his desk and checked his email.

"I have one here from you. What's this?"

"It's a link to a video on YouTube," Nicholas replied.

Rufus clicked the link. The browser launched and the video appeared.

"What is this?"

"It's just something I put together," Nicholas replied.

Rufus' heart sank as he watched the video.

"Nicholas, what have you done?"

"BioMedSyn are responsible for some of the worst medical atrocities in recent history, including clinical trials resulting in the death of eight people and further thirty–six with life changing abnormalities, the chemical leak at your manufacturing plant in Chile which poisoned a river, killed all the wildlife and caused cancer in all of the indigenous people that relied on the river to survive, the mercury vapour leak at your plant in Belarus which caused respiratory problems in the local communities. In addition to all that, there is the environmental damage, poor hazardous material handling and animal trials — even though some of those animal trials have been banned."

Rufus didn't reply — Nicholas continued.

"Then we have the really dodgy stuff like trading in banned biological weapons ..."

"That's just rumour planted by our competitors," Rufus added.

"... and ..." Nicholas went on "back–handers, corruption and bribes, you've already mentioned the Ethics Committee panel — and last but not least, burglary and kidnapping — which I have obviously experienced first–hand."

"So is that why you came to us?"

"I came to you to help fulfil my ambition."

"To bring the company down?"

"No — to help save the world."

"But you've ruined the world by making people infertile."

"Humans are the greatest threat. They poison the world. They ruin the animals' natural habitat. They're depleting its resources. They're systematically destroying the entire planet."

Rufus chuckled to himself.

"Good try, but we'll be fine. We'll contact Google and get the video pulled on the basis that it's slandering our organisation, and ..."

"It won't do any good," Nicholas interrupted.

"And why not?"

"Because it's already out there, on the web. It's also been posted to Vimeo, DailyMotion and a host of other services — clearly, I'm not going to tell you what they are."

Rufus started to lose his cool, "Nic, I am going ..."

"And, do you know what is best of all?" Nicholas cut him short. "At the end of the video I have explained how it was your intention all along to tamper with my original compound composition."

"You have no evidence," Rufus said.

"Oh but I do — I overheard you in your meeting. On the day I was with Craig."

"You what — but how?" Rufus was enraged.

"I have said in the video how it was originally your idea that you could make a great deal of money out of the drug. You were so disappointed to have to do it for free that it must have been your intention all along to make people infertile so you could then charge for the IVF treatment that you are also pioneering."

"What?" Rufus was shell–shocked.

"Give with one hand and take with another?"

"There is no way that will stand up," Rufus snarled.

"Well, I was there. I heard first–hand and I saw first–hand. So, although it might not have been your original plan exactly, I think the authorities will be convinced that you tampered with the levels of the compound. After all, with all the security measures you have in place there is no way an individual such as me would have been able to make those changes. And the evidence is on your computers. The template I worked on with Craig would have worked — you modified the template — BioMedSyn are finished."

"Nic, I am going to ..." Rufus almost exploded with rage. He fought to regain his composure.

"Nicholas — have the police left yet?"

Nicholas looked over the edge of the building.

"Yes."

"I have some friends parked in a black van who are going to come and pay you a visit. They will bring you to me and we can continue this discussion face to face."

"I don't think so," Nicholas replied.

"Well, I ..."

Nicholas hung up.

He dropped the phone on the roof.

He closed his eyes and sighed.

He thought of his Father and how much he missed him.

He wondered how his Father must have felt all those years ago as he prepared to take his own life.

Standing on the edge of London Bridge before jumping into the ice–cold Thames.

He hadn't seen him jump, but he had been told.

He'd had a recurring nightmare of his Father jumping and the ripples extending outward into the river. Just below the surface he could see his Father's face. He was desperately trying to talk but no words were coming out.

He couldn't imagine what his parents must have been going through at the time.

He just remembered his Father acting differently.

Originally, he'd been such a kind and gentle man, an artist with a hugely creative mind — but then he'd slowly transformed into a monster with mood swings, aggressive outbursts and very bad language.

He had been diagnosed with prostate cancer but instead of opting for an operation, he had decided to take part in the medical trial of a drug that helped reduce inflammation and would, over time, eradicate the cancer completely.

The final straw had been when he had hit his Mother.

Afterwards during a period of clarity, he must have felt he couldn't bear to live with what he'd done. He had written a note and given it to his Mum.

When his Mum was out one day Nicholas searched her bedroom and found it.

The note had said 'You and Nicholas are all that is precious to me and I could never forgive myself if I was to do anything to hurt you. I am a shadow of my former self and I don't want you to see me this way any longer. Please forgive me and I hope I will be forever in your hearts as you will be in mine.'

Nicholas had cried for hours that day. He locked himself in his bedroom cupboard for three days. His Mother had been so worried she had arranged for counselling, which helped.

She always blamed the demise of his Father on the medical trial.

***

He thought of his Mother and the blossoming relationship that she had formed with her new boss.

He thought of his Gran and how her mind had improved but how old age would soon return to take her.

He thought of his team and how he knew Rapture would be safe in their hands.

He thought of Leo and what a wonderful man he was to believe in him in the first place.

He thought of Paul and his tribe. He hoped they would be okay.

He thought of BioMedSyn and how they had manufactured the pills which had taken his Father.

He thought of Rufus and how the ruthless man would finally get his comeuppance.

He thought of the planet and what things might be like in a few decades' time.

He thought of the animals and how eventually their habitats would recover.

He thought how life would thrive and reclaim the planet.

It was time.

He stepped up onto the edge of the building and looked down.

He imagined the grey car park below was the grey water of the Thames.

Soon he would join his Father.

He jumped.

Epilogue

"Welcome back," Trevor said into the lens of camera two.

"Tonight, the Ethical Debate discusses the actions of one individual who has single–handedly changed the world."

As mutters began to erupt from the audience, he continued.

"You will all be aware of the high–profile court case involving BioMedSyn. Nic Savage, shortly before his death, produced a video that suggested BioMedSyn were responsible for changing the drug, SISA, so it would cause worldwide sterility. Evidence produced on the behalf of BioMedSyn seems to suggest that Nic Savage meddled with his own drug with the intent of causing global infertility."

"Tonight's debate is not a trial, it is a discussion and, with the court case still on–going, a final conclusion has yet to be determined."

"On that basis, let's begin," Trevor turned to the panel.

"Jenny, you are from Friends of the Earth, a group that has been around since 1969 which has been focussed on environmental issues, the key driver to the original intentions of Rapture, the charity formed by Nicholas Savage — what are your thoughts?"

"Thank you Trevor — well obviously can I first say that I do not condone or support what Nicholas Savage has allegedly done, but you're right, Rapture was working on some key environmental issues and in fact Friends of the Earth and Rapture were working on a number of projects together. The Clarion system has been a godsend to us and our productivity. Nicholas formed Rapture to help save the planet ..."

Trevor interrupted, "But isn't that what he has done?"

"I'm sorry?"

"Isn't that exactly what Nicholas has done, through his actions he has ultimately saved the planet?"

A wave of muttering began to spread across the audience.

"Well, as I said, we do not condone the actions of Nicholas Savage, but we have known for many years that the main contributor to many of the problems facing the Earth is man himself."

"So, technically, Nicholas has saved the Earth?"

The murmurs grew louder.

"Well, actually — probably — yes," Jenny said. Her expression showed her discomfort, but she had answered a direct question as honestly as she could.

The audience erupted. Hands waved from side to side and a few people stood up, before hastily being asked to be seated again by the studio ushers.

"We'll get to some of your questions shortly," Trevor said, "but in the meantime, I'd like to hear from our other guests."

"Jane, from the World Health Organisation, thank you for joining us, I know you only flew in from Italy earlier today."

Jane nodded — she felt a smile would have been inappropriate.

Trevor quickly referred to his notes.

"Nicholas took a slightly different direction after he came up with the SISA drug, a drug which was proven to treat and reverse the harmful effects of Alzheimer's and other forms of dementia and, by increasing the active ingredient, the drug has made many people infertile."

Jane shifted her position uncomfortably in her chair.

"Yes, well, as you said, the case is currently on–going and, yes, the levels of drug were increased. The impact of this is being felt by people in this country and many other countries all around the world."

"But you helped him didn't you?"

Jane adjusted her position again and raised a hand to cut off any further questions.

"We worked with Nicholas Savage, just as many organisations did across the world. He was bright, passionate, energetic, forward–thinking and convincing. His desire to make a difference was infectious and when you sat with him in a room, you came away wanting to help — which is what we did — there was no way we could have predicted these results."

"You said you worked with Nicholas Savage — in what capacity?"

"There were a number of projects where our interests overlapped and we worked together. We also use the Clarion system which has been invaluable for our collaborative work with other organisations."

"And it is also true that you helped distribute the SISA drug?"

Jane sighed, "Yes, we helped."

Voices from the audience shouted their disapproval but were quickly quietened down.

"It is important to remember ..." Jane said over the noise of the commotion, "... that we were just one of many organisations that helped Nicholas in all his endeavours, from the very good work we did with communities at risk of losing their homes to logging and even natural disasters, to helping distribute the SISA drug."

Jane looked down into her lap and composed herself. She sighed and looked back up.

"The SISA drug was proven to work, it was a miracle for one of humanities' biggest threats of the modern age — dementia. We had — no–one had — any idea it had been tampered with — whoever is responsible must be held to account."

The audience erupted. There were mostly cheers, clapping and whistles, but also a few boos.

Trevor jumped in.

"Despite the legal aspects of the current case, the SISA drug was successful in treating and eradicating Dementia from those who had it and also prevented it from ever happening to those who took the drug, correct?" Trevor said.

"Yes, yes — it is true — the SISA drug works and everyone who took it will have a better quality of life."

"Thank you Jane," Trevor said, raising his voice to be heard over the crowd.

"And last, but not least, I'd like to welcome Louise from the Research Ethics Committee, who was also present at the original hearing of Nic Savage."

Louise smiled, "Yes, that's correct — hello."

"The Research Ethics Committee oversees clinical trials— what happened, how did you let it get through?"

"Well, to be clear, we don't actually perform the trials ourselves. We ensure that processes and procedures are followed to ensure that clinical trials are carried out safely."

"But this wasn't safe?"

Louise sat upright and composed herself.

"And, as a result of the outcome of this trial, additional procedures have been implemented to ensure that drugs can't be fast tracked on the basis of another trial ..."

"But it wasn't so much the trial," Trevor referred to his notes. "The drug essentially works, the problem was due to someone tampering with the composition during the production process."

"Yes, as I was about to say — drug companies will also introduce additional processes during the production stage to ensure this can never happen again."

The audience were unusually quiet, obviously waiting for the next opinion–dividing comment.

Trevor was distracted for a moment by a voice in his ear.

"Turn it up a gear — it's the audience we want to hear from," the producer instructed.

"Thank you Louise. Someone tampered with the drug and, despite clinical trial procedures being adjusted to ensure this doesn't happen again, the fact is, it did happen and here we are."

Trevor obeyed the instruction in his ear piece to turn towards another camera.

"Nicholas Savage will go down in history as the man who

changed the world — but, what history will we have left if most of humanity have long since perished. Fortunately, there are some countries who didn't accept the drug or who were late to administer SISA to their citizens and there are pockets of human colonies and tribes in various parts of the world who wouldn't have had access to it."

Trevor turned back towards the previous camera.

"So, humanity certainly won't become extinct by any means, but it is true, the gradually decreasing human population will have a lessening demand on the Earth's resources and nature and the animal population should flourish without human interference or — 'humanity's rape of the planet' as one newspaper headline put it — but what do you think?"

"Now we would like to hear from our studio audience."

Even before Trevor had finished the sentence people across the audience were thrusting their arms into the air, willing Trevor to choose them.

"Yes, the lady in the purple top," Trevor pointed.

"Hello Trevor, my name is Helen. My Mother is eighty-three years old. She was only in the early stages of Dementia but she was deteriorating fast, really fast. She didn't know who I was, who her grandchildren were, she didn't even recognise the people in the home looking after her, it was —" her voice trembled, "— so upsetting to see my Mother basically disintegrate in front of my eyes. She was my strength, my rock, we had been through so much in life together — it's such a horrible way to go."

She wiped a tear from here eye. "When SISA came along, we were sceptical at first, especially as the doctors had said that nothing could be done. But we tried it and even after just a day you could see a sparkle back in her eyes. In no time at all it was like I got my old Mum back. It's a shame we had to sell her house to pay for care, but we've built her an annexe onto our house and it's like I've got my best mate back from the dead — it was — miraculous."

The audience erupted once again. The reaction was still mixed — people shouting over one another, either booing and hissing or cheering and agreeing with her.

Trevor gestured the audience to quiet down.

"Sir," Trevor said, "the gentleman near the end of the second row."

The man pointed to himself to make sure it was him being chosen.

"Yes, sir, what do you have to say?"

The man stood up. He was a slight man with a beard. He spoke very quietly.

"Sorry sir, we'll try and get the microphone a little closer but can you speak up."

"I used to be a very religious man but throughout my life I have seen things that raised doubts in my mind. The final straw was when I experienced a life event that caused me to question my faith. My Father suffered from Vascular Dementia, the onset was very quick and very sudden. Then he had a stroke. He took SISA and, although it took him a while to recover from the stroke, he was, to all intents and purposes, back to normal. I no longer believe in God, but I believe in Nicholas Savage. He has technically healed the sick and his actions will ultimately save the world."

The audience became volatile. A woman near the man who had spoken rushed out of her seat and tried to attack him.

"I wanted a baby!" she screamed.

An usher grabbed her and dragged her away.

The studio exploded with shouts and screams.

"Please, please ..." Trevor struggled to calm the audience, "Please calm down."

"I do appreciate that this is an incredibly divided subject and people have very strong views. We've never had to evict a studio audience before, but we will if this continues."

Slowly the audience began to quieten down.

"Now, the lady who rushed forward. What is your name and why did you react that way?"

The woman calmed down and the usher gently let go.

She stood back near her seat and looked up to make sure the microphone had reached her.

"My name is Sacha and I am 24 from Ealing. You may recognise me as the founder of the Mothers Without Babies campaign. My Mum had me when I was 24. Her Mum had her when she was 24. I wanted to carry on the tradition and have my child at 24 as well, but I can't — all because of Nicholas–bloody–Savage."

"And how does that make you feel?" Trevor asked.

"I'm absolutely devastated," she replied.

Jenny leant forward in her chair, "May I ask a question?"

Trevor nodded.

"Hi Sacha. What would you have felt like if you had been unable to get pregnant straight away and perhaps given birth to your child at 25 or 26?"

"Er, disappointed I guess."

"Why?

"Because I wouldn't have been able to carry on the tradition of having the baby at 24."

"Okay, and what if you couldn't have given birth at all?"

"What?"

"I ask because I had a similar experience. My Mother gave birth to me in her late thirties, her Mother also in her late thirties and I had planned to build my career and then have my child in my thirties, but I couldn't — I developed Endometriosis which made me infertile."

A few in the audience drew breath.

"I couldn't have a child, even though I was so keen to start a family — so what if you had found out that you were infertile?"

"Er, I dunno. I'd have been heartbroken, I suppose."

"But then what?"

The woman didn't seem to grasp the question.

"Having understood that you could never have children, what would you have done then?"

The woman thought about it for a moment.

"I guess I'd just have to accept it and move on with my life."

Jenny nodded and sat back in her seat.

The lady appeared unsure about what had just happened. The audience were strangely quiet as well, as though a pearl of wisdom had just been shared but not properly understood.

"He's a murderer!" a woman shouted. "A murderer."

A woman in a blue top caught Trevor's eye.

"Lady in the blue top — why do you say that?"

Mixed reactions erupted from the audience and Trevor waved it down.

"Let us remember that Nic Savage has yet to be found guilty of any crime, but what do you mean — a murderer?"

"All those poor unborn children, he killed them — he killed them all," the lady shouted.

"But, there were no children to kill. He made people infertile which means they couldn't get pregnant — there were no children."

The lady in the blue top sunk into her seat. Voices muttered around her, "He's got a point," — "That's right," — "Stupid cow," — Trevor quickly continued the debate.

"You sir — front row."

"Hello Trevor, panel. My name is Tom and I am thirty eight years old. I was diagnosed with a rare form of Dementia for which there was no cure. I should be dead by now but thanks to Nicholas Savage I am still alive, and I have a whole future ahead of me," the man said. "To be honest, I think the whole world owes a lot to Nicholas Savage. He might have prevented some people from having babies but he has given most of us a better quality of life and has saved many more lives with his actions."

Typically the audience erupted once more and Trevor calmed them down.

"The lady at the end of the aisle. Yes, you."

"My name is Marjorie and I am ninety–three years of age," the lady said.

Most of the audience cheered her age, a few did not.

"I was in a terrible state, apparently, I don't remember much about it — thank heavens. But apparently I couldn't remember names, faces, I couldn't even remember what had happened a minute ago — but look at me now," she said, standing up and performing a little twirl in the aisle.

The audience applauded.

She sat back down.

More hands went up in the air.

"The lady in the red dress," Trevor pointed.

"Thank you Trevor. I have recently come back from South America myself, near where Nicholas Savage was kidnapped. I saw for myself the extent of the problems with logging and population displacement, not just with people but animals too. Through Rapture Nicholas helped the world. With SISA he has saved the world," She said and sat back down.

The crowd erupted.

"It's interesting, we've heard from people who have been affected by direct experiences, but is there anyone in the audience who has a different viewpoint?"

Many hands went down, a few remained raised.

"You sir — with the pale blue tie."

"Hello Trevor, panel and the studio audience," he said looking around. "My name is Professor Rodriguez and I specialise in research analysis into the spread of disease. Throughout the history of nature it has been observed that, once a species outgrows its natural size, something happens. It is as if Mother Nature fights back by introducing disease to help control the population. Our own analysis showed that a worldwide pandemic was well overdue and could have happened any day. What would have followed would have been disease, global panic, horrible painful deaths, families losing loved ones and potentially many, many years of misery and hardship," He paused.

433

"I am just saying, and this is my own view as a scientist, that Nicholas Savage has most likely saved humanity from great suffering by organising the orderly process of population control — just my opinion."

The debate continued and Trevor chose other people to have their say before returning to the panel for a further discussion.

"Sorry, I am going to have to cut you off there, Frederick. I am afraid we've run out of time."

"It has been one of the most interesting debates that we have ever had and, whilst you may or may not agree with the actions of Nicholas Savage, one can't deny that he has had an impact on the world."

"Thank you for joining us and we'll see you next time, on The Debate."

The End

Acknowledgements

Thank you to Heather and Dottie, our Jack Russell Terrier, for your encouragement and support throughout this process.

Thank you also to my proof–reading team, including Tina, Josie, Dorothy and Alex.

Other Titles by Rob Wassell

Pearl of Wisdom
978-0-9569912-2-5
www.pearlofwisdombook.com

The Story of the Belle Tout Lighthouse
978-0-9569912-0-1
www.belletoutlighthouse.co.uk

The Story of the Beachy Head Lighthouse
978-0-9569912-1-8
www.beachyheadlighthouse.co.uk

The Story of Birling Gap
978-0-9569912-4-9
www.birlinggapsussex.co.uk